"Are you sure you won't have dinner with me sometime?"

Ashley shook her head, smiling. "I don't think so."

"Why?"

The bald question took her by surprise.

"Because."

"That's not an answer." Michael kicked at a stone on the ground before meeting her gaze. "I'm not looking for anything more than a friend I can talk to. My daughter's great, but sometimes it's nice to talk to another adult."

"I'm sure there are lots of adults you can talk to."

"But not you?"

She shrugged. "I won't be here that long. Just enough time to put my world back together again."

He nodded, his dark eyes full of empathy.

"Believe me, I understand that. If you want to talk, call me."

"And you'll make time in that busy schedule of yours?"

He lifted her hand, brushed his lips against her knuckles. "I'll make time for you."

LOIS RICHER

Sneaking a flashlight under the blankets, hiding in a thicket of Caragana bushes where no one could see, pushing books into socks to take to camp—those are just some of the things Lois Richer freely admits to in her pursuit of the written word. "I'm a book-a-holic. I can't do without stories," she confesses. "It's always been that way."

Her love of language evolved into writing her own stories. Today her passion is to create tales of personal struggle that lead to triumph over life's rocky road. For Lois, a happy ending is essential.

"In my stories, as in my own life, God has a way of making all things beautiful. Writing a love story is my way of reinforcing my faith in His ultimate goodness toward us—His precious children."

Apple Blossom Bride
Lois Richer

Steeple
Hill®

Published by Steeple Hill Books™

STEEPLE HILL BOOKS

Steeple
Hill®

ISBN-13: 978-0-373-81303-2
ISBN-10:   0-373-81303-1

APPLE BLOSSOM BRIDE

Copyright © 2007 by Lois M. Richer

This edition published by arrangement with Steeple Hill Books.

www.SteepleHill.com

Printed in U.S.A.

I am holding you by your right hand—
I the Lord your God—and I say to you,
Don't be afraid; I am here to help you.
—*Isaiah* 41:13

This book is dedicated to my dad. I love you.

Prologue

Seventeen Years Ago

"How can they do it, Pip?"

Ashley Adams scrubbed at her cheek, struggling to eradicate tears that wouldn't stop flowing. Sobbing made her hiccup. She had to pause to catch her breath before she could get out her next question.

"My parents promised to love each other until death parted them and now they're getting a divorce. How can they do that?"

"I don't know." Piper Langley sat down cross-legged beside her on the fresh spring grass, her forehead creased in a frown of perplexity. "I don't understand adults at all, Ash. I wish I did."

"Me, too. We'll be teenagers pretty soon. We're supposed to get smarter about this love stuff but I don't get it. I don't want to have two homes. I don't want to leave my dad or Serenity Bay." She wept. "I just want my family together."

Piper, good friend that she was, silently shared her grief.

"At Bible study last week Mrs. Masters said love is a decision." Ashley sniffed as she plucked the tumbling apple blossoms off her sweater. "My parents could *decide* to love each other, they could *decide* to stay married."

"If they told you about their decision today, it doesn't sound like they're going to change their minds," Piper warned. She checked her watch. "I've got to get home. Gran told me not to be late today. I want to stay with you," she hurried to explain, "but if I'm any later they'll worry."

"It's okay." Ashley sniffed, managed a weak smile. "I understand. You go on. I think I'll stay here for a little while."

"Don't stay too long or you'll be completely covered in apple blossoms." Piper jumped to her feet, black pigtails bobbing. She bent, hugged Ashley once in a tight squeeze, then grabbed her backpack, climbed on her bike and pedaled down the road toward her grandparents' home.

Ashley wished she could follow. Pip was so lucky. Her grandparents loved each other, and her. They would never make her choose between them.

You're away at school most of the year, anyway, honey. You'll spend the summers with me, and Christ-

mas and Easter with your mother. Or would you rather have it the other way around?

Who cared? The point was she wouldn't have a home. Not a real one.

A moment later her friend had disappeared from sight and Ashley was all alone in the churchyard with only the tumbling blossoms to listen to. Behind her, the woods rustled as the wind tickled newly sprouted leaves, but she paid no attention.

"I trusted you, God. I prayed and prayed, but they're still getting a divorce. I'm scared."

The words sounded worse when she said them out loud. She laid her head on her arms and wept for everything she was about to lose, uncaring that the afternoon sun weakened, unseeing when it let fingers of gloom creep in.

A rustle behind her drew her attention. But, before she could check it out, hard fingers locked on to her arm, pinching so tight she dropped her tissue.

"Get up. Slowly now. Don't make a sound."

Ashley blinked, startled by the command of a man who looked like a storybook hermit. She obeyed automatically, thinking she must know him. A friend of her father perhaps?

But when they reached the curb and he opened the door of a battered station wagon, her confusion gave way to uncertainty, concern, then full-bodied fear. She opened her mouth to protest but he thrust her inside, then climbed in beside her.

Panic gripped her so fiercely she couldn't breathe or make her legs work. The sensation of spiders crawling over her skin made her scratch at her arms. But that was nothing compared to the wave of dizziness that rose inside when she glanced over her shoulder and saw two suitcases on the backseat of the man's car.

You have to be careful, Ashley. Her mother's constant refrain accompanied the warning bells that were filling her brain.

She hadn't been careful. Now she was being kidnapped.

"Stop!"

But he didn't stop, and before she could scramble out of the car he'd already shifted into gear and roared past the church, past the apple blossom tree where she'd always found sanctuary.

"Let me out," she whispered, pressing herself against the door. Her throat was so dry so could hardly speak. "Please let me out."

He didn't seem to hear her. His attention was on his rearview mirror, his foot heavy on the gas pedal. He was moving too fast for her to jump out of the car.

They neared the center of town. Surely someone would notice that Ashley Adams was in a strange man's car?

But the stores were closing, the streets almost deserted. Only the coffee shop still shone its bright neon lights onto the street, welcoming people into its cozy interior.

"Let me go!" she pleaded. "I'm supposed to be at home now."

He ignored her. Perhaps he knew that her parents were too busy with their divorce plans to notice she hadn't been home all afternoon. Maybe that's why he'd taken her—maybe people could take one look at her and know that she was going to be like the kids in school she'd always felt sorry for.

As the car whizzed over the road Ashley tried to pray, struggled to think about God and those loving arms Mrs. Masters always talked about. But she couldn't feel them. All she felt was alone and very scared.

The man hunched over the wheel, his face set in a forbidding angry mask. Every so often he'd glance in his rearview mirror. Then his lips pinched together and his fingers squeezed the wheel so tightly they turned pasty-white. Anger emanated from him like smoke from a fire ready to ignite.

She had to get out of this car!

They approached the only traffic light in town, a yellow light which quickly turned red. It was now or maybe never. Ashley slid her fingers around the door handle and prepared herself. When he jerked to a stop she yanked the door open, hurled out of the vehicle and raced across the street to Mrs. Masters's coffee shop.

"Hey! Wait. I'll take you home," the man yelled after her.

Fat chance!

Ashley didn't look back nor did she stop running until she reached the coffee-shop door. Using both hands she dragged it open, burst into the pungent warmth that surrounded her as she drew deep gasping breaths into her lungs. She glanced from face to face, searching for an ally.

There were two customers at the counter. Mrs. Masters was laughing with them, but she stopped when Ashley locked the café door. By the time her sobs gurgled out, her Sunday school teacher was there, holding her.

"What's the matter, honey?"

"A man." Ashley clung to her capable hands as if to anchor herself. "A man tried to take me away. In his car."

"What man?" Mrs. Masters peered through the coffee-shop windows, shook her head. "I don't see anyone."

"He was there. I was at the apple tree by the ch-church and he grabbed me. He was trying to k-kidnap me." She was shaking and didn't know how to stop.

As if through a fog she heard Mrs. Masters speaking, felt herself being pushed down onto a chair. Someone pressed her hands around a cup. It warmed her icy fingers so she clung to it while people came and went.

"She said a man took her." She felt their stares and looked away, locking her gaze on the table, the chair, anything but the street in front. A while later her father came and took her home. To the home she wasn't going to have anymore.

That night the dreams started: nightmares so real Ashley could feel those bony fingers pressing into her skin, hear the gravel rattling beneath her feet as he pulled her across it, feel the biting odor of freshly cut spruce sting her nostrils and the hard metal pressure of the window handle against her back when she crouched in the car and waited for a chance to escape.

And every time she'd wake up, shaking, crying, knowing that some time, someday, somewhere he'd come back.

And that when he did, she wouldn't be able to leave.

Chapter One

Ashley shoved open the door of her Vancouver condo with her crutch and hobbled inside, absorbing the stale odor of a place too long uninhabited. She let the door swing closed behind her, made sure it was locked, then concentrated on inhaling deep breaths.

She was home. She was safe.

The mail sat neatly stacked on a side table, thanks to her landlord. But Ashley ignored it, coaxing her body to move a little farther into the room.

All she really wanted was to run. Which was sad when she'd spent so much time and effort dealing with her panic attacks, making this her safe haven. The accident with Kent had only proven what she already knew—there was no safe place. As if to emphasize that point, the fear that had assailed her in the elevator a few moments ago now ballooned and wouldn't let go.

The phone rang.

"Ash?" Piper's familiar voice soothed her fractured nerves. "I thought you'd be coming home today. How are you feeling?"

"Battered and bruised, Pip. My ankle's weak so I'm on crutches for a couple of days. But I'm okay." Would she ever be okay again?

"And Kent?"

"Walked away without a scratch. It was my side of the sportscar that was hit." She debated whether to explain, then decided there was no point in pretending. "He kept going faster, though I begged him to stop. He told me he could handle it, that he knew what he was doing with such a powerful car. He lied about that. He lied about everything."

"Oh, Ashley. I'm so sorry."

She couldn't handle the rush of sympathy. Not now. Not today.

"I'm not," she said steeling herself against the pain she knew would follow the words. "It wasn't me he really wanted. It was the money. It's better it happened now, before we're married, than finding out two years down the road."

"Yes, it is," Piper agreed quietly. "When do you go back to work?"

"I don't. Ferris let me go when I had to cancel out of the exhibition."

"The rat! You couldn't help the accident."

"I should never have believed Kent when he said

he knew how to drive a race car. He admitted at the hospital that he'd never even been inside one before."

"Yes, but—"

"Ferris was in a tight spot with the gallery expansion and he was depending on me to help. Being in the hospital because I was stupid and let myself get talked into something isn't an excuse."

"I suppose Kent left the bill for that car for you to pay, too, didn't he?" Piper waited a second then groaned. "Oh, Ash. The greedy—"

"Believe me, it was a cheap escape. Anyway I don't want to talk about him, Pip. I'm tired." Ashley leaned against the wall, rubbed the throbbing spot at the side of her head. "I guess I need to rest."

"Then as soon as you feel up to it, you should come here. The autumn colors are always gorgeous around the Bay." Piper's voice changed, softened. "Cathcart House is made for visitors. You know that. Think of it—you could sleep in every morning, take long walks when you're better, think about your next move. You could even help me plan my wedding. Or you can just relax if you want. Please say you'll come."

Piper sounded so happy, so at peace with her world. Ashley swallowed a tinge of envy.

"I should really be looking for a job, Pip."

"Don't tell me you've emptied your grandfather's trust account already? You were supposed to be recuperating in that hospital, not buying stuff online."

Piper and Rowena were the only two people Ashley would allow to tease about her recent inheritance. Piper's taunt brought back happy memories of other times they'd shared in Serenity Bay.

"You're awfully quiet, Ash. You'd better fess up. Just how many pairs of shoes can one woman buy?" Piper demanded.

"Since you're the queen of shoes, you tell me." Ashley glanced down at the scuffed and dirty sneakers she'd worn home from the hospital. Looked like she'd have to go shopping. She wanted no lingering memories—of Kent or the accident.

"Ash?"

"I'm here," she murmured. "Just thinking."

"Why not come visit me?" Piper pushed.

Ashley could picture exactly how Serenity Bay would look. The water always seemed darker, deeper in autumn. The sky switched to a richer shade of cerulean. The hills cloaked their rolling sides in the finest burnt orange, fiery red and forest green.

And the people—she doubted many of them would know about her broken engagement, even though Serenity Bay was so small everybody knew everyone else's business.

"Rowena's coming down for the Labor Day long weekend," Piper wheedled. "We'd have a chance to reconnect."

The last weekend of summer. It was too tempting.

"Okay I'll come," Ashley agreed. "But just for a

few weeks. I want to work, Pip. I don't want to be one of the idle rich."

The snort of disbelief carried clearly down the line.

"Like that would happen, Ms. 'Frenetic Pace' Adams. When can I expect you?"

Ashley glanced around. There was nothing to hold her here.

"A week—no, two. The doctor said I'll need a few days for my ankle to strengthen. It will take me about five days to drive there. Say…two weeks from today?" she suggested.

"Yes!" Piper cheered. "I can hardly wait."

"Listen, I know you're busy. I don't want to interfere with your work there, or get in your way."

"You won't. The busiest part of the summer is over. It went better than we could have imagined. Now if I could just get my winter plans to work."

"Winter plans?" Ashley yawned, suddenly tired.

"You're exhausted. I can tell." Piper chuckled. "Never mind my brilliant ideas. I'll tell you all about it when you get here. Go rest, Ash. Dream of all the things we'll do together once you get here."

"Yes. It'll be great." But she didn't hang up. Instead Ashley clung to the phone, needing to share what lay so heavily on her heart. "What's wrong with me, Pip?" she finally whispered.

"Absolutely nothing," her friend stoutly insisted. "You just made a mistake."

"Two of them. I thought I knew Parker. And yet I had no idea that he was in love with someone else."

"He should have said something earlier." Piper's voice wasn't forgiving.

"I should have listened better."

"Does it matter now? Your engagement to Parker only lasted a couple of days before you learned the truth and corrected things. It's not your fault. He wasn't honest about his feelings for someone else."

"Maybe. But what about Kent? I thought I could trust him. I thought he was everything I wanted in a husband." She hated saying it out loud. It sounded so silly, but why deny the truth when Piper knew it anyway. "All he wanted was my money, Pip."

"I'm sure that isn't so. But even if it is, he's gone now. You're starting over."

"Yes." She chewed her bottom lip. "Don't tell anyone, okay, Piper?"

"About the engagements?" Piper's soothing tones did wonders for Ashley. "Of course not. No one will care anyway. One look at you and the men will be knocking down my door."

"I doubt that." She chewed her bottom lip for a moment, then admitted what was really on her mind. "I suppose people know about my grandfather's oil money but I hope nobody asks about it."

"I can almost guarantee that someone will. After all, your dad lived here till he died. Some of the old folks will remember him, and you. What's wrong with that?"

"Nothing if that's all it is. But sometimes when people find out about it they change, ask me to do things, insist I help them. It can be rather scary." She felt silly admitting that but it was the truth. "Last week a woman who said she knew my grandfather came into the gallery and asked me to pay for her son's rehab. I was lucky Ferris came back from lunch early but even then he had to call the police to make her leave. I've been on tenterhooks ever since, hoping she won't accost me on the street."

"I'm sure no one here will do that. Mostly I've found that people here are as friendly as you are. Just like when we were kids. The only thing is I've already told Jason about Kent and all the rest," Piper soothed. Her soft voice brimmed with happiness. "We don't have any secrets."

"Jason's okay. You trust him, so I do, too."

"Yeah, I do trust him. Totally. Which is why I can hardly wait to marry the man."

"I'm happy for you, Pip."

They discussed how long it would take to drive from Vancouver to the cottage country two hours north of Toronto.

"It's an awfully long drive to make alone, Ash."

"It's the only way. I can't fly. Last time was horrible."

Piper sighed. "I was hoping you were getting over those panic attacks."

"Some days I think I am. Then something happens and it starts all over again."

"That's an even better reason to come to the Bay. You know you're safe here."

Not quite true, but Ashley wasn't going to get into it. She promised to call Piper every night she was on the road, then hung up. Because her ankle ached she sank onto the sofa she'd bought with her first paycheck, the one Kent hated so much—the one she loved because to her the pale-blue suede said *home*. She gazed at her watercolor of Serenity Bay.

Would she be safe there?

She was older now, had learned how to take precautions. Therapy had helped her deal with the panic attacks. But most importantly, *he* wasn't there anymore. She'd been back to the Bay several times and never once had she seen the man who'd grabbed her that spring afternoon so long ago.

Thinking about him made her anxious, so Ashley closed her eyes and let daydreams of happier times take over—until the familiar nightmare cut in. Then she rose and changed into her nightgown. From the vial in her purse she took out one of the sedatives that would guarantee a deep, dreamless sleep and swallowed it.

Snuggled into bed, she refocused on Serenity Bay and the good times she'd once found on its shores.

Michael Masters gazed at the cherubic face of his sleeping daughter. Tatiana was so small, yet she held his heart in that grubby little fist.

He touched a fingertip to the cloud of hair as dark

as his own, felt the silken texture of one fat curl wrap against his skin. He'd never imagined he would experience weak knees and palpitations all because of one four-year-old girl.

Lest he disturb her afternoon nap, he tiptoed from the room, monitor in hand. If she made a squeak he'd be back in here in three seconds. But he hoped she'd nap for an hour, long enough that he could get some work done.

His studio, if you could call it that, was at the back of the house, far from her room. It was an addition roughly thrown together, a place to work in his spare time.

Spare time. Ha! A joke. There was never any spare time, not since Tati had whirled into his life.

Michael stepped inside the room, breathed in. Pine, spruce, cedar—they mingled together into a woodsy blend that made his fingertips itch to get to work. Once he'd checked the volume on the monitor, he set it on his work table, picked up the oak piece he'd begun two weeks ago and grabbed a chisel. In his mind he visualized what he wanted to create, then set about releasing the face from the wood, bit by hardened bit.

He was almost finished the left side when it dawned on him that he'd heard nothing from Tatiana's room. He glanced at his watch, blinked.

Two hours? Tati had never slept that long in all the time she'd been with him, no matter how he tired her out.

He set down his chisel, touched the wood with one scarred thumb, then placed the carving on the table, too. As he made his way quietly through the house he chastised himself for not being a better father. Maybe Serenity Bay wasn't the best place for his daughter to grow up. Sure, his mom was here and she'd gladly offered all the mothering one small grandchild could want, but Serenity Bay was the back of nowhere. There was no ballet school or children's theater here. Maybe Tati was missing out on something.

He pushed open the door of her room, ready to tease her awake.

His heart dropped like a stone.

The bed was empty.

He scanned the room, noticed her shoes were missing, as well as her doll. The window was pushed up, curtains fluttering in the warm autumn air. Surely she hadn't gone outside by herself?

Oh, Lord, keep her safe.

He raced through the house, then outside around the back to the window of her room. Tiny footprints had rearranged the flowers he'd so painstakingly planted last spring, but Michael didn't care about that.

"Tati?"

His heart hit overdrive as he pushed through the woods, found her hair band on the other side of the bridge. Thanks to a dry summer the creek down here wasn't much more than a trickle, but farther up… He raced along the trail until he came to the old stone church he worshipped in every Sunday.

Where was she?

He stood for a moment, eyes narrowed, assessing the view. Finally his heart gave a bump of relief when he spotted the familiar dark curls beneath the apple tree. She had her doll with her, the one her mother had given her. A red wagon, the one Tati dragged everywhere she went, was turned upside down, forming a stool for her bottom.

Anxious not to scare her, he fought to control his breathing as he listened to her discussion with the beautiful bride doll she never let out of her sight.

"You mustn't run away again, Princess," she said in soft admonishing tones. "Daddy doesn't like it and Mommy can't follow you. I know the other children come here sometimes and you want to play with them, but you have to ask me first."

His words exactly. So she knew she was in the wrong.

"Tati?" He stepped closer, crouched down beside her. "What are you doing here?"

"Playing. Princess and I like to catch the leaves. You know, Daddy, for our book." She pointed to a stack of curled up reddish leaves spread out at her feet.

He remembered the big books she'd stacked on the floor. Ah. Presumably there were leaves between the pages. He'd have to take them off the shelf and put them back before she discovered he'd moved them.

At the moment there were more important concerns.

"Yes, your book is nice. But Tati, you know very well that you are not allowed to come here by yourself."

"I wasn't alone, Daddy. Princess was with me." She blinked that guileless expression that punched him right in the gut. "You didn't say Princess couldn't come, Daddy."

"I didn't say you *could* come. I said you had to ask me before you went anywhere. You didn't ask. That's disobeying." Michael struggled to keep himself from weakening when those big brown eyes met his. Staying firm with her was the hardest part of being a father. "I was worried about you when I saw that you weren't in bed, Tatiana."

"I wasn't tired anymore and a bird was calling. I'm sorry, Daddy."

"I know you are. But that isn't the point." He brushed the curls off her forehead, tipped her head up so he could look into her eyes. "It's dangerous to go through the woods yourself, especially in the fall. Sometimes there are animals around. That's why I said you have to ask me."

"Okay, Daddy."

He'd have to get a fence up around the yard, fast.

"That's not enough. I told you not to go outside by yourself."

She kept staring at him. Michael reached down, grasped the handle of her wagon, praying she'd move, that he wouldn't have to physically force her to comply. He wasn't good at the battle of wills she occasionally set him.

"Come on, now. We have to go home. And next time you may not come here unless you ask me first."

He hated bawling her out but many more disappearances and he'd be grayer than the oldest man in Serenity Bay.

"I'm *not* finished playing." Her chin butted out in that determined way that told him she was ready for a battle.

Michael's heart sank but he knew he couldn't give in.

"Yes, honey. You *are* finished. We're going home. Now." He waited a moment, and when she didn't move he gently lifted her off the wagon, turned it right side up and stacked her leaves in it. "Climb in. I'll pull you back."

Tati shook her head, curls flying. She began picking at her doll, tugging off the tiny socks. Before he could react she'd headed for the brook—and it wasn't a trickle there.

"Princess wants to wash her feet in the water."

"Stop!" He gasped as he fought to control his breathing. "Tatiana, you may not *ever* go in that water without me. Do you understand?" Panic assailed him in a wave that sent his hand out to grasp her shoulder. "Never. Come on. We're leaving. Now."

"No!" She jerked away from him, her dark eyes blazing with temper. "I don't want to go."

"I'm sorry about that but we have to. Get into the wagon, Tati. I'll give you a ride home." Before she could argue any further he wrapped his arms around her forearms and lifted her off the ground.

"No!" she bellowed, her face a rich angry red. "I won't. Leave me alone."

She struggled against him, her shoes making painful contact with his midsection while her elbows dug into his chest.

"I don't want to go with you. Let me go!"

"Stop this right now. You're coming with me if I have to force you—"

"Put her down!"

The fury in that voice commanded his attention. Michael glanced around, saw a tall, slim woman with a cascade of silver-gilt hair glaring at him. She stood a few feet beyond his reach, her stance alert as if she might race away any moment. Or attack him.

"Excuse me?" Michael frowned, noted the way her hands curled into fists at her sides.

"I said put her down. And I meant it. Do it now. Otherwise I'm calling the police." A cell phone appeared in her fingers, flipped open.

Tati had gone completely still. Michael took one

look into his daughter's curious face and knew he had to get this settled, fast. Before the little girl found a new way to create chaos in his once-normal world.

"Look, Miss Whoever You Are. You have no idea—"

"My name is Ashley Adams, if that matters." She stepped an inch closer, touched Tati's hand with a gentle brush. Her eyes rested on his child, softened for a moment, then returned to him.

The softness dissipated. Now her eyes glittered like rocks. Her other hand slid into her purse. She looked like a city girl, which meant she was probably carrying some kind of protection. He prayed it wasn't a gun.

"You're the one with no idea, buddy. Put that child down on the ground and do it fast. Then get out of here. I don't care how you leave, but you'll only take her with you over my dead body."

She was serious. So was the can of Mace in her fingers.

Michael took a step backward, opened his mouth to explain. Tati struggled against him. Deciding it might be wisest to argue his case without clutching her wiggling body, he set her gently down on the ground but clung to one tiny hand. After a moment, as if to emphasize her power, Tati dragged that hand out of his.

He would have held on, but the woman's stern glare warned him to let go. A puff of angry frustration boiled over.

"Look, er, Ashley. This isn't what you—"

She ignored him, crouched down to look into Tati's eyes.

"Hi, honey. Are you all right?"

Playing the part of the maligned child to the hilt, Tati nodded, thrusting one knuckle into her mouth in a way that always aroused sympathy in the grocery store. What chance did a mere man have against those wiles? Her thick dark lashes fluttered against her chubby cheek as if she was ready to burst into tears.

Michael almost groaned. Consummate actress. Just like her mother.

"What's your name, sweetie?"

"Tati—Tatiana."

"Why don't you come with me, Tatiana? We'll go get the police to help us find your mom. Okay?"

Tati frowned, shook her head. "We can't."

"Why not, sweetheart?"

"'Cause Daddy said Mommy's in heaven. Didn't you, Daddy?" Tati's hand slid back inside his as if she'd accepted that he was her main protector now.

"Daddy?" The woman's almond-shaped eyes opened wide. "You're her father?"

Michael nodded.

"Guilty," he admitted, amused by the look on her aristocratic face. Half belligerence, half embarrassment. Served her right.

"Well, for goodness' sakes, why didn't you say so?" Her sharp high cheekbones bore dots of bright red.

"You didn't actually give me a chance to explain." He squatted down, grasped Tati's chin. "Grab Princess and get into the wagon," he said clearly. "We have to go home. Now."

"Okay, Daddy," she sang agreeably, as if there had never been any other option. "Can I have one of the chocolate cookies Granny made?"

"After disobeying?" He gave her an arch look. His daughter had the grace to look ashamed. "Get in the wagon, Tati," he ordered quietly.

"Look, obviously I misjudged the situation. I'm really sorry." The woman followed his stare to her hand, shoved the Mace and her phone back into the peacock leather purse that hung from her narrow shoulder.

"No problem. I guess I should be relieved that you didn't call the police. I'm Michael Masters, by the way. You've already met my daughter." He thrust out one hand, shook hers, noticing the faint white line on the ring finger of her left hand where it clutched her bag.

He caught himself speculating about the reason she'd interrupted him and Tati, and ordered his brain to stop.

"Wait a minute—Masters?" She blinked. "Mick— I mean *Michael* Masters?"

"That'd be me." He hadn't heard that nickname

since high school. Which meant she knew him—but he couldn't remember anyone from those days who looked like she did.

"Oh." Her expression altered, her eyes widened. A moment later her mask had dropped back into place and he couldn't quite discern what had caused the change.

She drew herself erect. "I'm Ashley Adams. As you already know."

"Nice to meet you, Ashley Adams."

"Yes, well." She gulped, risked a look at him then quickly looked away, toward Tati. Her voice emerged low, with a ragged edge. "I'm really sorry. I shouldn't have butted in. It's just that I heard her yell and it reminded me of—never mind."

"It doesn't—"

"Sorry," she whispered. "I'm really very sorry." She rubbed her left hand against her thigh, half turned as if she wanted to race away. But she didn't.

Michael blinked. Instead model-long legs encased in cream silk pants covered the distance toward a sleek sports car at a careful pace. How on earth could she walk in those spiky shoes—with a limp, nonetheless?

"Why didn't you ask that nice lady to come for cookies, Daddy?"

Michael turned, saw the glimmer in Tati's eyes and sighed.

"You're not having cookies, remember? Anyway,

she didn't exactly give me a chance," he told her as he grasped the wagon handle and began tugging it toward home.

"Next time I'll ask her. I don't think that lady likes you, Daddy."

Too bad. Because Michael was interested in that lady. And in what had made her rush to Tati's rescue.

Most of all he wanted to know what made her stumble over his name.

Chapter Two

She was bored.

Ashley perched on the deck of Piper's gorgeous hillside home two weeks later and stared down into the smooth clear waters of Serenity Bay without really seeing a thing.

Her ankle still ached if she walked too much, her ribs weren't totally healed, but after two weeks of sitting around while Piper rushed off to work, she was sick of waiting for a return to normalcy—whatever that was. She'd expected to find peace here. Instead the same old sense of unease clung.

She needed to do something.

"Maybe I'll go into town," she told the crow perched on a deck railing.

Maybe you'll see Mick Masters again, a little voice whispered.

She pushed it away, but the damage had already been done.

A perfect likeness of Michael filled her head. Neither the brown-black eyes, nor that flirting diamond sparkle that dared you to smile, had been dimmed by the years. His hair was exactly as she remembered—maybe a little shorter now than it had been when she'd fallen for him in her fifteenth summer, but still a bit shaggy, emphasizing his rakish charm.

He hadn't recognized her. There was a lot to be thankful for in that. Heat scorched her cheeks remembering how she'd trailed after him when his mother had held parties for the church youth group at her house. Ashley had attended the group every week that summer just to catch a glimpse of Mick.

That summer shone golden in her mind. Her friends, the bay with its silken sand beach and Mick's teasing grin to hope for—a thousand girls would have envied her. But they didn't know that she was only pretending to be normal.

Ashley rose, walked inside, sweeping away the memories in a rush of busyness. But dusting Piper's pristine living room was a wasted effort and soon she was gazing out the windows again.

"Might as well go into town and get it over with," she told herself.

She hadn't been back since the first day when she'd embarrassed herself. Grabbing that little girl— what was she thinking?

Simple. She'd been thinking about the past, about

the day anxiety took over her life. Over the past ten years Ashley had consulted counselors, psychologists, medical personnel of all kinds, but no matter what she tried, the panic attacks continued. They'd grown worse lately.

A Bible study leader in one of the small groups she'd attended suggested that the sense of fear Ashley had asked them to pray about was a result of not trusting God, that she had to let go and let Him handle things. Like she hadn't tried that a thousand times!

The woman meant well but she didn't understand. How could she? Ashley couldn't explain where the fear came from. She'd carried it around with her for so long it had become part of her. So she found a way to deal with it.

Everything in her life was deliberately planned, carefully organized and carried out, minimizing the chance for that paralyzing terror to swamp her. That she'd let her guard down with Kent and endangered herself was too scary. That's why she'd been so ready to leave Vancouver. It didn't feel safe anymore.

Ashley remembered the look on Mick's face when she'd ordered him to put his daughter down. It would have been funny if it hadn't been so pathetic. Well, she'd just have to run the other way if she saw him. She was thankful that he hadn't seemed to recognize her. Maybe he wasn't aware of her teenage crush, or he had forgotten how she'd hung on his every word. She hoped.

Serenity Bay looked the same as it always did after the summer cottagers had gone back to the city. Barrels of flowers still burgeoned with cascading blossoms, fairy lights hung from red-gold maples in the town square, a few balloons clung limply to the lamppost outside the ice-cream shop. The welcome banner still stretched across the main road.

The biggest difference was the abundance of empty parking spaces on either side of the narrow streets.

Ashley pulled in front of the Coffee Pot. Through the huge glass windows she could see Mrs. Masters, her round face as unlined as it had always been. A spurt of warmth bubbled up at the welcome Ashley knew she'd find inside. She pulled open the café door with a flutter of excitement.

"Ashley? Ashley Adams, is that you?" Strong arms pulled her close, enveloping her in a cloudy aroma of yeasty bread and summer's last roses. After a minute, Mrs. Masters drew back, peered into her face. "My goodness dear, you look like a New York model. If it wasn't for those big gray eyes of yours I'm not sure I would have recognized you."

They chatted for a few minutes. Mrs. Masters insisted she share a cup of freshly brewed coffee and a piece of fresh apple pie which Ashley picked at.

"Is there something wrong?" her hostess asked, frowning at the mangled pie. "You used to like my apple pie."

"No. It's delicious. And I still do. I'm just not very hungry, I guess."

"You really need to take care of yourself, my dear. You're so thin. And there are dark circles under your eyes."

"I was in an accident. I guess it's taking longer to heal than I thought." She smiled to ease the other woman's concern. "I'm going a little stir crazy just sitting around at Piper's. It was very kind of her to invite me, but I'm used to being active and Serenity Bay isn't exactly buzzing at this time of year."

"A museum or something—wasn't that where you worked?"

"Actually an art gallery," Ashley corrected. "But I'm not there anymore."

"No, I don't imagine you're up to working after crashing a race car." Her eyes twinkled. "All right, I'll confess. I had heard about the accident. Remember, there are no secrets in a small town." Mrs. Masters paused, tapped one finger against her bottom lip. "I wonder."

"What are you wondering?" Ashley murmured, then questioned whether she should have asked. Mrs. Masters was a busybody—a nice one, but a busybody all the same.

"The art teacher up at the high school was in for dinner last night, bemoaning the fact that the school board can't afford to provide the students access to galleries to see the new styles today's artists use.

She's got some creative souls in that class who she thinks would flourish if they could just have their interest piqued. I don't suppose you still carry around your slide collection?"

Ashley nodded. "Yes, I do. In fact, they're in my car. I brought them specifically to show Rowena when she was here for Labor Day. We had some wonderful things come through the gallery this summer and you know how she loves to scout out unusual pieces for those landscapes she designs."

"Yes, I do. I also think I know some high school kids who'd appreciate seeing those slides." Mrs. Masters scanned Ashley from head to foot, nodding. "One look at you and I know they'd sit up and listen. You are what they aspire to be. Talented, gorgeous, smart, interesting."

"Me?" Ashley raised one eyebrow. "I don't even have a job at the moment."

"That's not important right now. Your health is what matters most. But if you're bored, helping at the school might fill your day." Mrs. Masters pulled out a pad of paper and a pen. "Take this to the school. Jillian Tremaine is the teacher's name. Tell her I sent you."

Three men pushed through the doors of the coffee shop. Ashley gave them a quick check, her heart racing. Nope. Not him.

"You've got customers. I'd better go." But Ashley couldn't leave until she'd learned what she really needed to know. "How is your family, Mrs. Masters?"

"We're all fine. My girls have moved to the east coast for their jobs but Michael's back in town. He lives below the ridge with his daughter. She's a darling." A fond smile tilted her generous mouth.

"I didn't know he'd married." Understatement of the year.

"Yes, but he's single now. Tati is a godsend." Her eyes lit up. "We love that little sweetheart so much."

"I'm sure."

Mrs. Masters's attention wavered to her now-seated customers.

"Excuse me, dear. I've got to get back to work. You be sure to talk to Jillian." She patted her shoulder absently. "I hope you're feeling better soon."

"Thanks for the pie."

"Oh, *pfui!* You take care of yourself."

Ashley waggled her fingers and left, mulling over the idea of showing her slides. A few hours a week at the high school—it might just keep her busy enough to prevent getting involved in Piper's winter festival plans.

Not that Ashley had anything against a winter festival in Serenity Bay. Her father had been part of a group who'd self-published a community history book on the trappers, hunters and fishermen who'd originally settled the bay. Piper's plan to resurrect some of those old skills into a modern-day festival sounded like loads of fun.

But Ashley wasn't ready to tie herself down here. Not yet. Not since a tiny sprite with black curly hair had demanded to be free, stopping her heart and reminding her that the past wasn't dead and buried.

Her focus shifted to what Mrs. Masters had said about Mick. So he'd been married. Hardly surprising given that half the tourist girls that had visited the Bay every summer went gaga over Mick's bad-boy grin and heart-melting winks. Ashley had come back to visit her father every summer after her parents had split, and her fifteenth summer had been spent hoping and praying Mick would notice her.

It had never happened.

Mick never chose one female over another. He preferred hanging out with a group of friends—both boys and girls. Of course she'd never really been part of his set. He was three years older for one thing. And employed. While she'd played with Piper and Rowena, Mick had helped out his dad in the garage and his mother in her coffee shop. Then one summer Ashley arrived to find he'd left the Bay. She'd never seen him again.

Until the other day at the apple tree when she'd let the past intrude.

She was more certain than ever that Michael had probably never noticed her gaping at him from afar. Good thing, because it meant she wouldn't feel doubly embarrassed if she met up with him again.

Which she had absolutely no intention of doing.

Ashley started the car, shifted into first and headed toward the school.

"I can't tell you how relieved I am that Mrs. Masters asked you to talk to me." Jillian Tremaine pressed a hand to her upsweep, pushing a pin in place.

"Oh?"

"I've been at my wits' end trying to get these kids interested in expressing themselves with visual arts. Unless it has to do with computers they tune out, you know. And somehow the curriculum books just don't cut it. But you and your slides—" She smiled. "They're going to enjoy their time with you and I'm going to enjoy putting those busy little minds to work."

"I hope you're right—about the slides, I mean."

"I am."

Ashley chatted with her for another few minutes, agreeing to show up Monday after lunch. She left as the bell rang for the next period.

Students filled the halls, laughing, talking and shoving each other good-naturedly as they went. One or two of the boys gave her the once-over. Ashley had to smile.

She was almost to the front door when a hand closed around her arm. Every nerve tensed as she jerked free, whirled around, prepared to defend herself. Her jaw dropped.

"You!"

"Yep. Sorry if I hurt you." Brown eyes melting like chocolate in the sun lit up Mick's face. His mouth tilted into a crooked smile. "I didn't mean to grip so hard. I called out a couple of times but with this mob I don't suppose you heard."

"No, I didn't." Why had he stopped her? "Are you leaving, too?"

His nose wrinkled. "I wish. I have a class this period."

"You're teaching here?" She couldn't believe it. The last thing she'd expected Mick Masters to become was a teacher.

"Started this month. Shop class for grades ten to twelve. You don't want to know how dangerous it is to pair up a teenager with a saw." He grinned. "Most of my students are accidents waiting to happen."

Ashley honed in on the bandage covering his thumb. "Apparently not only the kids."

He had the grace to look embarrassed.

"A misbehaving chisel. I chastised it thoroughly, don't worry."

"Uh-huh." She zipped her jacket. "Good to talk to you again, Michael. I'd better not keep you."

"You're not. The kids aren't allowed to touch anything unless I'm in the room. For that reason I try always to be late." He said it without any sign of an apology, but his eyes danced with fun. "Can we have coffee sometime?"

"Why?" She held the door open, wishing her brain would function. She wasn't prepared for this, not at all.

"Why?" He frowned, tilted his head to one side. "Well, because I've never had coffee with a fashion model and because it would greatly improve my status with the two terrors watching us from upstairs."

"I'm not a fashion model." Ashley glanced up. Both boys were ogling her and Mick.

She shifted uncomfortably, her fingers tightening against the metal.

"Besides, I wanted to thank you for going out of your way to make sure no one was hurting my daughter. Not everyone would pay that much attention to a child's cry," he said quietly.

"It was a mistake. I should have minded my own business. I have to go now. Goodbye." She scooted through the door and strode down the steps toward her car. Seconds later she'd left the school—and Mick—far behind.

When she saw the sign for Lookout Point, Ashley pulled into the parking area, shut off her motor and sat there, staring across the valley, the sound of her heartbeat echoing in her ears. She hadn't answered him about the coffee but no doubt he'd gotten the message. Mick wasn't stupid.

And yet, it wasn't Mick she'd met again.

This was no boy, definitely not the teenage heartthrob she'd spent hours daydreaming about. Michael Masters was a grown man, with a daughter and responsibilities.

He'd been married once, now he had a child.

That alone was a good reason not to go with him for coffee. She'd already made two mistakes trying to achieve a relationship where she completely trusted her partner. One where her heart wouldn't be at risk.

Young Mick Masters had been anything but safe. Michael Masters the man would be no different.

"I don't know how you do it, Mom." Michael savored the last bite of apple pie his mother had saved for him. "You work a much longer day than I do yet you still manage to make a home-cooked dinner and entertain Tati when I can barely keep one foot in front of the other. Amazing."

"No, honey. It's just years of practice. And owning a restaurant." She chuckled as she picked up his plate, set it in her dishwasher. "Things will get easier for you, I promise. When you and your sisters were little your father and I were walking zombies. But we learned how to cope. You will, too."

"The difference is you had Dad. I sometimes wonder if Tati's suffering without her mother."

"Has she said something?"

"No. She seems fine at the daycare. But it's hard to leave her there with strangers all day. Thanks." He accepted the tea she handed him, watching out the window as Tati climbed the old slide and whizzed down it just as he and his sisters had done.

"Tatiana is adjusting well. She has a stable home now, a daddy who loves her. That has to be better than gallivanting all over the globe with Carissa. Children need security. You're providing that. Cut yourself some slack."

"I guess." He mulled that over as he got up, dried the pots and pans she had washed, then resumed his seat. Tati was busy in the sandbox so he had a few minutes to talk. "I wanted to ask you about someone I met. A woman—tall, blond. She looks like a movie star or something. Her name is Ashley—"

"Adams." His mother nodded. "You should remember her. She used to live in the Bay. She was in my Bible class before her parents separated. Her mother moved away, but Ashley came back every summer to stay with her father, Regan Adams. Remember him? He died several years ago—a salesman who traveled a lot. Ashley's a good friend of Piper Langley's."

"Wow. Do you also know her shoe size?" He stared at her in admiration. "Nothing gets past you."

"Remember that," she teased.

"She was at the school today."

"Of course she was. I sent her there to talk to Jillian about showing her art slides." His mother stored the last of the pots away. "Ashley used to work in a fancy gallery in Vancouver. She keeps a collection of slides from noteworthy work she's handled. If what I've heard is correct, they're perfect for Jillian to show to her students."

"A gallery?" He sat up straight. "You said 'worked,' not 'works.' She's not there anymore?"

"She was in an accident. She came to Cathcart House to stay with Piper and recuperate. I don't know if she's going back or not." His mother gave him "the look." "If you'd spoken to her, you could have asked her."

"I tried. If I'd known about the gallery gig, I might have tried harder." He checked the backyard, saw Tati hovering by the fence. "Uh-oh, she's restless, which can only mean trouble. I'd better go. Are you sure she didn't ruin your tablecloth? That juice is a pain to get out."

"After surviving you three my linens are inde-structible to childish spills. Besides, it wouldn't matter a whit if she did," his mother insisted. "I can buy another tablecloth. But that sweet child will only be four years old for a very short time."

"True. The question is whether I can last till five." Michael rose, massaged the tense cords in his neck. "Thanks again for dinner. I appreciate not having to cook."

"Are you going to work tonight?" his mother asked. She tapped one knuckle on the window to get Tati's attention, shook her head. Apparently Tati obeyed.

"Tonight I have to check over some homework I stupidly assigned last week." He groaned. "Teaching takes up so much time. I never imagined I'd be spending so many hours at it. It makes it hard to find time—" A squeal from outside drew his attention. Michael sighed as he went to investigate. "We'd better go. It's almost bath time."

Teaching, Tati and trivialities—that's what took up his time nowadays. Frustration ate at Michael as he fastened her into the car seat, but a pat on his cheek from her little hand tamped it down. He'd choose Tati over his silly dream every time.

His mother waved them off while Tati chatted merrily about her friend Wanda at day care. Tales of Wanda filled the entire drive to the house he'd purchased a few short months ago. The place had seemed the right decision then, but on days like this he wondered about all his choices.

Michael struggled to engage Tati in their nightly bubble war. Though she was up to her eyebrows in the iridescent globes and only too willing to douse him as well, she wasn't entirely happy about something. He didn't press. She wouldn't tell him until she was good and ready anyway. At least he'd learned that much about her.

His attention strayed too long. The bubble bottle slipped and it took ages to clean up the slippery mess. Another half hour to clean Tati off, get her into pajamas and dry her hair.

But once she was tucked in bed, pressed against his shoulder as he read her a favorite story, Michael couldn't begrudge her one second. This was worth everything.

"Wanda says daddies and mommies are supposed to live together. Is that right, Daddy?"

"That's the way God planned it, sweetheart. But sometimes things don't work out like that."

"Because my mommy is in heaven?"

"Uh-huh." He so did not want to get into this tonight.

"Well, I don't like it. I want a mommy to do things with me like Wanda has. Do you know her mommy made her a pretty dress for her birthday? I want to have a pretty dress, Daddy. One that's white with frills and lots of ribbons. Just like Cinderella's."

Tati wouldn't last two minutes in frilly white, but Michael only smiled and nodded. "Very pretty, honey."

"Can I have a dress like that, Daddy?"

He studied the picture she indicated, wondering what the right answer was.

"Those dresses are for special occasions. Like Christmas and stuff. They're not very good for finger painting, or for playing in Granny's sandbox."

"I know." She flipped through the pages until she found the one she wanted. "Can I have a dress like this for Christmas, Daddy?"

He stared at Snow White's layered organza perfection and wondered if children's clothiers even made such a thing anymore.

"Tell you what, Tati, we'll have a look in the store when they get their Christmas clothes in. But that's a long time away. You might change your mind. How about if we think about it till then?"

"I guess." She tilted her head back to study him. "Wanda says 'We'll think about it' means her mommy won't do it."

"I'm not Wanda's mommy," he told her wishing the four-year-old fount of wisdom his daughter played with would, just once, run out of answers. "We'll both think about it. And when it gets nearer Christmas we'll talk about it again. Okay?"

"Okay, Daddy. I love you." She reached up to encircle his neck with her arms and squeezed as tight as she could. "This much," she grunted as used all her strength to show him.

Michael closed his eyes and breathed in as he wrapped his own arms around her tiny body. "I love you more, Tatiana," he whispered.

They outdid each other in hugs for a few minutes until he caught her yawning. She said her prayers then hugged him once more.

"Goodnight, sweetie. Sleep tight. Don't let the bed bugs bite."

She gave him one of her old lady looks. "Wanda says there are no bed bugs in Serenity Bay."

"Oh, yeah? What's this then?" He gently pinched

her leg under the covers, grinned at her squeal. "You tell Wanda she better watch out."

"You're silly, Daddy."

Michael leaned down, brushed his lips against her forehead. "I love you."

"G'night." She yawned, then curled into a ball under the pink bedspread covered with ballerinas. "Tomorrow for dress-up I'm going to be a lifesaver," she murmured just before her eyelids dropped closed.

"You already are." He flicked off the lamp so the nightlight shed its pale glow. He checked the window, made sure it was locked, cleared a path in case she got up in the night. Then Michael left the room, pulling the door almost closed, so he could hear if she called out.

He reached out to get the monitor from the dining room table, realized he'd left it in his studio. Again.

Michael unlocked the workroom door, pushed it open and flicked on the light. He paused for a moment, studying his work.

His critical focus rested on the last two carvings he'd done. These faces were his best. It had taken more than four years to get comfortable with his own particular style, but it had been worth the effort and time he'd spent to perfect his craft. His carvings now were nothing like those from his New York days, ones his mockers had called kindling.

He'd need another six or seven months to get

enough of them to mount a showing in the city. Of course he had no idea how to go about something like that, but Ashley Adams might. Maybe that's why God had sent her here, put her into his path— so he was one step closer to make his dream of working as a full-time carver come true.

The telephone rang.

He hurried to answer it, praying it wouldn't wake Tati and regretting the intrusion, but happy to hear Piper Langley's voice.

"Hello, Piper. It's nice to hear from you. I enjoyed the fireworks display you organized for Labor Day. You received high praise from my daughter, too."

He listened as she spoke, outlining a plan that, even for her, was big.

"Sounds like fun," he agreed when she'd finished describing her winter festival ideas.

"I'm hoping I can persuade you to get more involved."

"Me? How?"

"I'm using the history book of the area as a resource guide to organize some of the events. It was done several years ago and though we don't have many trappers or woodsmen around anymore, I'm bringing in some people who can show folks what it was like."

"Sounds like a lot of work."

"Eventually we want to have dogsled races, trapper contests, the whole thing. For this first year, though, we're counting on a few big names, maybe make some spectator events like snow sculptures and dogsled pulls for kids."

"Okay." He still didn't get how it involved him.

"As a windup for the week of the festival, we plan to have a live theater event in the school auditorium on the last night."

"Piper, I can't act worth a hoot. And when it comes to costumes—"

"We need a set builder," she interrupted. "For the play. There aren't a lot of sets to be built and the hardest work will be painting them, for which I've already found volunteers. But we need someone to put them together. Jason and I thought that since you're the shop teacher and already at the school, you might be able to help."

"Harmon McTaggert would be a lot better at it than me," he muttered.

"He's willing to help you whenever he can, but a recent health scare has him taking things easy."

"Morley French?"

"He's organizing two of the events. And Steve Garner is working the publicity end." She sounded apologetic. "I've exhausted my list, Michael. The only person I haven't asked is you."

"It's a great idea, Piper, and I'd really love to help."

"Great!"

"But I'm going to have to refuse," he added quickly, before she got started thanking him. "I'm sorry, I wish I could take it on but it's just not possible."

"You're sure?"

"Sorry, but yes."

"I see. I'm sorry about that. I'd really hoped to persuade you." She sounded tired. "I was just telling Ashley about the bins you helped the kids put together for the recycling program. It's a great project."

"Thanks."

Ashley. Her name kept coming up. In his mind's eye he could see her, slim and elegant, her hair looking tousled and windblown around those big gray eyes, though it had probably taken a salon hours to create the effect.

"Really, I wish I could do it, Piper. But with Tati to take care of and working at the school—I think I've bitten off just a little more than I can chew."

She laughed, a soft musical sound that carried across the wires.

"Tati's a sweetheart. One look from those big brown eyes and I'd be lost. I don't know how you can ever say no to her."

"I can't," he admitted.

They traded a few more words then Piper let him go, but not before asking him to dinner after church on Sunday.

"Nothing big, just a few of our friends. Jason and I want everyone to meet Ashley."

"Oh, we've already met," he told her. "Didn't she tell you? She was going to call the cops on me."

When they hung up Michael was grinning.

Let Ms. Ice explain that.

Chapter Three

"Everything for the winter festival is coming together so well. If I could just figure a way to get those sets built."

"You will."

Piper tossed her briefcase on a chair, flung off her shoes and smiled at Ashley.

"Such faith. Thanks, pal." She sniffed. "Something smells wonderful. I love it when you cook on Fridays. Jason says it's like the kickoff to a great weekend."

Jason says this and Jason says that. During the month Ashley had been at Cathcart House, barely a sentence had left Piper's lips that didn't include her fiancé. Ashley felt a faint prick of envy for the couple. Theirs would be a wonderful marriage.

"Shrimp cocktail for starters. Prime rib and roasted potatoes. Corn from the farmer's marker.

Coleslaw from the cabbage in your garden, and apple betty crumble for dessert. How does that sound?"

"Like I should have brought another three guys." Jason walked through the door, kissed Piper, then waved a hand. "Come on in, buddy. Hey, Ashley, I found Michael heading for his mother's coffee shop and invited him to join us. Since he missed our Sunday get-together, I figured we owed him. Is that okay?"

Like she could say no now, with him standing there, grinning at her.

"Of course. The more the merrier." Ashley sent a half smile in Michael's direction then busied herself thickening the gravy. "It won't take a minute to get everything on the table. I made some punch if anyone's interested."

"I ask you, could I have found a better roommate than this?" Piper poured four glasses, handed them round, then walked out onto the deck with Jason, laughing over something that had happened that day.

Ashley prayed Michael would follow, but God apparently had other plans. Michael leaned one hip against the end of the counter and took a sip of his drink.

"Cranberries, raspberries and a bite," he guessed, licking his lips. "Cinnamon and bitters?"

She nodded.

"For some reason the changing leaves always make me think of cinnamon. Is it too strong?"

"It's perfect. Like you." He ignored her uplifted eyebrow. "I mean it. Look at you, after slaving all day in the kitchen your hair looks as if you'd spent the day at the spa. Your dress hasn't got a spot of grease on it and as far as I can tell you haven't broken a sweat."

She had to laugh.

"It's not exactly hard labor you know. All I did was cook a few things and set the table."

"To me that is hard labor. Mostly I hope my mother invites us for dinner so I don't have to go through the agony of cooking. Tati even asks Wanda to invite her so she won't have to eat it."

It was hard to tell if he was joking or serious. She began to dish up the meal. Without being asked, Michael carried each porcelain container to the table. When he saw her lift out the meat, he went to the door and called the other two.

Jason helped Piper be seated. Michael winked at Ashley as he held her chair, then promptly sank down in the one closest to her.

"Honey, do you want to say grace?" Piper asked, reaching out for Jason's hand on one side of the table and Michael's on the other.

"Sure." Jason held out his hand for Ashley's, watched Michael take the other one, then bowed his head. "Thank you God for friends and food and your love. Bless us now we ask. Amen."

Jason released Ashley's hand immediately but Michael held on so long she had to tug her fingers from his. He made a face.

"Couldn't you think of a longer prayer, Jason?" he asked.

Piper and Jason chuckled. To hide her red cheeks, Ashley rose to retrieve the carving knife. As she handed it to Jason her gaze rested on Michael.

"It's very sharp," she said clearly. "You'll want to be careful it doesn't slip and hurt someone."

Michael inclined his head. "She means someone like me," he explained in a loud whisper.

Ashley pretended to ignore him and concentrated on her meal, listening as Piper expounded on her winter festival plans.

"Things are falling together so well. So far we've had a great response. It looks like we'll have entries in every category. The trapper's dinner has been taken over by two women who used to run a catering business, which is a huge relief." She leaned back in her chair, her forehead wrinkled. "If it wasn't for that play—"

"Still nobody to build the sets, I'm guessing." Michael sipped his water, looked at Jason. "How about you?"

Jason's head was shaking before he'd finished asking.

"Give me a motor and some tools and I can do great things. But with a hammer I'm a liability."

"He's telling the truth," Ashley vouched, trying to smother her smile. "If you look above the piano you can see where he was going to hang a picture."

They all turned to stare at the damaged plaster. Jason endured their teasing good-naturedly until Ashley cleared the dishes and served dessert. The subject changed to the timing of the festival.

"It's got to be in January," Piper explained. "We need the ice and snow to carry off the ice-sculpture contests. And the lake will still be frozen, which will allow us to have our family skating day and the community bonfire out there."

"Not to mention the ice-fishing tournament." Jason set down his fork. "I don't know when I've enjoyed a meal so much. Thank you, Ashley."

"Me, too," Michael added, scooping up the last bite of apple betty. "You should sell this recipe to my mom. She'd pay a lot to serve this."

"It has to be the spices," Piper decided, savoring the taste on her tongue. "I know there's cinnamon, but you've added something else that makes me think of apple trees just starting to form the apples. It's delicious."

"A hint of nutmeg. Thank you all." Blushing, Ashley rose, began removing the dessert dishes.

"Oh, no. You cooked. We clean." Jason lifted the plates from her hands. "Isn't that right?" he asked Piper.

"Absolutely. Why don't you take your coffee out

on the deck, Ash? It's a gorgeous evening. Jason even lit a fire in the firepit, just in case it gets cool."

"I'll go with you to make sure you won't have to stand out there alone and stare at the stars by yourself," Michael offered, grasping her elbow as if to lead her. "You understand, don't you, guys?" he said over one shoulder, winking at Piper and Jason.

"I'll let it go this time because I get to spend some more time with my girl, but I'm warning you, man." Jason shook his head. "There will come a day when that smooth tongue of yours is going to fail."

"Envy is a terrible thing." Michael let Ashley tug her arm out of his grasp, and poured two cups of coffee from the decanter she'd left on a side table. "After you, madam."

She went with him, because to refuse would be to create a scene. Besides, Piper and Jason needed time together without her in the room.

"You and Jason sound like you've known each other forever."

"That's what it seems like. Jason could be the brother I never had," Michael admitted. "We clicked the day I arrived back here and he offered to help me move in."

"He is a nice guy. I'm glad he and Piper found each other."

"You two have been friends for a while, I take it?"

"The three of us, Piper, Rowena and I, were inseparable as kids." She smiled. "We all came from here, went to boarding school together and stuck by each other through thick and thin. We still try and get together as often as we can. And we phone a lot."

"Nice." Mick handed her a cup. "This deck has the most fantastic vista." He remained beside her, staring across the treetops. "Years ago people considered the view and built accordingly. Now it seems like we raze everything to the ground and then try to recreate nature. Most of the time we don't do nearly as good a job."

"Why won't you help Piper with the play sets?" she asked, refusing to dance around the issue any longer. "She's worked so hard on this, trying to get Serenity Bay on the map so people can live here year round and earn a good living. It can't be that hard to build a few sets."

Michael kept staring outward, as if he were ignoring her.

"Are you against the winter festival or against bringing more tourists to town?"

"Neither." He did look at her then, surprise covering his face. "I'm for both. The more the merrier. I think Piper's done a fantastic job of developing Serenity Bay."

"But you're against development, is that it?"

"Not at all." He shook his head, frowned at her. "Why do you say that?"

"Well, you're not helping, so—"

"It's not that I don't want to. I think the winter

festival is a great idea. Bringing back some of the old ways to teach the kids, showing them firsthand how trappers worked—all of it is going to be very educational and fun. That's the way kids learn best."

"Not to mention the people it will bring to town just to see the contestants," she murmured. She kept her focus on him. "So what's the problem?"

"The problem is time. Actually a lack of it." He sipped his coffee, then reached out, plucked a tumbling leaf from her hair. "I don't have enough of it. I teach full-time. I have a young daughter to raise and a house to clean. I'm already struggling to keep up in all three of those areas, Ashley."

It wasn't the answer she wanted, and Ashley had a hunch it wasn't the whole answer, either. There was something Michael wasn't saying. What was he hiding?

"I finally remembered you," he said quietly.

"P-pardon?"

"From when you lived here before. Ashley Adams. You lived in that big silver-gray house on the waterfront. I used to envy you."

"Me?" Ashley turned to look at him. "Why would you ever envy me?" You had parents and sisters who loved you, a stable home.

"That's easy. You could get up in the morning, walk a hundred feet and dive into the water," he explained.

"So could you. Serenity Bay is almost surrounded by water."

"Ah, yes, but I had to bike to get to the beach. You lived right beside it. You could swim anytime you wanted. For someone like me who is addicted to water, your house was perfection. It's up for sale, did you know?"

"No, I didn't." The house she'd once loved had become a cold empty place. Her father wasn't home much during the year so he'd only kept the sparsest of furniture. Summers he spent in the backyard or on his boat. By an unspoken mutual agreement, neither of them spent more than the necessary amount of time inside.

"Well, it is. I looked at it when I moved here last spring. It might need a bit of work but the location is still its biggest asset."

"You weren't tempted to buy it? Access to water and all that?"

"I wish." Michael shook his head. "I couldn't afford it. Anyway, it's a place meant for a big family to enjoy and right now there's only Tati and I."

"She's a beautiful child."

"Yes, she is. Beautiful and headstrong with a tendency to spill stuff."

Ashley remembered her own childhood. "Aren't all kids clumsy, to some extent?"

He snickered. "You don't know Tati very well. *To some extent* doesn't begin to cover my child."

There were several comments Ashley could have made just then, but none of them seemed kind. So she kept her mouth shut and after a couple of minutes of silence Michael described his daughter's attempt to "help" him make dinner two nights before.

"Every smoke alarm in the place was ringing. I had to toss the toaster outside eventually. That's when I found out she'd put cheese slices on the bread she'd buttered before she put it in the toaster. The house still smells."

"Accidents happen," she told him, suppressing her laughter.

"Once could be called an accident but yesterday I had to take my DVD player apart."

"She put something in it?" Ashley asked, trying not to stare at him as his expression changed from chagrin to laughter.

"My socks. Tati claimed she was trying to make a video for her grandmother."

"A video of socks?" Ashley frowned.

"To show Granny the holes so she could get me new ones for Christmas," he admitted. "Tati's a little focused on Christmas at the moment. She has her special Christmas dress all picked out."

"Smart girl. It's good to be prepared."

His shoulder brushed hers. Since Ashley was in the corner of the railing she could hardly move away. Leaving would only prove—to herself most of all—how much he affected her. So she stood there.

"It must be fun to have a child in your life."

"Fun, yes. Also very scary. Since you knew me

back when, you might remember I was never an A student when it came to responsibility. Being the youngest kid does that, I guess." He studied her. "Are you cold? Would you like to move nearer the fire?"

Ashley nodded, followed him to the lounge chairs. He waited till she'd sunk into one, then sat down on the end of it.

"What about you? Do you want children?"

"Someday." She panned a look. "I'd like to get married first, though."

"Smart lady." He flicked her cheek with one finger, chasing away a mosquito. "If I remember correctly, you were always popular with the boys."

"You remember incorrectly," she chided, peeking up through her lashes. "Or you'd remember me hugging your mother's ficus plant in the corner at her parties. I was usually the wallflower. Too shy, I guess."

"You don't seem the shy type."

"But then you don't know me that well." She reached for the soft shawl she'd dropped on a side table earlier.

"I'd like to," he said simply, meeting her gaze. "Know you better, I mean. Maybe we could go out for dinner one evening."

"You're too busy," she reminded archly. "You can't even find a moment to work on the sets."

"Tati and her grandmother have a standing date on Friday nights. I'm free as a bird then."

Ashley shifted uncomfortably. "I'm not really interested in dating right now," she murmured, feeling hemmed in. "I came to Serenity Bay to relax and recuperate for a little while."

"After your accident. My mother told me. Do you want to talk about it?"

"No."

"Okay, then." Michael folded his hands together in his lap, stretched out his legs and glanced around like an eager tourist taking in the sights. "Nice weather we're having, isn't it?"

She couldn't help but chuckle.

"Now there's a sound I haven't heard in a while. Ashley laughing. I like it." Piper walked onto the deck behind Jason who was carrying a tray with two mugs and a plate of cookies on it. She sat down on the swing, patted the seat next to her then accepted her cup. "What are you two talking about?"

"The weather."

"Ashley not dating."

Their simultaneous responses had the other two grinning.

"Maybe we should go back inside and let them settle this," Jason said.

"Oh, I'd rather let them continue. We'll just listen in." Piper leaned back against Jason's arm, slung across the back of her seat and passed the cookies. "Ashley needs a challenge, Michael. She's kind of stuck in her ways. That's why I've been begging her to help me with the festival. Did you know she contacted her former boss about setting up a gallery to display local artists' work in town?"

Michael shifted, his attention intent on Piper.

"I didn't know," he said. He turned to Ashley. "Any luck?"

"No. He turned me down without even seeing some of the things that are produced here. But that's okay. I'll find someone else. I'm good at getting backers for artists who need to get their work to the public."

"Are you?"

"Have you heard of Terrence Demain?"

"Who hasn't?" Michael nodded, eyes wide. "Mosaics. Gorgeous walls of fantastic color."

"Exactly. A friend of mine commissioned his first wall. The critics couldn't get enough of his work and he took off."

"That's what Ashley does, you see. She finds the talent and then brings it to the light. Her former boss could tell you how good she is if he hadn't fired her." Piper smiled at Ashley. "How many times has Ferris begged you to come back, Ash?"

"I've lost count."

"You don't want to go back to your old job?" Michael studied her.

"Maybe. Sometime." Ashley kept her face expressionless as she scrambled for excuses. The intensity of his stare was unnerving. "I need a break first. I'd been working nonstop for ages. It feels good to relax, putter around a bit. And Piper's a peach for letting me come here. There's nowhere like the Bay for re-orienting yourself."

"Mmm." Michael tilted his head to one side, shrugged. "I guess."

She watched him closely, framing her next words with care.

"You probably thought the same thing yourself. I mean, isn't that why you've come back, after all these years? To start over with your daughter?"

"I guess you could say that."

If she hadn't been watching Ashley might have missed his wince. As it was, she couldn't help but wonder what had caused it and why he was staring at her as if she held some secret he needed.

"Anyway, I'll probably leave in a couple of weeks."

"But you have to be here for our wedding, Ash," Piper protested. "You and Row are my bridesmaids and I'm not getting married without either of you. I've got your dresses all picked out." She threaded her fingers through Jason's, her engagement ring flashing its fire. "Christmas isn't all that far off, you know."

Michael choked on his coffee. One look at his face and Ashley burst into laughter.

"What is so funny?" Piper asked.

"Apparently you're not the only one who's looking forward to Christmas," Ashley told her.

"Or thinking about fancy dresses," Michael added.

"Oh." A furrow appeared across Piper's forehead. She glanced from him to Ashley, then shrugged. "I'll assume it's a private joke."

"It is," Ashley assured her.

Michael winked at her, then rose.

"I'd better get going," he told her, holding out one hand to Ashley. "Walk me to my car?"

She could hardly refuse. Ashley placed her hand in his and rose. "I thought you said you had Friday evenings free?"

"I do. I gave my students a test last week and promised I'd have their marks ready on Monday. People think teaching is nine to three but they have no idea about the overtime."

"I guess not."

"Thanks for hosting me, Piper. And Jason, anytime you want another dinner guest, give me a call."

"Will do." Jason and Piper stood together, arms wrapped around each other's waists. "You know you're welcome. Bring Tatiana next time."

"We'll see." He walked toward the door. Ashley followed. "Good night," he said as he stepped outside. "Thanks again."

They waved. Ashley walked with him to his car without saying anything. Dusk had fallen. Across the road, some sixty feet away, a doe and her fawn were enjoying an evening lunch on a patch of grass. She touched his arm, pointed.

Michael watched for a while. Then he faced her.

"It was a great meal," he said. "I enjoyed talking to you. Are you sure you won't have dinner with me sometime, so I can repay your generosity?"

She shook her head, smiled. "I don't think so. But thank you."

"Why?"

The bald question took her by surprise.

"Because."

"That's not an answer." He shoved his hands into his pockets, kicked at a stone on the ground before meeting her gaze.

"I'm not trying to trap you into anything, Ashley. I'm not looking for anything more than a friend I can talk to." He shrugged. "Tati's great but sometimes it's nice to talk to another adult, discuss something other than her friend Wanda at day care."

She smiled at the frustration that gilded his voice.

"I'm sure there are lots of adults you can talk to."

"But not you?"

She shrugged. "I won't be here that long. I'm going to spend some time helping Piper while I search for another job." She struggled to explain. "I'm sure your mother told you I broke off my engagement recently. I guess what I'm saying is that I need time to put my world back together again."

He nodded, his dark eyes melting with empathy.

"Believe me, I understand that." He thrust out his hand. "If you get a moment and want to talk, phone me."

"And you'll make time in that busy schedule of yours?" she murmured as her fingers slid into his.

He held her hand, stared down at it cradled in his bigger rougher one, then looked at her. Ashley stared into his eyes, unsure if the zip of current she felt was only her imagination.

"I'll make time for you," he answered quietly. He lifted her hand, brushed his lips against her knuckles. "Good night, beautiful. I hope we cross paths again soon."

Then he was gone and Ashley was left with the imprint of his lips on her skin. But it wasn't only that he'd touched her physically. Something in her spirit recognized that he was seeking solace, just as she was.

She didn't understand how or why she knew that, but Michael Masters's effect on her was no different than the first time she'd visited the Louvre. Her knees were weak, her palms damp and she couldn't quite catch her breath.

Sort of like a panic attack. Only better.

All the more reason to stay away from him.

Chapter Four

"**W**ill you get me another mommy?"

Michael jerked out of his thoughts, found Tati staring at Carissa's picture in the silver frame he'd placed on a shelf in her room. He regrouped quickly, picked up his daughter and hugged her.

"I don't know if I can do that, sweetheart."

"'Cause my mommy was special." Tati nodded like a wise owl. "I know. She danced the best *Swan Lake.*"

She never failed to amaze him. "How do you know about *Swan Lake?*"

"Wanda." Tati's busy fingers brushed through his hair. "She said her mom didn't believe my mommy was a ballerina so she looked on the Internet. Wanda's mom said my mommy had rave reviews. Are rave reviews good, Daddy?"

"I'm very sure they are," he murmured, kissing her

cheek. But they didn't compare to holding your child in your arms. "Did you get all your toys put away?"

"Uh-huh. Can we go to the Dairy Shack now?"

"We can." He swirled her around until the giggles he loved to hear burst out of her, then he set her down. "How about getting your jacket?"

"Daddy." Her eyes brimmed with scorn. "It's boiling outside."

"It is now," he agreed, brushing her nose with his fingertip. "But it might not be so warm on the water later."

Tati squealed with delight. "We're going on a boat?"

He nodded. "The houseboat. Like we had for Granny's birthday, remember? We've been invited to go for a ride with Piper and Jason."

Her face glowed with excitement, but she said nothing more, simply headed for her room and her sweater. Moments later they were on the road and Michael was fielding her incessant questions, punctuated by expressions of delight. Tati would finally have something interesting to talk about at show and tell.

"Can I catch a fish?"

"I don't know, honey. We'll have to see."

"I hope it's a giant fish. A whale."

"We don't have whales in Serenity Bay, honey."

"It could happen," she insisted stubbornly then turned to stare out the window. "Wanda says lots of strange things happen."

Wanda would know. Michael drove through the shedding trees, crunching over dry red and gold leaves toward the ice cream shop. His mind grappled with the same old problem. Assuming he could get some pieces finished by next summer, how and where could he arrange a showing? And was that God's will or his own?

"Look, Daddy. Aren't the flowers pretty?"

"Where?" He followed her pointing finger to a shiny convertible sitting next to a gigantic plastic cone advertising fifty-one flavors. Something about that car seemed familiar.

"In the window of that car. The nice lady's there."

Michael pulled into a parking spot, turned his head and saw Ashley Adams seated behind the wheel of her black sports car, facing straight ahead. A transparency of Van Gogh's big yellow sunflowers had been stuck on the back side window.

"Let's go say hello." Michael released Tati from her car seat, took her hand as they walked toward Ashley. Though the roof was down, all her windows were rolled up. He tapped on one.

Ashley jerked, slowly turned her head to face him. Her face was a pasty white, her eyes stretched wide with fear.

"Are you all right?" He waited, and when she didn't respond, reached over the window to unlock the door. He opened it, touched her shoulder. "Ashley?"

Her whole body jerked at the contact.

"Yes?" Her voice emerged a thread of sound.

"Is something the matter?"

"Is she sick, Daddy?"

Tati's squeak of inquiry seemed to break the bubble Ashley had been trapped in. She drew in a deep breath and released her fingers from their death grip on the wheel.

"I'm fine. Thank you for asking."

"You don't look fine," he told her bluntly. She cast furtive glances to the left, then right, as if searching for someone. Or something.

"What's wrong?"

"Wrong?" She blinked, swung her legs from the car. "Nothing's wrong. I came to get a carton of ice cream. I'm going for a boat ride with Piper and Jason."

"So are we!" Tati squealed in delight. "What kind of ice cream are you going to get?"

"What kind would you like?"

Her recovery happened faster than he expected, but it wasn't complete. Michael knew from the way she closed the car door then checked the street that she was looking for something. Or someone.

"I like chocolate chip cookie dough. And tiger-tiger. And strawberry cheesecake and pistachio and—"

Ashley laughed. "Maybe I should have asked what kind you *don't* like."

"Oh." Tati frowned, grasped Michael's hand. "What kind of ice cream *don't* I like, Daddy?"

"I don't think there is one." He motioned to the store. "Shall we go inside and look?"

"Sure." Ashley walked along beside him. She wasn't wearing her usual high heels but the cream linen pants and matching silk sweater still screamed money. Even her toes, poking out of woven rope sandals, were perfectly manicured and polished a soft blush pink.

Michael held the door, waited for her to pass in front of him.

"Your hand is shaking," he said, softly enough that Tati couldn't hear. "I wish you'd tell me what's wrong."

"It's nothing." She tipped her head back to stare into his eyes. "Just some bad memories that won't go away."

Her hair was bundled onto the top of her head and held there by a silver comb, though wispy ringlets broke free and framed her face. A few longer tendrils caressed the long smooth line of her neck like an expensive pewter frame. She was gorgeous.

"I didn't realize you'd be going on the houseboat today."

"Or you would have begged off?" He smiled at her faint blush. "I can cancel if it will bring back that killer smile of yours."

"Don't be silly. Tati would be devastated." She inclined her head toward the little girl peeking over the ice-cream freezer trying to choose her favorite. "You have a beautiful daughter."

"Yes, I know. I thank God for her every day." Since they were early Michael insisted on buying them each a cone, then suggested they wander across the street to the park to eat them.

"Color coordination down to a T," he murmured, watching as she nipped at the top of her ice cream.

"What do you mean?" Ashley blinked, stared at him.

"Just thinking aloud."

"Oh, no, you don't," she said. "Tell me the truth. What did you mean by that?"

"Okay, but just remember, you asked me." He wrinkled his nose, glared at her ice cream. "Vanilla? Of all the flavors you could have picked you chose boring old vanilla? I assumed you chose it so that it would blend in with your clothing."

"You think my clothes are boring?" She lifted one eyebrow like an imperial queen questioning a servant.

"No." Michael shook his head. "See, I knew I'd blow this. Your clothes are perfect. You're perfect. But vanilla ice cream is boring. Not like you at all. I would have thought you'd choose something subtle but definitely flavored, like butter pecan."

She glanced over at Tati who seemed happy to sit on the bottom of the slide and lick her double chocolate chip ice cream.

"I'm not big on pecans. See. You don't know me that well."

"Sure I do. You're the girl who used to hide behind my mom's plant."

"You didn't remember that." Ashley shook her head, her smile faint. "I told you."

He tried again, scouring his brain for some other memory. "You never used to say much. The silent type."

"I told you that, too." She looked him straight in the eye. "You don't remember me at all, do you, Michael? Not that you should. I don't think I ever said more than fifteen words to you. We never had anything in common."

"Of course I remember. You came here to spend summer with your father after your parents split. You and Piper and another girl used to hang around together a lot." He struggled to recall some detail his mother had let slip. "Anyway, you had the best house in the neighborhood."

"You said that before." She glanced down at her cone, dabbed at the white glob that dripped on her wrist. "It really doesn't matter. Just accept that I chose vanilla ice cream because I like it."

"Why?"

Ashley gave him a testy look, shrugged her shoulders.

"I don't know. It's simple, uncomplicated. The way I want my life to be."

He almost laughed—until he saw how serious she was.

"Ashley, unless you're a monk in a monastery, I don't think that's going to happen."

"Why not?"

"Because life isn't like that. It's messy and challenging and full of surprises. And that's good."

"Why? I don't like surprises."

From the dark clouds scudding across her face, Michael got the distinct impression she'd just made the understatement of the year. He waited, hoping she'd expound further.

"I like my life organized, not chaotic. I like to wake up knowing what I've planned for the day and then do it. I don't like wondering what tomorrow will bring."

"It scares you," he guessed quietly. "I suppose an accident, losing your job and breaking an engagement can do that to a person. But you'll get past it. You'll want challenges in your life again."

She tilted her head to one side.

"Are you analyzing me?"

"Hardly." Like he was qualified to help anyone when his own life was such a shambles. "I'm just saying, why not cut yourself some slack? You've obviously gone through a lot. You need some time to just let the wind blow the cobwebs away."

"Is that what you do?"

He glanced around, found Tati kicking sand in the sandbox. "Not lately," he admitted.

"But you'd like to spend more time with your daughter?" Now she was analyzing him.

"I spend as much as I can with her, but sometimes

the mornings are so rushed." He shrugged. "As the days get shorter, daylight comes later and it feels more and more like I'm dragging her out of bed at the crack of dawn to ship her off to day care."

"Doesn't she enjoy it there?"

"Oh, yeah." Michael smiled. "Tati's always been around a lot of people. Keeping her at home alone wouldn't be an option."

"So why the guilt?"

He studied her wide gray eyes, found only empathy. That was probably why he let the words pour out.

"I want to give her everything," he explained softly. "I don't ever want her to think back and feel like she missed out on something because of me or remember that I wasn't there when she wanted me. I don't want to be too busy for her, but—"

"But you have a lot of things to do and it's not easy to divide your time between them. I understand. And I really wasn't going to press you about the set building again." Ashley tossed the rest of her cone into the trash can, dabbed her fingers against a napkin and tossed it in, too. "Piper's very good at recruiting people. She'll find someone else. I hope."

He laughed at her last remark.

"Hint taken. I'll think about it, okay? Now no more guilt," he decreed. "Let's go for that boat ride and enjoy the afternoon. It'll be something to look back on in January when it's twenty below and the snow's up to our ears. Come on, Tati."

She came trundling across the leaf-covered grass, legs churning as fast as they could carry her, chocolate smears covering her face, her T-shirt and her jeans.

"You need a bath," he told her, grimacing at her grungy fingers. He glanced at Ashley. "Could you watch her while I run across to ask for some damp napkins?"

"No need." Ashley reached inside her cream purse and lifted out a small zippered bag. She removed two small packets, handed them to him. "Wet wipes. They should do the trick."

"Thank you." Michael sighed. She's a lot better prepared than you. One step at a time.

Once Tati was as clean as they could manage, they trooped back to the cars. Michael couldn't miss Ashley's surreptitious scan of the area.

"I wish you'd tell me what's wrong," he murmured quietly as Tati climbed inside her car seat and buckled herself in.

"Why do you keep saying that? I'm fine."

"Is that why you keep checking over your shoulder?"

She stared at him for a moment, bit her lip. "I thought I saw someone." she finally admitted.

"Someone you don't want to see, I assume."

Ashley's spun-silver hair jerked as she nodded. "Someone I never want to see again."

The vehemence in her voice stunned him. Who did she mean?

"Your former fiancé?"

"Kent?" Surprise filled her eyes. She shook her head, her smile lopsided. "No worries there. He's off looking for other fish to fry."

"You don't sound upset by that." He studied her face, searching for the remnants of pain. He found none.

"I'm not." Her eyes hardened for a moment, then she shrugged. "I made a mistake. A marriage between us never would have lasted."

Since she didn't seem averse to sharing, Michael dug a little deeper. "Why not? Didn't you love him?"

"I thought I did. Turns out he loved something more than me."

"You mean *someone*, don't you?"

She chuckled. "Actually I don't, Michael. I mean some*thing*—as in money. My fiancé wanted to be kept in the style to which he'd become accustomed. When I objected to being his meal ticket, he decided it was time to cut all ties." Ashley's indifference to that decision was visible. She pulled her sunglasses off the dash of her car and twiddled them in one hand. "He's probably found someone else by now."

"And you don't care?"

A tiny flush of color tinted her pale cheeks. "It's a little embarrassing, but once I get past that, no, I really don't care. Actually I think I'm glad I found out when I did. I can't imagine living the way he wanted. I like to work, to be busy. I'm not good at lounging."

"I wouldn't mind trying it for a while," he admitted.

"Are we going now, Daddy?"

Michael raised his eyebrows, inclined his head. "See what I mean?"

"Yes," Ashley laughed, her gray eyes agleam with fun. "And I think it's wonderful. She's a great little girl. You're very lucky."

"Then maybe you'd like to share my good fortune and ride with us to Jason's marina? I could bring you back afterward."

He thought she'd refuse but after a moment she nodded.

"Sure. Just let me put up the top and lock my car."

Michael stood back and watched, envying her the luxury of such a beautiful car. That meant she had money, right? Must have, to afford something like this.

"She's a beaut," he told her, sliding one hand over the fender, unable to decide if it was last year's model or not. "You have good taste in cars."

"Oh, I didn't choose this," she told him, her eyes wide with surprise. "I don't know anything about cars. My grandfather bought it just before he died. He left it to me."

"Nice grandpa." By comparison his old wagon was an oxcart, but Michael held the door for her, waited while she stepped inside, her long legs swinging in with a grace he admired.

"Are you a car afficionado?" she asked once he'd started the engine.

"Mostly I admire them from a distance." He caught her stare and grinned. "I like nice cars but I also like having a roof over my head and three square meals. In the scheme of things I guess a new car isn't all that important to me."

"Daddy had a nice red car but it got made into lemonade." Tati's chirping voice carried clearly.

"Lemonade?" Ashley twisted to study him. "Did you crash?"

He burst out laughing. "No, nothing like that. I had a sports car, but I sold it, bought this one and pocketed the extra cash. It wasn't roomy enough for Tati and her friends and this one will be more practical when the snowdrifts come. Besides, it gave me a bigger deposit on the house so my payments aren't as high."

"But how—"

"Lemons make lemonade," Tati explained, reaching forward to pat her shoulder. "Daddy says that's just how life is."

"Okay." Ashley smiled at the little girl but it took her a few minutes to make the connection. "When life hands you lemons," she said eventually. "I get it."

"Exactly." He grinned as if they'd just shared the formula for world peace. They arrived at the marina to find Piper waiting for them.

"I'm so glad you could come but there's been a hitch," she explained. "Jason had one of his rentals break down and he's had to go after it. Since there's nobody to stay at the shop in case they come back, I have to wait here. But you three can go on your own. You've handled the Zephyr before, haven't you, Michael?"

"Yes, I rented it when we took Mom out for her birthday in July. But are you sure we shouldn't wait for Jason? He won't be that long."

"Oh, yes, he will. He said at least three hours and by then the sun will be cooling. You go ahead. Take Ash with you. She hasn't done anything but hang around the house and show her slides at school." She wrapped her arm around Ashley's waist, hugged her. "You can trust Michael. He's good at everything he does but maybe you can help with Tati."

"I don't need help." Tati planted her hands on her hips. "I'm a big girl."

"I know it. I think you've grown two whole inches this summer." Piper swooped Tati up into her arms and hugged her. "You've got spots," she said, wrinkling her nose.

"Choc'late chips from the ice cream. Daddy thinks I'm a mess."

"A very pretty mess."

Tati wiggled free, moved beside Ashley, her fingers grasping the long slender ones. "Can you help me with my life jacket?"

"Um, sure. I guess."

Michael watched a silent message flutter from

Ashley to Piper and wondered if she'd back out. Not if he could help it.

"Is everything ready to go, Piper?"

"Jason said to tell you the tank is full and everything's operating perfectly. I tucked a picnic in the galley for later and there are some CDs next to the stereo. Just get back before eight. It gets dark fast lately."

"Wait!" Tati tugged her arm. Ashley leaned down so his daughter could whisper something in her ear. Ashley listened, smiled, nodded then straightened.

"Ready now?" Piper asked with a grin.

"Ready." Tati wore the happiest grin he'd seen in hours, which made Michael just the tiniest bit nervous.

What was she up to?

"Well, ladies, shall we?" He waved a hand toward the vessel hopefully. He'd spent months trying to figure out God's plan for his future and since wisdom hadn't yet arrived, he'd no doubt spend plenty more. But surely God wouldn't begrudge him an afternoon with a beautiful woman on this glassy lake.

"We shall," Ashley said as if she sensed his thoughts. Then she pointed her nose in the air and strode across the deck as if she were a princess. Tati followed, copying her snooty stance.

Michael looked to Piper who was trying to conceal her grin.

"Come along then, Captain. Let's get this rig moving." Ashley tilted one imperious eyebrow as if questioning his hesitation.

"You have your orders, sailor." Piper saluted him smartly.

"Yes, ma'am." He saluted back then marched across in proper servant form. He started the engine, waited till Piper cast off, then eased them out of the berth and across the still blue water.

"Ta ta," Ashley called, offering a queenly wave. She and Tati both wore life jackets and sat in the front of the boat on the most comfortable chairs.

Michael pushed the throttle a little harder, watching as the two heads, one silver-bright, one dark as night, pressed together. Even over the sound of the motor he could hear their singing.

So that was the secret. Tati loved to sing.

He shoved his sunglasses down over his eyes and smiled. Life didn't get much better than this.

"It was a great afternoon," Ashley murmured as Michael lifted Tati from her lap and carried the sleeping child ashore. "Thank you very much."

"Thank you for coming. It wouldn't have been nearly as much fun without you." He'd already tied off the boat, so he handed her the keys. "If you could take those into the marina, I'll put Tati in the car."

"Sure." She strode to the store well aware that his eyes followed her progress. Only when she was inside did she peek over one shoulder. He was heading for his car.

"Everything okay?" Jason asked as he took the keys.

"Everything was lovely. Tell Piper—" She stopped, smiled as she saw her friend sitting behind him. "The lunch was lovely, Pip. I don't know how you managed to find fresh strawberries at this time of year."

"I have my sources." Piper raised one eyebrow.

"What's the look for?"

"Oh, nothing." Piper's dark eyes sparkled with interest. "So you enjoyed your afternoon with Michael? And Tatiana, of course."

Suddenly Ashley got it.

"No, Piper. Don't get any ideas. It was a nice afternoon, but I'm not interested in becoming anyone's mommy." As the last word left her lips, Ashley heard a noise behind her. She turned. Michael stood there, his face tight.

"Excuse me. Just wanted to say thanks for a great afternoon." Michael didn't even look at her. "Tati and I both enjoyed it." He turned and walked out of the building, toward his car.

"Rats!" Ashley glared at Piper. "This is your fault. I'll talk to you later."

"I look forward to it," Piper said with a knowing glint in her eyes.

As she followed Michael to the car, Ashley

searched for the appropriate apology. But how did you apologize for a faux pas like that?

He held her door, politely waited until she was inside, then closed it with great care so as not to waken his daughter. But as he walked around the hood and got into the car, she saw that all the fun had drained away.

"It won't take a minute to get back to your car," he said quietly.

"Look, I'm sorry you heard that." Ashley bit her lip, tried again. "I didn't mean it exactly the way it sounded."

"No?"

He wasn't cutting her any slack. Ashley tried again.

"No. Piper's in this blissful state because she's in love with Jason and she thinks it should be the same for me."

"Uh-huh." He kept his gaze straight ahead.

She could almost feel the ice.

"Look. I'm sorry. Really. But your life is full with your daughter and your work, Michael. You told me that yourself."

"Yes, I did." He glanced at her. "I don't recall suggesting I was looking for a mother for my daughter. Or anything else."

"No, you didn't." She shifted uncomfortably. "But Piper's thinking that way. I was just trying to stop her before it went too far."

He turned the corner, pulled up beside her car, then turned to face her.

"What's too far for you, Ashley? Friendship? An afternoon on a boat?" His mouth tightened. "I'm not going to abduct you, you know."

She blanched at his words, pressed her spine against the seat. "I know that."

"For your information, just so we've got everything straight—I was divorced. Her idea, not mine, but our marriage ended shortly after it happened. Several years ago actually." He glared at her, a self-mocking, sardonic smile twisting his lips. "I guess I wasn't as bright as you. I didn't see the problems early enough to bail."

"Michael, please. I didn't mean—" She stopped. The hole was only getting bigger.

"You see, that's the problem, Ashley. I don't know what you mean. I don't understand you at all. One minute you look like you're enjoying yourself, the next you've thrown up this iron fence around yourself as if you're scared you might let go and let somebody see the real you." She opened her mouth, but he held up a hand. "Don't bother to deny it. You were laughing and enjoying yourself today. What's wrong with that?"

"Nothing." She glared through the windshield, irritated by his manner.

"Then why do you act as if you're afraid?" His voice dropped. "For a little while you forget. You poke your head out into life for a few minutes, let yourself enjoy what's happening. But then something changes and you pull back in like a scared turtle. Can't you tell me why you keep freezing up?"

"I'm not doing that," she insisted.

"Yes, you are." He held her gaze, his own solemn. "I thought we could be friends, but you put up barriers, like you expect something bad to happen. As if you expect *me* to do something. What did I do to make you think that?"

"Nothing."

"Then…" He opened his eyes wide, waited for her to speak as he parked beside her car.

She wanted to pretend, but Ashley knew exactly what he was talking about. Because she *was* afraid, she had been for years. But she wasn't going to admit it here and now. Especially not to him.

A flickering memory from the past reminded her that he'd always championed the underdog. He would want to help, to give her advice or reassure her. But Ashley did not want to be Michael's next project.

"I've ruined everything and I never meant to," she apologized quietly. "I was trying to stop Piper from matchmaking and I blurted out the first thing that came to mind. It was rude and I regret it. Your personal life is entirely your own business."

"Sounds like there's a *but* coming."

"I had a wonderful time with both of you. It was fun. Tell Tati goodbye for me, will you?"

Before he could say a word Ashley eased out of his car, closed the door and unlocked her own. A moment later she drove down Main Street, headed in the wrong direction, but who cared? Anything to get away.

But as she drove the familiar streets, Ashley realized she was driving toward her childhood home, the one she'd returned to each summer to live in with her father. She paused, prepared to turn around and then suddenly, she changed her mind.

Maybe it was time to face the past. Part of it, anyway.

She drove slowly, savoring the maple-lined streets, the big spacious lawns with bikes on the sidewalks. Then she was home.

Home. What an odd word. She hadn't really felt at home for years.

There was a sign on the lawn. Open House. She stared at the sign, let the idea spark into life. What could it hurt—just to look?

Ashley climbed out of the car, walked up the cement sidewalk her father had put in when she was about four.

"Hello. Are you here for the open house? You're just in time. I was about to close up. Come on in."

The agent held the door. Ashley walked inside.

It was different.

It was the same.

The entry was big, showcasing an oak banister she'd slid down more than once. Someone had painted the wood a gruesome shade of green and covered the hardwood floors with broadloom, but otherwise the layout was the same.

"It's a beautiful house. Needs a little work, of course. No one's lived in it for several months."

"The owners moved out?" Ashley asked, pausing to study the living room and the huge bay window where she'd sat mooning over Michael all those summers ago.

"They separated in the spring. Here's the study."

Ashley followed her, listening as the woman described features already engraved in her mind.

"It's a gorgeous study. There's a little fountain outside that window that the birds just love. And here's the dining room. Perfect for entertaining. You'll love the kitchen, too. Updated, but without ruining the views and the layout toward the family room. The lake view is perfect, isn't it?"

"Yes, it is." Ashley stared out the wall of windows toward the jetty her parents had built together. It had probably been repaired over the years, but if she cleared her mind, she could almost see her mother standing there, calling her, Piper and Rowena to get out of the water and eat supper.

"There's a back staircase tucked under here providing access to the bedrooms from both ends. It's well laid out." The woman led the way upstairs. "Here's the master bedroom. Very spacious. And the bathroom's been refinished."

Ashley gave it only a cursory look then moved on to the room at the back, her room.

"I think this is the best room in the house. Just look at that view."

Ashley was looking, drinking it in like someone dying of thirst.

"The window seat is perfect, isn't it? Water view, hills, the garden below. See the tree house?"

"Do you mind if I spend a few moments here? By myself," she added when the woman looked as though she'd stay. "I know you want to close but I'd just like a bit of time to think."

"Take all the time you want. There are two other bedrooms to see, as well. I'll be downstairs."

"Thank you."

Two other rooms that should have been filled with brothers and sisters that had never happened. Her mother had claimed one as her sewing room. Ashley had used the other for her paints and watercolors.

In the blink of an eye her surroundings became her room from the past. White organza curtains billowing at the windows, white carpet on the floor, a white eyelet spread on the bed. Even after she'd left to come back each summer, it had stayed the same. Piper and Rowena had lounged on the red chairs while she stretched out on the bed.

For a few moments the happy times flooded back, but then the pain intruded. With a wistful sigh, Ashley turned and walked downstairs.

"Are you interested? I'll give you my card, just in case. Feel free to call at any time. Here are the specs if you need them."

"Thanks for letting me look." Ashley tucked the paper into her purse, then walked back to her car, the sadness of the place haunting her.

Why am I still here, God? What is it I'm trying to find in Serenity Bay that will let me get back my life?

She could easily find herself another job. She had the experience and the credentials—it wouldn't be hard. And yet a tiny tug in her heart told her she should wait. A verse Mrs. Masters had taught them echoed back from the past as it had twice before.

Be still and know that I am God.

Be still—Was He trying to teach her something?

But before Michael came, at the ice-cream shop— I saw him. I know I did. She'd never forget that face, no matter how long she lived.

Which meant that either her abductor had returned or he'd never left.

"How can I stay if he's here?"

As she drove to Piper's, Ashley heard only one answer.

Know that I am God.

Chapter Five

After three weeks of using every possible excuse she could find to avoid running into Michael Masters again, Ashley's luck ran out the Friday an early snow-storm sent school students home ahead of schedule.

"Hello, Michael," she said when she had to pass by him to get her coat from the staff room.

He nodded, stepped back to allow her to pass. "Ashley."

She retrieved her coat, wound her scarf around her neck, buying precious minutes until he left. But Michael didn't seem inclined to leave quickly. He thrust his arms into his jacket, waited until the other teachers left the room. Then there were only two of them.

"How are you?"

"Fine." She risked a look at him, found his focus centered on her. "You?"

"Can't complain." He kept watching her. "You're still here."

"Yes." She shrugged. "I promised Piper I wouldn't leave until after her wedding. Except for Christmas. I'm going to Hawaii for that."

"Nice."

"My mom lives there." Ashley drew on her gloves, wishing he'd move away from the doorway. She didn't want to push past him and there really was little more to say.

"What's keeping you busy?"

"Nothing much."

"Somehow I don't see you content to think about nothing much which means you've been up to something." Michael's mischievous grin flashed then disappeared. His voice grew edgy. "Sorry. It's none of my business."

"It's not a secret." She sighed, pressed the strap of her purse over one shoulder. "Look. I messed up. Big-time. I offended you and I know it. If I say I'm sorry again will you forgive me and forget about my big mouth?"

"It's *why* you said it that bugs me."

She'd known that was coming. Ashley met his gaze and admitted the truth.

"You make me nervous, Michael."

"Nervous? Me?" He blinked. "Why?"

"Shades of the past, probably. I guess I still think of you as the most popular boy on the Bay and I feel like the dumb klutz I was, hiding behind your mother's plant. Sometimes my mouth gets going before my brain is in gear, like that day when I—you know. I feel stupid."

"Then we're even," he murmured.

Ashley frowned. "What do you mean?"

"I look at you and see a classy polished woman who's traveled around the world, wears designer clothes, has mingled with some of the twentieth century's best artists, and I feel like a country bumpkin. And then there's the connection."

Connection? What was he talking about?

"I know it probably sounds cheesy to put it like that, but there *is* a connection between us, Ashley. You must have felt it."

She might have told herself he was teasing but for his serious expression. And for the fact that she had felt a zing of electricity the moment she'd first seen him. That had grown stronger with each meeting.

"You're not saying anything. That's a bad sign."

"I don't know what to say," she admitted.

"Just talk to me."

"I like you, Michael. I like Tati very much. But coming back to Serenity Bay—well, it's brought back a lot of stuff I'd rather forget. None of it particularly pleasant." She hoped he wouldn't press for details.

"So where do we go from here?"

"What if we just agree that you're no country

bumpkin and you say you'll forgive me saying and doing the wrong thing at the wrong time."

"Done." He thrust out his hand and grasped hers, shaking it as if they'd struck some deal. "So what have you been doing lately?"

"If I say you're like a dog with a bone, will you be offended?" She chuckled at his growl. "If you must know, I've been assembling a sort of inventory of the artists in the area."

He frowned. "Why?"

"Probably because of all Piper's talk about getting Serenity Bay on the map. She thinks there could be a real explosion of interest here once tourists find out there are so many talented people doing such a variety of work. Frankly, I think she's right. But nobody's going to know unless the artists get some exposure."

"You know a way to do that?"

"I know some gallery owners," she said, wondering what had put the glint back in his eyes. "I've contacted a couple of them who are willing to look at some pieces on spec."

"You don't look pleased by that."

"I guess it's a first step, but I was thinking more in terms of setting up something here. If a well-known gallery had a satellite place in Serenity Bay, they'd have first shot at the pieces and the city galleries might accept that the work that's produced here is worth coming to see." She rubbed her neck, aware that a tiny headache had begun there. "A win-win situation."

"But your gallery people don't want that."

"To them a place here would be a money loser. The area's tourism isn't built in yet so they say what's happened so far might be a flash in the pan. Piper's plans for the winter look good on paper but until the Bay starts attracting people and revenue, I don't think anyone is going to sink that big an investment for return that only lasts a few months in the year."

"I see."

She ducked her head to look outside. "The snow's getting worse. I'd better go."

"Yeah." Still he didn't move. It was almost as if he wanted to say something but couldn't quite get the words out.

"Would you let me pass, please?"

He opened his mouth as if to say something, but after a moment shook his head and stepped aside. "Of course. Drive carefully."

"I always do." She eased past him, catching the scent of his aftershave that made her think of a summer long past when she'd seen Michael riding his motorcycle. Her heart skipped.

Oh, yeah, there was a connection between them.

"Have a good weekend."

Ashley fluttered her fingers then hurried down the hall, pushed open the door. Noon's brisk autumn breeze had become a raging gust that ripped at her hair and dashed snow against her cheek. If this kept up, it wouldn't be long before the roads were covered with snow drifts. She tossed her purse onto the passenger's seat, saw a slide fall out and remembered that she was supposed to have given it to a student in her class who was studying that artist's work.

"Blast!"

Ashley pulled out her cell phone and called Jillian to get directions to the girl's home. Then she eased out of her parking spot and onto the street. The sky darkened to lead as the wind caught falling snowflakes and hurled them into the air, making visibility difficult.

"Just give me enough time for one stop," she begged, peering through the windshield. "Just one, then I'm home."

She found the outlying street without any trouble, but the house was set far back on the property and she had to drive the car down snowy ruts. She could have waited, of course. But the essay Jillian had assigned was due next Wednesday and Ashley had already forgotten once.

She left the motor running, grabbed the square of film and trudged to the door. After a hurried explanation she handed it over to the girl's mother. As she hurried back to her car, she slipped twice. The temperature had dropped. The storm was getting much worse.

Back on the street Ashley found her exit blocked by two cars that had hit each other head-on. She backed up, took a side road, biting her lips as the undercarriage of the car rubbed over the ice and snow ridges.

"Just get me home, baby. That's all I ask."

The road Ashley turned onto wasn't familiar. These houses were set on larger plots of land, far back from the road, hidden from view.

"They must all drive four-by-fours," she muttered to herself as she corrected yet another swerve of the car. A truck behind her moved in a little too close so she eased to one side, hoping he would pass and let her to drive at her own speed.

He didn't pass.

Ashley gripped the wheel tightly as she steered. The truck stayed on her tail, only now the driver was honking. The familiar quaver of panic began in her stomach, pinching its way to each nerve as she crept along, her wheels slipping and sliding over the icy surface, trying to find traction.

What if? What if—

Finally, at a crossroad approach, the truck roared up beside her.

He was going to pass. Ashley drew a calming breath, felt the pressure ease. Everything was fine. She was safe.

"Good riddance to you, too," she agreed when the truck blasted one last honk before it roared ahead of her.

But the flurry of white it left behind caused her to lose sight of the road. Too late, she realized she was heading for the ditch. Trying to correct, she over-steered. The car spun round and round and all she could do was hang on as memories of another crash took control of her mind.

Except this time there was a soft *poof* as the car slid into a pile of snow.

She wasn't hurt. She was fine. Nothing had happened.

Ashley pressed the gas pedal. The tires spun use-lessly. She tried Reverse—to no avail.

Great. She was totally stuck on the side of the road in the middle of a freak snowstorm.

"Wonderful," she grumbled, reaching for her purse. "Not only don't I know exactly where I am but my cell phone probably doesn't work out here."

It didn't. Hills loomed on either side. Which, of course, blocked the signal.

"Perfect." Reminded of warnings against carbon monoxide poisoning Ashley switched off the engine. Immediately the howl of the wind whistled around her. The rag-top wasn't built for this.

At least she had on her low-heeled boots, a warm sweater and her heaviest wool coat. She could walk if she had to. Somebody had to live at the end of the lane across the road—which meant there should be traffic on this road. She turned on her flashers and decided to wait it out.

The heat from the car dissipated in minutes. Ashley drew her collar up around her ears, tightened her scarf around her neck. She'd give it ten minutes. If no one came by then, she'd get out and walk. Locking the doors made her feel a little better.

Time ticked by so slowly.

A forgotten sweater lay on the backseat. She reached back to grab it, heard someone rap on her window. Heaving a sigh of relief she struggled to unroll it, trying to see through the misted glass.

Her breath caught in her throat as a face she'd never forgotten loomed before her.

"Get out." Same words, same gruff tone.

The terror of those moments rushed back, snapping the paralysis that had kept her silent.

"Go away," she screamed as she grabbed the handle and rolled up the window. "Leave me alone!"

He tapped on the window twice more but Ashley ignored him, her body shaking as she prayed for help. She pressed the horn, once, twice. He yelled something, rapped one last time then finally left. She tried to see where he'd gone as her heart pounded furiously. Finally a rusty truck pulled onto the road and passed her.

It wasn't the same vehicle she'd been pushed into so long ago, but then it wouldn't be, seventeen years later.

Ashley clutched the wheel, closed her eyes and fought against another wash of fear by pulling in slow deep breaths, just as she'd been taught. It took a while but finally she felt able to critically assess her situation.

No way could she get out and walk now. He could be the one who lived down that lane. But neither could she wait here forever. The radio said the storm could last all night. She'd be buried by morning. Already the light was fading.

Fears that had hung in the wings of her mind tiptoed forward, encouraging a host of worries to follow.

Piper and Jason were away. No one would miss her. If the snow and wind continued, her car could be buried, or hit by a snowplow. She could die out here!

Oh, God, I'm scared and alone and I need help. Please send someone.

"That's Ashley's car."

Michael frowned, dared to glance away from the road for a second. "Where?"

"Up there. See, Daddy. The sunflowers."

"Yes, I see, honey." He followed her pointing finger, saw the car half buried at the edge of the road. What was Ashley doing out here? "I'm going to talk to her. You stay in your seat and keep your belt buckled," he ordered as he edged over onto the side of the road. "Don't get out of your seat, Tati. I mean it," he emphasized as he set his hazard lights.

"Yes, Daddy."

Michael tugged on his gloves then stepped out of the vehicle, struggling through the accumulation of snow to reach her. The car was going to need a tow truck.

He rapped on her window.

"Leave me alone!"

Uncertain that he'd heard the words correctly, he tried again, pulling on the door handle as he spoke.

"Ashley, it's Michael Masters. Are you all right?"

The window rolled down a crack. "Michael?" she whispered.

"Yep, it's me. Unlock the door and I'll help you out."

"I'm stuck."

"I can see that. You're going to need a tow truck and they're really busy with the storm. You can come to my place to wait. It's just down the road."

"Okay." But she didn't move.

"You have to open the door, Ashley." He checked to be sure Tati was still safely inside his car as another vehicle approached.

"Need any help?" a man in the other car called out.

"Not unless you can pull this out." Michael already knew the little import he was driving would be no help.

"Sorry. Haven't got enough power."

"Thanks anyway."

As the other car drove off he heard door locks

click. A moment later Ashley opened her door. In the light of her car Michael thought he saw tears on her pale cheeks.

"Are you hurt? Anything broken?" he asked, checking her face, her clothes. But aside from the tear tracks, Ashley Adams looked as immaculate as she always did.

"I'm fine. It was a soft landing." She stood staring up at him, her big gray eyes filled with shadows, her voice trembling. "I'm so glad you came."

"So am I." He took her arm, helped her over the crust of snow and onto the road. "Go get in my car. I'll lock up here. Do you have your keys?"

Confusion filled her face. "I don't know."

Something was obviously wrong, but he wasn't going to question her now. Michael bent, glanced at the ignition.

"They're here. I'll bring them. Can you make it to the car or do you need help in those boots?"

"I'll wait for you," she said, so softly he barely heard. She sounded terrified. Utterly unlike Ashley.

Frowning, Michael removed the keys, locked the doors, then turned to grasp her elbow. "Okay, let's go. Tati must be wondering what's taking so long."

"Tati. Yes." She hurried along beside him, glancing over one shoulder, then the other as if expecting something to jump out of the bush.

He helped her inside his car and closed the door. A shot of surprise filled him when she quickly locked it. Something was definitely wrong. Michael unlocked his door, climbed inside, glad for once of Tatiana's chatty voice.

"Did you get pushed in the snow? Wanda says lots of people will have trouble in this storm. She says people never drive with the proper equ—" She paused. "What's the word, Daddy?"

"Equipment."

"Yes. Equipment. Anyway, that's what Wanda says. Is that what happened to you, Ashley?" Tati leaned forward, tapped her on the shoulder when no immediately answer was forthcoming.

"Uh, yes. I guess it is." Though Ashley managed a smile, her color had still not returned.

"We passed a number of people who'd gone off the road and there are only two tow trucks in Serenity Bay so you'll have a bit of a wait. But you're welcome to stay with us as long as you like," he told her, concentrating on turning the slippery corner. "I'm sure you'll want to phone Piper and let her and Jason know you're okay."

"They're out of town."

"Oh. Well, good thing we came along then."

"Yes, it is. I tried my cell but it wouldn't work." She huddled in the corner as if afraid he'd bite.

"Service is iffy when you get down in the valley here," Michael explained, unable to rid himself of the feeling that something else had happened to shake that reserved manner she usually clung to like a cloak. "We'll be home in a minute. You can call the service station from there."

"Thanks."

Tati chatted about her day the rest of the way home, leaving little space for any other discussion. Michael hit the remote for the garage door, then pulled inside, glad to be off the road.

"We made it." He climbed out, helped Tati down from her seat. By then Ashley was out of the car, standing beside him. "Come on inside."

He unlocked the door for them before rescuing the pan of lasagne his mother had placed in a box in the trunk. After sliding it into the oven and setting the temperature as she'd directed, he shed his coat, helped Ashley out of hers and hung all three on the pegs by the door. Tati's boots took a little longer. By the time he had them off Ashley had slid her feet out of her own smooth calf-leather footwear. Her feet were bare.

Michael grabbed a pair of his socks from the laundry room.

"You'd better put these on or your toes will freeze on these cold floors."

She didn't argue. "Thanks."

"The phone's over here. The number is on the wall above it. At least that's the one I've used. The book is in the drawer if you'd rather try someone else."

"I have an auto club," she told him. She drew her wallet out of her bag, took out the card and dialed the number on the back. She gave the information then turned to him. "I don't know where to tell them I am," she said quietly.

"I'll explain." He took the phone, gave the directions then asked that the truck call them just before arrival so they could meet it. "How long?"

"At least a couple of hours, I'd imagine. We've got a whole list before you. Everyone's working as fast as they can."

"Okay, thanks." He handed the phone back to Ashley who spoke for a moment then hung up. "All right?"

"Yes, thank you. She said to expect a long wait." She looked at him through her lashes, her gray eyes shaded. "I'm sorry to intrude on your evening like this, Michael."

"Don't be silly. My mother sent supper. I'll just get the rest of my stuff from the car and when everything's ready we'll eat. Tati, you show Ashley the living room. Maybe she'd like to watch the news."

"I don't like news. I like to paint. Do you want to see my paintings, Ashley?"

"I'd love to."

At least she'd warmed up to his daughter, Michael mused as he lugged in the groceries he'd stocked up on. His mother had insisted on sending along a full meal. Garlic bread, a Caesar salad, fresh blueberry pie and a bag of lemon coconut cookies for Tati. A perfect dinner and no cooking.

As Michael set the pie at the back of the stove to

warm, he glanced into the living room. Ashley was seated on the floor, a crayon in her hand as she followed Tatiana's directions for drawing a butterfly. Whatever had bothered her out there seemed to be gone now.

Tati switched on the lamp and it shone down on their guest's blond head. A burgundy turtleneck hugged her curves. She wore matching wool slacks. When she moved, a faint tinkling at her waist drew his attention to the golden belt cinched around it.

Ashley was every bit as gorgeous as he'd remembered her. Better than that, she was at his home for dinner and couldn't leave even if she wanted to.

Michael smiled at the irony.

But his smile quickly disappeared when she rose, went to the windows and pushed aside the drapes to peer outside into the yard. So she wasn't totally in control. Which meant that she was still afraid. He made up his mind to find out what had caused this reaction.

"Dinner's ready. Wash your hands, Tati."

His daughter grumbled all the way to the bathroom, but she skipped back happily enough, presenting her palms for him to sniff. "I used soap," she told him.

"I can smell it. Good girl. Ashley, have a seat there, if you'd like."

"Thanks."

"We hold hands to say grace. Is that okay?"

Ashley said nothing but when he stretched out his hand, she paused before sliding hers into it. Her skin felt like silk against his work-roughened fingers. He tried not to notice when she grasped Tati's little mitt with no apparent hesitation.

"God is great, God is good. And we thank him for this food. Amen."

The words barely left Tati's mouth before Ashley tugged her hand out of his, her cheeks a bright pink.

"We haven't got any food to eat, Daddy."

Michael gulped, told himself to get a grip. He rose, slid the lasagne from the oven and set it in the middle of the table.

"If you can reach the salad, Ashley, I'll get the garlic bread."

She placed the salad on the table, then smoothed her napkin in her lap. Michael passed her the bread, then began serving the lasagne.

"How did you go off the road?" he asked to break the silence.

"A truck was behind me. It was following too close so I edged over to let it pass. When it passed me it kicked up snow flurries and I lost sight of the road. By the time I realized I was off-kilter, the damage had already been done. I slid off."

"A big red truck?" he asked. "Wheels high up off the ground?"

She nodded, wide eyes luminous. "How did you know?"

"Tommy Cliburn. He just got his license. For some reason his parents thought that truck would keep him safe." Michael watched her pick at her food, noticed that the color in her cheeks had returned to its usual pale translucence. "You do realize that you can't keep driving that car in the winter?"

"I'll have to get snow tires."

He shook his head. "It's not the tires. The undercarriage isn't built for these kinds of roads. Every drive from Piper's down those switchback roads will be a nightmare—worse if it's icy. You need something safer."

"I'll be fine."

Not wanting to belabor the subject, Michael changed the subject.

"You said you went to boarding school. Why?"

"My mother thought it would be a stabilizing influence." She sipped her water. When she spoke again her voice had lost the quaver. "She hated winter in the Bay, so after Thanksgiving, she stayed with my grandparents in Hawaii. Since I would have had to change schools in the fall and spring, she thought boarding school would be a better option."

"That must have been hard for you."

"Actually it wasn't. There was a very constant routine, I knew exactly what was happening from day to day, what to expect." She shrugged. "I really liked it. Pip and Row were there, too, so that made it even better."

Constant routine? The comment struck him as odd.

"I'm afraid I don't remember much about your father."

"No, you wouldn't. He traveled a lot with his job. We were always here for the Christmas holidays, though." She plucked the soft center out of her bread just like his daughter did.

"Where's Hawaii?" Tati asked.

"I'll show you on the map after dinner," he promised.

"What's it like, Ashley?"

"It's an island. It has water all around it and it's lovely to swim in. They never get winter in Hawaii." Ashley smiled as the child's eyes grew. "I used to love playing on the beach."

"I like beaches." Tati reached out for her milk, hit the edge of the glass and knocked it over into Ashley's plate, spattering droplets in an arc across her sweater and pants.

"I'm sorry." Fat tears welled on Tati's cheeks as the milk spread across the table and dripped onto the floor.

Sighing, Michael rose, fetched a damp cloth for Ashley. "Here," he offered. Then he began to mop up the spill.

"I didn't mean to do it," Tati sobbed.

"Don't worry about it, honey. I'm sure Ashley will forgive you."

"Of course I will. It was an accident. Everybody has them. I had one tonight, remember?" Ashley dabbed at the table, made a face at her drenched plate. "I think I'm finished my lasagne."

"Here, I'll take care of that."

This was not exactly romantic. But then who'd said anything about romance? Ashley was simply waiting for a tow truck.

"Do you need another cloth?" he asked, wondering if her clothes were ruined.

"I'm fine." She sat down, giggled at the croutons floating across Tati's plate. "I think she's finished, too."

"Mom sent over some pie, if you're interested."

"Maybe later."

"My hands are icky." Tati held them up for inspection.

"Yes, you may be excused. Go and wash them off."

"Okay." Having been forgiven, she dashed out of the room, banging into a stool as she went, which sent the cat's dish flying.

"I'm seeing a pattern here." Ashley chuckled at his pained glare. "Don't be such a grump. She'll grow out of it soon enough."

"I hope so," he muttered. What had seemed so appetizing before now looked like leftovers. Would a meal ever be just a meal again? Michael began clearing the table. Ashley helped, scraping plates and stacking them in the dishwasher.

He stored the leftover lasagne in the fridge, knowing he'd be glad of it tomorrow. Anything not to have to cook. He wanted every extra minute to work on his carving.

"Okay, that's enough cleaning," he told her when she finished scrubbing the counter. "Let's have some tea."

Ashley checked her watch, glanced out the window. "It's taking quite a while for the tow truck, isn't it?"

"All the more time for the grader to clear your road," he said quietly.

She nodded but the faint line of worry across her brow didn't disappear. "I guess."

"Can we play this?" Tati emerged from her room holding a game she loved that involved hippos and marbles.

"Want to play?" he asked, watching Ashley's face for signs that she was bored.

"I haven't played this for years!" She helped Tati open the game, ran a finger over the hippos' backs. "But I used to be quite good."

It was asking for trouble to let Tatiana play it now when she was tired. He'd probably spend the rest of the night hunting for marbles but Michael figured that would be worth it for the pleasure of watching Ashley relax, even giggle as she tried to beat Tatiana.

"Okay, sweetie," he said when all the marbles were safely stored inside the last hippo. "I want you to get ready for bed."

"I don't want to sleep when Ashley's here!"

Her indignant words made him smile.

"I didn't say you had to go to bed, but I want you in your pajamas. When the tow truck calls we'll take Ashley to her car."

"In my pajamas?" she asked, wide-eyed.

"Uh-huh. Until then you can stay up—as long as you can stay awake."

"Wait till Wanda hears about this!" The little girl dashed from the room.

"I'm sorry I'm keeping her up. I never intended to be here so long." Ashley picked up two stray marbles from the floor and tucked them into the box. "I must be ruining your evening, too."

"Not at all. It's nice to have the company." Normally he was loathe to give up a second of his free evenings once Tati was tucked in, but Ashley being here was different. "Do you like mint tea?"

"Yes."

He carried it through to the living room, poured her a cup and handed it to her. She stood in front of the fireplace, holding her mug, but Michael knew it wasn't because she was cold. Her gaze kept straying to the window.

"What really happened out there today?"

She turned, frowning. "I told you."

"Not all of it." He sat, waiting.

Ashley's gray eyes rested on him for several minutes. Finally she drew a deep breath, nodded. "After I went into the snowbank, a man frightened me," she admitted quietly.

"What man?"

"I don't know his name."

"What did he do?" he asked as a spurt of anger

bubbled up inside, right beside the wish to protect her.

"It's not so much what he did today," she said, her voice halting. "He just…scared me."

"I see." But Michael didn't see, not at all. She'd been terrified, had kept looking around during the entire ride home. There was more to it than she'd admitted, but he could see by her expression that she wasn't going to tell him. Not now anyway.

Tati came racing into the room in what she called her ballerina pajamas just as the phone rang. He answered, agreed to meet the tow truck in ten minutes.

"I guess it's time to go." Ashley rose, returned her cup to the kitchen and pulled on her boots. "I'm sorry to make you go out again, Mick."

"It's no problem." He bundled up his daughter, pulled on his own things and waited while Ashley drew on her kid gloves. "Ready?"

"Yes."

They drove back to her car, saying little save for Tatiana's chatter and even that didn't last long. Soon her head drooped against her seat and soft snores emanated from the back.

Michael pulled in behind Ashley's car, parked and left the motor running.

"I know it wasn't the nicest experience for you but I'm glad we could spend some time together."

"You've been very gracious." She tilted her head

to peer through the windshield. "It's getting quite cold. I'm glad I didn't have to stay out here for long."

"Ashley?"

"Yes?" She turned her head to stare at him.

"You can tell me the truth you know," he said softly. "I only want to help."

"Thank you." But she said no more.

Behind him Michael could see the tow truck coming, its lights flashing over the snow. He bit back his frustration.

"Stay here. I'll talk to him." He got out, used her keys to unlock the door and set the gearshift into neutral. Then he returned to his car, waited by the hood as the little sports car was winched free.

Ashley joined him as soon as her car broke free of the snow's embrace. Michael didn't miss her quick scan of the area nor the way she hurried toward her vehicle just a shade too fast, as if she couldn't wait to get away. He followed, waited while she climbed inside and started the engine.

"Let it warm up for a couple of minutes. I'll follow you to the end of this road, just to make sure everything's okay," he said as the truck driver removed his chain. "I'd appreciate it if you'd call me when you get home. Otherwise I'll worry that you're stranded somewhere else along the way."

"That's not necessary, really. I'll be fine. And it will take me a while to get there. You have things to do."

There it was again, that quick inspection. As if she thought someone was tailing her.

"I'm sure you'll be fine, but phone me anyway." Michael placed his hand on the door, stopping her from rolling up the window, then bent to look straight into her gaze. "Please, Ashley?"

After a moment she nodded. "Okay. Thank you for everything. Say bye to Tati for me."

"I will. Take care."

There were a lot of other things he wanted to say, but Ashley rolled up the window. As soon as she could see through the windshield she shifted into gear then moved off. Michael could do little more but follow her to the end of the road and watch as her taillights faded into the night.

Michael drove home, put Tati to bed and went to his studio. But he couldn't work. He kept seeing Ashley's face when he'd first confronted her. She'd been white, shaking. Who was this man, what had he done to her?

Michael grabbed the phone on its first ring.

"I'm here. I'm sorry it took so long. Piper phoned just as I got in the door. She was frantic and it took a while to explain."

"Is everything okay?"

"Yes, it's fine. The plow had already been through so I had no trouble."

"Good." He waited, hoping, praying she'd explain.

"Thanks for rescuing me, Mick. It's nice to have a friend." The soft words were barely audible.

But Michael heard every word and a rush of sweet joy filled him at the implication. At least they could be friends.

It was enough. For now.

Chapter Six

"We've invested so much time and effort in planning this winter festival. It's going to seem anti-climactic without the final event."

"I wish I could do something."

"Thanks, Ash. But you're doing enough." Piper folded her legs beneath her as she glared at the fireplace. "I don't understand why it's so difficult to find someone to build those sets, but without them we can't do the play."

"Are you sure?" Ashley felt sorry for her friend. Piper devoted hours of time outside of work to make sure every detail of her various publicity campaigns went off without a hitch. But despite her best efforts, this one just wasn't working out.

"The play needs those backdrops to make it fit the time period and we don't have enough in the budget to pay someone to build them." She sighed, leaned back and closed her eyes. A moment later she'd regained her equanimity. "Guess I'll have to keep praying about it. What are your plans today, Ash?"

"I have the art class at school. And there's a weaver I want to visit—Tracey. Have you met her?"

"Oh, yes." Piper's eyes sparkled. "She does excellent work. Are you still pursuing the idea of a show for the artists?"

A rush of excitement filled Ashley as she thought about the works she'd seen in the past few weeks.

"I suggested it to the art guild and they decided to sponsor an indoor sale and show during the winter festival. And why not? Their work is fantastic—so much innovation and ingenuity. It's not just the same old thing with these people. They've tons of talent and use them very creatively, but with the Bay being so isolated, they are each locked away in their own little world." She sighed. "I just wish I could get someone from the city to come out here and see what I see."

"Maybe you'll have to organize a showing yourself." Piper swallowed a last mouthful of coffee, rose and stretched before putting her cup in the dishwasher. "I've got to go for a fitting for my dress today. Want to come?"

"Yes!"

They agreed to meet at noon. Piper paused before she left.

"The panic thing—is it any better now, Ash?"

"That night—on the road, it was worse than it's

been for a while," she admitted. "In the back of my mind I think I figured I'd feel safer when I got here. It's so isolated that I guess I thought there wouldn't be any surprises in good old Serenity Bay. It's not turning out that way."

"Not all surprises are bad, Ash." Piper hugged her, then held her back, meeting her gaze. "You probably won't like me saying this, but I don't think you came here looking for safety. I think you came because you need answers and because a lot of your questions are tied up with the Bay. Can I give you a piece of advice?"

"You will anyway."

"Yes, I will." Piper smiled. "I think you have to stop looking around you and begin searching inside. God doesn't let things happen to us randomly. There's always a reason and if we let Him, He will use them to teach us. Maybe you should start asking what He's trying to teach you."

One more hug then Piper hurried off to work. Ashley pondered what she'd said, refilled her coffee and opened her Bible. But she couldn't seem to dig into any of the verses she read. They were just words, some of them she'd even memorized. But nothing spoke to the apprehensive feeling she couldn't quite suppress.

Dissatisfied, she finally closed the leather cover. A small bookmark fell out: Perfect love casts out fear.

"Either I don't have perfect love for You, Lord, or

I don't understand this verse." She thought about Michael, his quiet request for her to trust him. But she couldn't. She didn't dare, and she wasn't exactly sure why. He wasn't like Kent and in her head she knew that, but it didn't seem to matter. She had to deal with her recurring dread in her own way.

Ashley prayed for peace, but though she felt better when she'd finished, the angst, the underlying sense of disquiet remained hidden inside her heart and she knew why.

Because no matter how she wanted it to be finished, no matter the ways she'd learned or devised to chase away the fears, pretend they didn't exist, or attribute them to something else—the truth was that the man who'd abducted her all those years ago was still out there.

For years she'd kept that night locked away in her mind, refused to face it. She'd never told Rowena or Piper until recently because her parents had insisted that she'd imagined it all and she wasn't certain they were wrong.

Ashley admitted she'd been upset. Her parents' breakup, teen hormones, her grandmother's sudden death—her emotions had fluctuated wildly that year. Eventually she'd taken a psychologist's advice, which coincided with her parents', and convinced herself she'd let her too-vivid imagination take over back then, that it had all been a horrid dream. That there was no man.

Until she'd returned to the Bay, and the face had reappeared. Twice.

Now, no matter how she denied it, she had known that face, recognized his voice when he'd rapped on her window. And that couldn't have happened if it was her imagination.

So what was she supposed to do about it?

Piper would be shocked if she knew Ashley had spent the last two weeks scanning newspaper files for reports of missing or abducted children. She'd found a couple of incidents, both of which police claimed were parental abductions. But no record of another child being taken.

So was her case a fluke? Had he changed his modus operandi? Moved? Gone farther afield?

So many questions, so few answers.

Thinking about it only added to her tension, so Ashley whispered a soft plea for help, then headed for the weaver's house.

"I feel like I've hit the mother lode," Ashley exclaimed as she stared at the pieces displayed around Tracey's room. "Haven't you ever shown these?"

"I tried once. But the galleries prefer artists who've already had good showings. Except, how do you get a good showing if you can't show?" Tracey made a face.

"Vicious circle"

"It's not just that. It's such an effort to pack everything up, take it in there, then try to display it properly. Then there's the expense of finding a sitter and staying in the city while they evaluate everything." Tracey glanced at her toddler. "It's so much easier to sell them on the Internet. At least while the kids are small."

"I understand, believe me." Ashley watched her cuddle her little boy. "These times are special. You don't want to trade them for the off chance that someone will maybe let you display."

They talked about Tracey's plans for the winter festival show and about her other two preschoolers playing just outside the big picture window.

"It must be nice to allow them the freedom to play in the yard alone." Ashley watched the pair digging holes for a snow cave. No worries there.

"They're always up to something," Tracey giggled. "I have to keep my eyes on them every moment, but I will say I like living here a lot better than living in the city. I feel safer. Here everyone's so friendly. We know all our neighbors and they are only too eager to pitch in whenever I ask."

"Serenity Bay's a great place. I should know. I grew up here."

"And now you're back."

"For a little while. Until Piper's wedding and the winter festival are over. I agreed to stick around that long. Then I need to get back to work."

"But I thought you said you'd lost your job?" Tracey asked, tapping on the window and shaking her head. "See what I mean? Always into something."

"I'll get another job." After the freedom of calling her time her own, Ashley couldn't quite reconcile herself to going back to a stuffy gallery, but by the end of February she'd probably be over trekking through snow and only too ready to go back to mild Vancouver.

"Why don't you stay here? You could open a gallery, hold weekend showings when the skiers come down."

"I don't think that's going to be possible," Ashley told her.

"No, I suppose it takes a lot of money." Tracey grinned. "Can't blame a girl for trying, though. I notice you're driving a new car."

"I rented it. A friend helped me realize my other one just couldn't handle the winter roads around here." She glanced at her watch. "Speaking of roads, I'd better get on one. I'm meeting Piper for lunch. Can I take this piece?" she asked, lifting a beautiful tapestry from the table.

"If you like."

"I know exactly where I want to place it to get some shots. Then I'll contact someone I know. I promise I'll return it in mint condition."

Tracey wrapped the weaving in tissue and set it inside a box.

"Feel free to stop by anytime," she said as Ashley left. "I'm always glad to have someone older than five to talk to."

Ashley tossed a snowball at the kids, then scrambled to get into her SUV before they sent a volley of missiles back. Michael had been right, she admitted as she headed for the seamstress Piper had hired. She did feel safer driving in this bigger vehicle.

She paused at the stop light, glanced to the right. A stray sunbeam drew her attention to a rusty truck parked in front of the post office. The same truck that had stopped the day her car had gone off the road.

The horn behind her roused Ashley into action. She drove around the block for a second look, but by the time she arrived back at the spot, the truck was gone and the church bell was signaling twelve noon.

It wasn't him. She was imagining the similarity. But her hands were clenched around the steering wheel as she pulled in next to Piper's car. She sat for a few moments forcing herself to calm down before she stepped out of her vehicle and went to the door.

"Come on in," someone called.

Ashley opened the door and stepped inside the snug cottage. Emma Dickens loved everything about fabrics. Her home bore the stamp of her passion from soft yellow curtains to plump coordinated cushions to the suedelike cover on her sofa.

"It's just me," Ashley called, doffing her coat on a kitchen chair before she walked into the living room. "Wow!"

Piper stood on a stool, her white velvet dress glistening like ice crystals on snow.

"It's gorgeous, Pip."

"Isn't it?" Piper smoothed a hand over the nap. "Emma's done an amazing job."

"Well I'm glad you both like it but you're going to have to hold still if you want me to get this hem right." Emma peeked around the skirt to wave at Ashley. "Have a seat and talk to her. She's been as nervous as a kitten."

"I don't know why." Contrary to Emma's advice, Ashley moved around Piper, taking in the details. "The high waist fits like a glove, Pip. And that scooped neck is adorable."

"Do you think the sleeves are all right?" The bride-to-be wiggled to get a better look at the long sleeves. "They're not too full?"

"No. They're perfect. So is that bit of train." Ashley sank onto the sofa, thrilled by the glow that lit Piper's face. "You'll be a beautiful bride, Pip."

"Thanks. Emma made something so I'll even be cosy outside. New Year's Eve is never warm around here, and since Jason wants some pictures outdoors—" She grinned. "Show her, Em."

Emma draped a full-length, soft white, fuzzy cape lined with pure white satin and trimmed with silken ribbon around Piper's shoulders, then handed her a faux fur muff.

"Gorgeous!"

"We all have one of these," Piper explained, holding out the muff. "Aren't they cute?"

"But they don't all have one of these." Emma disappeared into a room and returned with a tiny white hat, which she set on Piper's head. A fluff of veiling tacked onto the back was perfect.

"Emma, I commend you." Ashley blinked, stunned by how well everything went together. "It looks as though Piper shopped in Paris."

"I've always wanted to do a winter wedding. Most brides seem to think summer is better, but I've always thought winter was perfectly suited to a wedding."

"I agree."

Piper glanced at her watch, shrieked. "I've got to get back to work. I've got a conference call in fifteen minutes."

"Ashley, help us," Emma commanded as she unzipped her creation.

Moments later Piper was free to dress in her street clothes.

"Now, I'll need a fitting for your dress, Ashley. I don't know what I'm going to do if you keep losing weight. I've already taken out two inches."

"Then I'll look very chic," Ashley demurred.

"You'll look like a scarecrow if you lose much more." Emma was always blunt. "Put this on." She held out a dress in midnight-blue velvet.

The style was patterned after Piper's, long and sleek as it draped around her feet.

"Look at this!" Emma scrunched up fabric at the

waist. "Can't you get this girl to eat?" she complained to Piper.

Piper had one arm in her coat, but she stopped to frown at Ashley.

"You've lost more weight? Ash, you're supposed to be getting better, not starving yourself. You'll get sick if you continue like this."

"I never was a big eater."

"You don't eat anything! You spend hours cooking for us and then poke at your own meals. What's wrong?"

"Nothing's wrong. I'll soon be eating you out of house and home, it's just taking a while to get my strength back, that's all. Hadn't you better go?" she asked, tilting her head toward the mantel clock.

"Yes. But I'm not letting you off the hook. I'll be on your case tonight, Ash, and you will eat. You can't miss my wedding."

"I won't. Now go." Ashley stood silent as Emma measured, pinned, tucked and adjusted. Then she waited a little longer while the matching cape with the iridescent white lining was fitted. "It looks wonderful, Emma. Beautiful."

"Well, I'm not unpinning this velvet again so you get some good food into you."

"You have to take the waist in. It's too big!"

"Maybe I'll do one last fit just before Christmas to make sure. Until then, get some meat on your bones, girl!"

"Yes, ma'am." Ashley changed, agreed to eat the remaining half of a chicken sandwich Emma had made for Piper. "Happy now?" she asked Emma, who made a face at her.

"I won't be happy until I get the go-ahead for those costumes for the play Piper's always talking about. It takes time to get period pieces right and if she doesn't soon get that play nailed down, I'm not going to be able to do them."

"Oh, no! But that's what makes the play come alive. We have to have your costumes."

"Then you'd better find someone who can build those sets."

Ashley mulled it over as she drove to the school to give her weekly slide show. If only Michael would do it. He kept claiming he didn't have time, but she'd seen him playing football with Jason the week after the big snowstorm had melted. If he needed help with Tati she could help.

Maybe it was time to confront him again. Maybe if he knew the play was about to be cancelled.

The boisterous but interested art class was always a fun hour, but there were so many questions that Ashley ended up entering the staff room to get her coat ten minutes after the last bell of the day had gone. Michael bumped into her on the way out.

"Hi," she said brightly, wondering how to broach the subject of the sets.

"Hey, beautiful. How'd art class go?" He grabbed his coat, thrust his arms into it.

"Don't leave yet, Masters," the principal called. "We have a staff meeting today."

"I've got to pick up Tati. I hope you don't mind if I bring her back here because it's either that or I miss the meeting. I couldn't get a sitter."

The principal frowned, but after a moment she nodded permission. "Get back fast," she ordered. "We've got a full agenda today."

"Right." He matched his step to Ashley's. "She has no idea what she's in for," he mumbled as they walked down the hall.

"What do you mean?"

"Principal Zilk likes lots of debate on everything. Tati's not good at either sitting still or being patient. I can only imagine the disaster that's about to befall Serenity Bay High. Today's skating day and my daughter does not like missing her skating."

"Why don't I take her?" The offer popped out before Ashley could even think about it, but now that it was said, she wasn't sorry. She liked Tatiana.

"You skate?" He raised one eyebrow as if he found the idea utterly impossible.

"I used to. Fairly well, actually." She could see he didn't believe her. "In fact, I started figure skating when I was five and finished at boarding school. I was a soloist for several winter carnivals and played the Sugar Plum Fairy once at Christmas."

"Well, good for you. But Tati—" He stopped, shook his head.

"Look, how hard can it be to get one little girl on the ice, Michael?"

His eyes opened very wide as he came to an abrupt halt in the middle of the hall. Teens flooded around them on either side but Michael seemed oblivious.

"You have no idea," he told her softly.

"Don't be so melodramatic. She's a little girl. I'm an adult. I can do it. You go to your meeting. I'll take care of Tatiana. When you're finished, you can come and pick us up. Around five?"

He looked stunned, but after several seconds he nodded and told her how to find the day care.

"I'll phone the lady in charge of the day care so she knows you're coming," he said.

"Good." She grinned. "You look worried. Don't. I won't let anything happen to Tati."

"Tati will be fine. It's you I'm worried about. You look like dandelion fluff that a good wind could pick up and toss across the bay. And Tati is a lot more than a mere wind."

"Oh, stop it. You're just trying to scare me." She laughed, but noticed he didn't join in. "I'll see you later," Ashley promised before turning to leave.

"Ashley," he called, just loudly enough for her to hear. She glanced over one shoulder. "Try to keep her away from the other kids, will you?"

Hard as she looked, Ashley couldn't see a glimmer

of humor in his eyes. She walked out of the school, changed from her high-heeled boots to a pair of lower ones in the car, then drove to the address Michael had given her. Tati was dressed and waiting at the door, her skates zipped inside leather bags slung around her shoulders.

"Are you really taking me skating?" she asked excitedly.

"Sure."

"Are you going to skate, too?"

"I might try. If there are some skates my size."

"They have big girls' skates at the sporting goods store. Wanda's aunt got some. Can we go there first?"

"Why not?"

Half an hour later with the white skates tied on, Ashley lifted her foot to step delicately onto the ice.

"Please don't let me embarrass myself and fall on my behind," she prayed as the blade slid out of her control.

She thought she heard God laugh.

Michael stepped inside the rink to the sound of raised voices. His protective instincts zipped up like mercury on a hot day as he rushed toward the ice. In one glance he assessed the problem.

With her usual penchant for accidents Tati had apparently taken down an entire chain of skaters— and they were not happy about it. Ashley sat on the ice as well, a pained look on her face.

"Oh, boy." He laced up his skates and took off across the ice, rushing in behind Tati to lift her off her feet and out of the path of a boy her age who looked ready to push her down—once he got back on his feet. "Hi, kiddo."

"Daddy!" She smiled and his heart sang. "Ashley and I are skating."

"I can see that." He checked Ashley's face, knew he'd arrived in the nick of time. He offered a hand to pull her up then glanced around. "You guys playing bowling or something? Why's everyone sitting down?"

"Very funny," she muttered as she dusted herself off.

Michael forced himself not to stare at the length of her legs displayed so elegantly in the black jeans. He turned instead to survey the group. "Let's try Crack the Whip. Anyone interested?"

It was a favorite because even the little ones could cling on to someone else as they formed a long chain that circled round and round the ice. Loud agreement greeted his suggestion. He set Tati down, grabbed Ashley's gloved hand and placed it into his daughter's.

"Hang on," he advised as he started the circle. More and more children grabbed on until they were turning in a giant pinwheel. Fifteen minutes later the group had completely forgotten about Tati's misadventure and he judged it safe to leave the ice.

"That was fun, Daddy."

"It was, wasn't it?" He scooped her off the ice onto a bench and began unfastening her skates until he noticed that Ashley hadn't moved an inch after sitting down. "What's wrong?"

"Nothing yet." She shifted positions gingerly on the hard bench and winced. "But I have a hunch there will be by tomorrow. Contrary to my earlier boast, I'm not quite ready for the Olympics. Ow." She closed her eyes, groaned.

As soon as Tati's feet were tucked inside her boots, she wandered over to watch the other skaters. Michael set to work on Ashley's skates, unlacing them, then easing them off her feet. A soft sigh slipped from her lips as he massaged her toes.

"Don't think this will wipe the slate clean," she told him softly, that diamond glint back in her gray eyes. "You still owe me. Big-time. You realize I probably won't be able to walk tomorrow?"

He chuckled, slid her other foot free. "Which part of you hurts the most?"

"Never mind." She drew her foot away, bent to put on her boots. "Being in a car accident doesn't even begin to compare to this."

"Are you comparing my daughter to an accident?" he joked as he put his own shoes back on.

"I refuse to answer that for fear of self-incrimination." She glanced at Tati, kept her voice low. "You might get a call tonight. A woman was here teaching her daughter to skate. Tatiana apparently knows them. She kept trying to help but—" Ashley chuckled "—I don't think it was appreciated."

"I'll handle her." He picked up the skates, slung them over his shoulder. "I can't thank you enough, Ashley. It was a boring meeting. Tati would have driven them crazy. How about if I buy you supper as a down payment on my massive debt?"

He thought she'd refuse. But after staring at him for a moment, Ashley finally nodded.

"Dinner would be nice—if they have very soft chairs."

A rush of satisfaction filled him, until she continued.

"It's about time Piper and Jason spent an evening alone together, without me playing third wheel."

Slightly deflated, he collected Tati and walked outside beside her, not realizing until they stopped that they would have too many vehicles. Ashley clicked a button and the locks on a big SUV opened.

Michael gulped.

"Boy, when you take advice, you really take advice," he said, studying the latest features on her brand-new model.

She grinned, a quick flash of humor that did amazing things to her beautiful face. "I'm a quick study," she told him. "One dump in a snowbank is enough for me."

"Can we go in Ashley's new car?" Tati asked, dragging on his hand.

Michael couldn't have said it better himself.

"Do you mind? According to the rental agreement

I have tons of mileage available and I probably won't make a dent in it." Ashley started the motor and the heater. "I could drive you back here after dinner."

He nodded. "I'll get Tati's car seat."

"Don't bother. There's a child's jump seat in the back. It's good enough to go to the restaurant and back, isn't it?" Ashley blinked. "After all, she rode over here in it."

Good point.

He nodded. "Okay. In you go, honey." He boosted her up, made sure the belt was securely fastened, then pulled open his door. "It's a great vehicle," he told Ashley, buckling his own belt.

"Where do you want to eat?"

"Pizza!" Tati chirped from behind them.

"Pizza it is." Ashley pulled out from her parking spot and drove toward the town's favorite pizza spot.

"It's not a bad choice," Michael told her. "They've got a play area for kids. She can burn off her excess energy while we talk."

"Excess energy?" Ashley blinked. "I don't think so."

"Wait. You'll see."

"What do you want to talk about?" A small frown hit her mouth.

He shrugged. "Anything." Everything about you.

They were a bit early for the supper crowd. Michael chose a table where he could see Tati, but where their conversation wouldn't be overheard.

"Is this okay?"

"Perfect." She allowed him to take her coat and hang it up with Tati's, then eased onto the plush seat.

"Soft enough?" he asked, tongue-in-cheek.

She blushed. "Yes, thank you. Doesn't it smell wonderful?"

"Trying to change the subject?"

"Yes."

Tati hurried off to play. An awkward silence fell.

"I really want—"

"You have a wonderful—"

He grinned. "Ladies first."

"I was just going to tell you how much I enjoyed being with Tatiana. She's a lovely child. So inquisitive and open to new experiences. And she just plunges into life, doesn't she?"

A crash emanated from the play area. Michael glanced over, made a face as his daughter's head appeared poking out of the ball pit.

"Like that, you mean?" He loved Ashley's smile, the way it encompassed her whole face.

"I envy her the freedom to be so abandoned."

The softly murmured words surprised him. "Why would you envy her? You're free to plunge into whatever you want, aren't you?"

She stared at him for a long moment. Finally she nodded. But a second later she changed the subject.

"What is your shop class working on now?"

"Finishing up their individual projects. There are

those students who get everything done ahead of time, those who meet the deadline and those who leave everything to the last minute. I seem to have a majority from the latter group. Hurry isn't a good thing when you're working with tools so I like to allocate some extra classroom time, just in case."

"What about the ones who are already finished?"

"They can start something new, or work with one of the others." He held her gaze, shook his head. "I do not want to talk about school, Ashley."

"Why not? Don't you like your job?"

He waited until they'd given their order to the server before answering.

"It's okay. For now."

"What would you rather be doing?"

He couldn't very well explain without looking as if he wanted her help, and at this moment in time, Michael wasn't ready to talk about his carvings. He'd read a verse in his devotions this morning about trusting God for the perfect timing. Maybe it was a hint to stop worrying about a showing next summer. He needed time to think about what that would mean to his dream.

"Michael?"

"Sorry. Got sidetracked." He pushed the doubts away. "Let's talk about you instead of me. What did you do today?"

"School. Went with Piper for a dress fitting. Went skating." She sipped her coffee. "Oh, yes, and I went to see a weaver this morning. I'm going to look for a gallery to display her work."

His heart rate quickened but Michael ignored it. "Do you think they'll agree?"

"No one has so far." She played with her spoon, her face pensive. "I'm finding a certain reluctance among many gallery owners to feature artists who don't have some previous gallery experience, or who don't come from one of the schools that teach textiles, painting, whatever. It's frustrating because the work here is so innovative. It's going to take someone with vision and commitment to see the potential. So far I haven't run into that person."

"Sounds to me like you're her, Ashley."

"Tracey said something like that, too." She leaned forward. "Why did you say it?"

"You obviously have an eye for exceptional work. You have gallery experience, I'm told. And you have an insight into how to market an artist." Michael shrugged. "Maybe you should think about starting your own gallery."

The pizza arrived, followed seconds later by Tati who was red-faced and glowering. "There's a very bad boy over there."

"Well, he can play by himself while we eat. But first you need a wash. Let's go clean up." Michael took her by the hand and headed for the bathroom. When he returned, Ashley gave him a quizzical look he couldn't interpret.

The server refilled their glasses and left extra grated cheese.

"I'm starved."

"So am I."

They finished all but the last piece. Tati begged for another go at the play area now that the miscreant had left. Michael agreed, hoping it would wear her out so sleep would come quickly tonight. He hadn't done anything in his studio for days.

"Today one of the art students showed me drawings she'd done for the sets for the winter festival play," Ashley murmured after sipping her coffee.

Uh-oh.

"She said some of your students thought they could build them with some leadership. From you."

"Ashley, I can't. I explained all this."

"I'd be willing to help you, watch Tatiana if you needed it."

He found himself considering it. Not because he needed help with Tati, though that would be nice. But he wanted the chance to know Ashley better. She intrigued him, made him think life might hold something he hadn't dared dream of again, something he never planned to risk.

He couldn't walk away from her offer.

"While we were skating, Tatiana told me about her mother. I didn't realize she was a famous ballerina."

"Carissa would have liked to hear that," he mused

aloud. "Her goal was to be a household name around the world. She hated being ill, not being allowed to dance. It was her reason for getting up in the morning." He clamped his lips together, afraid he'd said too much.

"How long has she been gone?"

"Five months." He studied her, decided it was better to get the truth out now. "Ashley, I never knew I had a daughter until six months ago."

"What?" She looked stunned.

"Carissa and I were married only a few months when she was offered a six-month contract with the Bolshoi Ballet. My dad was ill, I was in the middle of—" he looked for the right word "—studies in New York. I couldn't drop everything and follow her, but Carissa promised she'd be back as soon as the contract was over. Two months after she left, I got a letter telling me she'd made a mistake, that she wanted a divorce, that all she wanted was to dance."

"Oh my." Her eyes grew huge. "She never told you she was pregnant?"

He shook his head.

"I tried to get in touch with her, to phone her. I wrote dozens of letters. They all came back. I learned her contract with the company had been suspended, but that's all I could find out." He pushed a hand through his hair as the memory of those dark days returned. "Dad died and everything else got pushed to the back burner for a while. Then the divorce papers arrived."

"So you signed them?"

"It had been over a year. I couldn't reach her. I had no access, other than through her former lawyer." He swallowed, looked down at the table. "Besides, by then I knew she was right. We'd made a mistake."

"I'm sorry." She reached out, touched his hand.

Surprised by the voluntary contact from such a reticent person, Michael covered her hand with his, and glancing up, found only compassion on her face.

"Thanks." He sighed. "I thought it was over, that the only people we'd hurt were ourselves. I was living in New York when I happened to read a small newspaper article that said Carissa was there convalescing. I decided to visit her, to make sure she was all right, you know?"

Ashley nodded, removed her hand from his grip.

"I phoned, but her manager said she didn't want to see me. I decided to go anyway. I figured I owed her that." It still rankled. "A friend who worked at her hotel got me up to her room. I knocked on the door and this little sprite answered. It was Tati. I would have known my daughter anywhere."

"Oh, Michael." She sounded as if she understood what he'd missed, the pain that had gutted him at what he'd never been allowed to experience.

"Carissa wasn't going to let me know until after she

died. She'd married again. A man she met in Russia. Vlad was nice, rich, adored the ground she walked on, but he couldn't buy her the cure she needed."

"Cure?"

"When I saw her she was in the last stages of lung cancer. It was very aggressive. She wanted Tati with her as long as possible. Vlad was to bring her to me after Carissa died."

"But how did you— I'm sorry. It's none of my business."

"No, it's okay. It's kind of nice to explain instead of watching you imagine all kinds of weird scenarios." He checked to be sure Tati was still busy, that she couldn't overhear. "Carissa kept hoping, right to the end, that she would go into remission, find a cure, something. Vlad got her to come to New York on the pretext of seeing a specialist, but I think it was more because of Tati. He was afraid there would be problems with her custody and he wanted to honor Carissa's wish for me to take care of her."

It galled him to say it even now, months later. He pushed away his coffee cup, stretched his legs and drew several breaths to ease the tension gathering at the back of his neck.

"But why wait so long?"

He smiled but felt no mirth. "We weren't married very long but Carissa knew that if I'd known I had a daughter, I would have insisted on being with her.

If she hadn't fallen sick I'm not sure I'd ever have known about my daughter."

"I'm sorry."

"So am I. Fortunately for all of us, Tati is very accepting. She'd always called Vlad by his first name. From the moment Carissa introduced us I was Daddy."

"I'm sorry she got sick, but I don't understand her actions at all. To deny a child her father—it's awful."

"You have to understand Carissa. No one ever said no to her. She'd pushed herself up through the ranks, made herself a household name. It was hard to match wills with her." He stared at the little girl who'd lit up his life so sweetly. "But I'd have done it and more if I'd known."

"Of course you would have." She summoned a smile. "You're very lucky to have Tatiana."

"I think so, too," he said warmly, appreciating her staunch defense. "So now perhaps you'll understand why I was so defensive about being a father that day we were on the boat. I'm trying to forgive Carissa, but the whole thing still rankles a bit whenever I think of what I missed."

"No wonder." She shook her head. "Now I'm doubly sorry I said it. How thoughtless!"

"You couldn't have known." He took a deep breath, decided to risk it. "Maybe knowing our history will make you feel more comfortable. I'm not looking to dash into anything, to make another mistake. I learned that lesson the hard way. But I am looking for a friend. Can we be friends, Ashley?"

She studied him for a moment, eyes large and luminous in her pale face. He held his breath, waiting. Finally she nodded.

"I've made mistakes, too," she said softly. "I've been engaged twice, both times to the wrong man. I don't trust myself not to make another mistake, that's why I said what I did."

Michael could tell it was a big admission for her. Delighted that she'd shared as much with him, he decided to press a little further, especially since Tati was happily involved with another little girl in the ball pit.

"But your mistakes—that's not what has made you so afraid, is it?"

The soft rose flush that had tinted her cheeks a moment ago faded to white. "No."

"Can you tell me about it?" He touched her arm, turned her hand over and slid his fingers between hers. "I'm a good listener."

"It's hard to explain."

"Just start at the beginning," he encouraged.

"Something happened to me a long time ago." She stared at their entwined hands, briefly explained the almost-abduction. "It's not just that. I don't think I've ever really felt secure."

"What does that mean? Is someone after you now?"

"I'm not—"

A loud squeal interrupted. Tati. With an apologetic look, Michael withdrew his hand and went to find out the problem. His sobbing daughter stood in the middle of the ball pit, a bruise forming at one corner of her cheek.

"She fell against the edge," a woman explained. "I'm sure it won't leave a lasting mark, but according to my son's experience with the same thing last week, it hurts a lot more than it shows."

"Thanks." He picked Tati up, hugged her close after inspecting the damage. "It's only a bruise, sweetie. You're fine. And it's way past your bedtime."

"But I wanted to play some more," she sobbed against his neck.

Recognizing the signs of overtiredness, Michael didn't argue, simply carried her back to the table.

"I'm sorry, Ashley. I think it's time we went home. Can you drive us back to the rink?"

"Sure. Is she okay?"

"Just a bump."

They left quickly, arrived at the rink with little more being said. Once Tati was settled into her own car seat, Ashley leaned in to kiss her goodnight, then closed the door. She tilted her head to one side as she studied Michael.

"I enjoyed this evening," she said quietly. "Thank you."

"No, thank *you*," he said, admiring her ethereal beauty. "I'm sure falling on the ice wasn't part of your plan for today."

"It had its moments."

Michael knew what he was going to say and didn't even try to stop the words.

"Tell Piper that if she really wants, I'll build the sets. I'll make it a project for the kids. Extra marks."

"You will? Really?" At his nod Ashley grinned, reached out and hugged him. "Thank you, Michael! Thank you very much."

"You're welcome." He hugged her back, relishing the touch of her silky cheek against his.

"Oh, sorry." She drew back, her face a soft rich pink.

"Anytime," he told her with a grin. And meant it. "Maybe you could get copies of those drawings from your art student and bring them to the school shop tomorrow. We'll need to order the wood right away."

"Sure. I'll do that. Thanks, Michael." Her smile flared again. "This is so great."

Then she looked at him and her eyes held a thousand secrets as a tiny smile kicked up the corners of her mouth.

Michael wanted to prolong the moment but he needed to get home, to do some work.

"I'll see you tomorrow, then."

"Yes. See you." She climbed into her vehicle, waited for him to precede her out of the lot.

As he drove home Michael suddenly realized that only once during their time outside the rink had Ashley checked over her shoulder or scanned the lot.

Did that mean she trusted him?

Chapter Seven

"Did you have a happy Thanksgiving, Ashley?" Tati stood in the doorway, surveying her visitor. Orange icing was smeared above one eyebrow.

"Yes, I did. Thank you, honey. How about you?"

"I had two pieces of pumpkin pie."

"Two, huh? You must have been stuffed. I'm surely glad all the snow melted so we could see the pumpkin display at the library. Aren't you?"

"Uh-huh. I liked the scarecrow best."

"I liked the roosters and the sunflowers. Can I come in?"

"Sure."

Ashley followed her into the house, sniffed and wrinkled her nose. "Is something burning?"

"Don't ask," Michael told her sticking his head out of the kitchen. "We're decorating cupcakes for her class. The teacher got sick and missed their Thanksgiving party." He frowned.

"Really?" She couldn't imagine that.

"Really. But these things—" he pointed to a dozen round brown blobs perched on the counter "—aren't nearly as funny as I remember."

"What are they?" she asked, pondering the misshapen lumps.

"I think it's bad if you have to ask."

She grinned. "Sorry."

"They're pumpkins, of course." Tati looked offended. "We're going to decorate them when they cool off."

Michael winked at her. "Want to try one? I'll even ice it for you."

"Thanks, anyway, but I just had lunch."

"Hey! They're not that bad. Even I can bake a cake mix."

"I'm sure they're delicious," she offered reassuringly. "It's just that orange icing does odd things to my taste buds. Especially that particular shade of orange. If you ice them, you'll have to watch how you wrap them."

"Huh?"

"The plastic wrap will stick to the icing."

"At school the teacher uses toothpicks."

Ashley smiled. Tatiana believed she was far too old for day care so she called it school and reprimanded anyone who termed it otherwise.

"Wanda doesn't think I can bring pumpkins but I told her Daddy would do it. He builds lots of stuff."

"He sure does. And he's very good at it, too." Ashley chuckled at Michael's preening. "I was talking about the sets, not your current, er, construction."

"Be nice, Ashley." He winked, held up the spatula and let a blob of orange drop off it into the bowl. "Or I'll make you taste this."

"Eww!" She glanced at Tati who was mucking about in the sink. "Hey, what about our trip?"

"Oh, we're still going. I was just soaking the dishes. Now I'll get my jacket." She raced out of the room.

"Soaking the dishes, her clothes, the floor, the curtains."

"She's a sweetie."

"Yes, she is. And she has such faith in me. It's scary."

"Why? Every little girl thinks her daddy is invincible."

"Yeah, but what happens when she finds out I'm not?" Michael made a face at his creations. "I'm afraid I'm going to disappoint her at this tender age because other than plastering this icing on top, I don't know how to make these things look a bit like pumpkins."

"Hmm. Do you have any chocolate chips?" Ashley accepted the bag he retrieved from the cupboard, arranged a stem on the one he'd iced. "Buy some green gumdrops for leaves and you're done. The kids will probably pick them off but it looks good."

"Yeah. Good idea. Thanks." He grinned at her as if they'd achieved an impossible feat, then covered the icing and stored it in the fridge. He glanced down, grinned. "Ah, new boots for our ride on the quads. I liked your other ones better."

"I thought you said you liked the heels I had on yesterday."

"I did."

"And my sandals that I wore that day on the houseboat?"

"I liked those, too." He deadpanned an innocent look.

"You seem to notice my footwear a lot, Michael. Why *is* that?"

"No comment. Except to say that given a choice, I prefer the heels." He grinned a wolfish smile that did nice things for her ego. "Though I do understand you couldn't wear them today."

"Well, hardly." She shook her head at his teasing and tried to quash the ripple of warning that told her to be careful. Stifling it, she checked to make sure Tati had not yet reappeared. "You have heard about the cougar, haven't you?'

"Sure." He nodded. "There have been lots of stories at school about one coming down from the hills. But we've had cougars in the area before. They seldom attack people."

"Still—" She didn't want to say anymore, not with Tatiana liable to appear at any moment.

"We'll be fine, Ashley. I wouldn't endanger my daughter."

No, that was true, but it didn't help much. When Tati reappeared, Michael sent her to the basement on an errand, then walked around the counter to face Ashley. He pressed his forefinger under her chin, tilting it up so she had to look at him.

"You worry a lot, don't you?"

"I don't know what you mean."

"Really?" It was clear Michael saw right through her pitiful defense. "Your footwear isn't the only thing I notice, Ashley. When we were on the boat that afternoon, you kept checking Tati's life jacket. And your own. Over and over, as if there might be some-- thing wrong with them."

"Did I?" She looked away.

"Yes, you did. And the night you went off the road you kept looking around."

"I explained that."

"Uh-huh." He touched her arm. "But there's something you haven't told me, isn't there? That night at the restaurant you said you've never really felt secure. I've been thinking about that. It seems so out of character."

"It does?" She wondered if he'd spoken to his mother, heard her story of crazy Ashley's abduction.

"You're a strong confident woman who's lived and worked in a big city. You've handled compli- cated showings, done your job with people coming and going all the time. So I'm guessing your anxiety level went up about the time you came back to Serenity Bay, right?"

"It was already up. But, yes, something like that."

"You're *still* talking?" Tatiana stood in the doorway, hands on her hips as she glared at them. "Are we going or what?"

"We are definitely going. I'll just get us a couple of drinks and some snacks," Michael told her.

"Don't bother. I have some stuff in my backpack." His surprised look made Ashley chuckle. "Seems only fair. You provide the wheels. I take care of the munchies."

"I'm good with that." He grabbed his jacket and a couple of thick wool blankets from a closet.

"What are those for?" she asked, following him outside and watching as he tucked them into the box on the back of his quad.

"You're not the only one who can surprise."

"Oh?" Ashley swallowed. He couldn't know but she wasn't big on surprises. "It might be better to prepare me."

He shook his head. "You'll just have to wait and see."

She could hardly stamp her foot and demand to know. Besides, Michael was clearly delighted with his little secret. A crooked smile tugged at his lips and his eyes glinted with mischief.

Ashley shoved back the apprehension. Michael was one of the nice guys. He didn't pretend to be what he wasn't. His confidence in himself extended to his relationships with other people. He gave and expected honesty. Pretty soon he was going to press her for details and she'd have to explain or push him away.

But just as she hadn't told him the whole truth about her fears, Ashley was beginning to realize there was something he hadn't shared, either. He'd taken the plans for the sets and she knew the kids had begun to work on them, but Michael didn't spend weekends at it, as she'd expected.

Not even when Tati had gone with his mother last weekend to see a puppeteer.

So what had he been doing?

"Ashley?"

"Yes?" She blinked, realized he'd been speaking to her.

"I asked if you'd ridden one of these before."

She glanced at the machine, shook her head.

"It's really quite easy." He demonstrated how the controls worked, then moved so she could take his place. "Go ahead, try a practice run. Just don't accelerate too fast."

Michael took Tati's hand, waiting with her on the side of the yard while Ashley practiced using the levers to start and stop around the yard. She'd assumed turning would be difficult but was able to manipulate the vehicle in sharp angles with little trouble. A silly sense of achievement rushed through her as she pulled to a stop in front of him.

"I did it!"

Michael grinned. "I'm guessing you're ready to go, then?"

"Yes."

"I want to ride with Ashley," Tati squealed, trying to squeeze in behind. Her father grasped her by the waist and set her on the ground.

"No, honey. We'll give Ashley a chance to get used to riding before we put a wiggling bundle of energy behind her. You ride with me. We'll talk about changing later."

For one rebellious moment her chubby face squinched up tightly and she opened her mouth to argue.

"Or I could ask Wanda's mom if you can stay with them while Ashley and I go by ourselves," he added.

Knowing how Tatiana and Wanda competed, Ashley suspected the little girl had been bragging to her friend about the planned outing. Sure enough, Tati climbed onto her father's four-wheeler without another word. Michael winked at Ashley.

"Ready to go?"

"You're sure we have lots of gas?"

He rolled his eyes. "Ashley, Ashley. When will you learn to trust me? There's a spare can on the back of your bike, just in case. Satisfied?"

Feeling chastened, she nodded.

"Try to keep up. You don't have to be right on my

tail, but don't get too far behind, either. I'll try to keep an even pace, but sometimes there are rocks or branches I can't go over. Keep your eyes peeled in case I have to stop quickly. Also, watch for branches. They could snap back and catch you."

"Got it."

They set off following a winding path out of the yard, moving at a steady clip. After several miles Ashley pushed her sunglasses to the top of her head. There was no need for them here in the forest where the sun barely skimmed the forest floor, thanks to massive pine and spruce boughs overhead. She inhaled the fresh scent, ordered her brain to relax.

After they'd crossed a particularly rough part, Michael pulled into a glade near a bubbling stream. Ashley drove in beside him, realizing as she climbed off that her legs were a bit stiff from pressing against the center of the seat. "I thought we'd take a break," he explained as he lifted Tati off.

"I want a drink, Daddy."

From her backpack, Ashley removed two thermoses of hot chocolate, a container of cookies and several disposable cups which she set on a huge stone by the water. As a table it worked perfectly. Better yet, it sat in the middle of a warm pool of sunshine.

"Here, Tati," she said as she poured a cup half full. She waited until the little girl was seated on the boulder then handed her the cup. Pulling napkins out of her bag, she laid one on the stone and set the cookies on top.

"Thank you." Tati munched away happily. "It's just like a picnic."

"Yes, it is." Michael accepted his cup and cookies, sat down beside her. "Hot chocolate was a great idea. It's cooler than I realized out here."

"I thought maybe we'd see some animals," Ashley admitted after sipping her own drink. "But I suppose the sound of the motors scares them away."

"We might see something yet." He had that twinkle in his eye again.

"I didn't spill anything," Tati said happily. She held out her cup. "May I please have some more?"

"Sure." Ashley refilled the cup half full. "But spills don't really matter out here, honey." It wasn't the first time she'd wondered about Tati's fretting over accidents. Now that she knew some of her history, she suspected that living in hotel rooms and moving among ballet costumes would have offered an open invitation to accidents for such an active little girl.

"Spills don't matter anywhere," her father championed. "We just clean 'em up and move on. Can you hear that blue jay calling?"

Tati listened, nodded, her brown eyes bright. "And a robin, Daddy. How come they haven't flown away yet?"

"They will pretty soon. It's getting cold at night and robins don't hang around for snow."

"Do they go to Hawaii, like Ashley did?"

Michael laughed. "Not that far."

"Oh."

Silence fell, save for the twittering of birds high above them and the forest sounds that Ashley couldn't identify. Noticing that Michael had closed his eyes and lain back against the warm stone, she took the opportunity to scour the area for a sign that someone or something had followed them. She saw nothing.

Ashley leaned against a tree and allowed herself to relax just the tiniest bit. With Michael nearby she was safe.

"Mommy didn't like snow, either. She said it's messy. Is there snow in heaven, Daddy?"

The yearning underlying that query touched Ashley's heart so she knew it had to hit Michael hard. To his credit he didn't show anything but love as he lifted Tati off the stone and cradled her in his arms.

"I don't know, sweetheart. But I'm positive Mommy's not cold. Heaven's a beautiful place and God wouldn't let your mommy get too cold or too hot."

"Just right. Like the little bear's porridge, right, Daddy?"

"Exactly right!" He tickled her until she was wiggling with delight, her squeals echoing around them. "Now finish up that cookie because we've got to show Ashley the secret, but don't tell!"

Tatiana shook her head, her eyes huge. She stuffed the rest of the cookie into her mouth as if to keep herself from talking, then held up her hands, palms outward.

"Sticky," was the only part Ashley understood.

"Fortunately for you, Miss Tati, we have the means to fix that." Michael carried her to the stream, held her so she could dip her hands into the water. She dried them against his pants, leaving brown streaks from the chocolate chips.

"Sorry. I should have rethought the cookie choice," Ashley murmured as he helped her gather their things.

"Why? It's a trip into the woods." He glanced down, shrugged. "I can wash my jeans later."

Five minutes later they were back on the trail, penetrating deeper into the forest. The gloom, the shadowy undergrowth, the flick of branches against her legs—all of these things contributed to Ashley's unease. She struggled to concentrate on her driving. Michael was there, she reminded herself over and over. He could be counted on if needed.

Finally they stopped at the edge of a clearing. Michael climbed off his bike, motioned with one finger across his lips for them to be quiet. He took Tati's hand. Ashley followed as he led them to the base of a tree and pulled on something. A rope ladder cascaded down.

He helped Tati up the first rung, waited till she'd climbed all the way, then motioned for Ashley to go next.

They were standing beneath some kind of a platform. Obviously they were going to sit up there. But why? She frowned at him.

"You wanted to see wild animals. If we're very quiet we may see a bear or two today. A friend of mine told me about a big brown mother that's been bringing her cubs here to eat the berries." His words brushed against her ear so softly she doubted Tati heard a thing. "Wait. I'll get your backpack. We can't leave any food down here."

He retrieved the pack and the blankets, passed them up, then swiftly followed Ashley up the ladder. Tati, who'd obviously been there before and knew the rules, stood quietly as she waited for him to prepare their seats. Then she snuggled into her father's lap.

It wasn't just a platform. It was a sort of box with a wide window that offered a perfect view of the clearing. The roof extended to give protection from the elements, the plywood sides kept out the wind. They could sit up here and observe without being observed.

"Look!"

Ashley followed his pointing finger, saw a big brown bear ambling out of the woods beyond. Twigs and branches snapped under her massive paws but she paid them no mind. Her attention was on a bush loaded with dark purple berries.

"Babies!" Tati's gasp burst out as two chubby cubs twice her size followed their mother.

Mama Bear paused a moment, glanced around as if to check on their safety, then went back to eating the berries, joined seconds later by her greedy children.

The animals were fascinating to Ashley who'd never experienced them in a setting like this, perched up high with no fear for her safety. It wasn't until the cubs moved away and began tumbling on the ground that she noticed a gray shadow lurking behind the trees.

Without thinking she grabbed Michael's arm, pointed.

"Yes, I've been watching him," he murmured. "He's checking out the cubs. He's downwind, so that Mama can't smell him yet."

The cougar remained crouched, frozen in position. Ashley's nerves stretched tautly as she waited for something to happen. A memory flickered, her father's quiet voice. *She was only eight, no contest for a hungry cougar.*

A child had been attacked on the outskirts of Serenity Bay one year, causing an uproar in town. Search parties had combed the hills trying to find the cat and put it down before it claimed another victim. But Ashley couldn't recall whether or not the cougar had been found.

Suddenly the cat moved—just slightly, but it was enough to alert the cubs' mother. She swung around, tilted back on her hind legs and let out a yowl of anger. Her giant paws, claws extended, swiped through the air as the cubs darted behind her.

Tatiana's eyes grew huge as she watched the drama before them. For her sake Ashley hoped the cat would leave.

It didn't. Not immediately. But after prowling the edge of the glade, the cougar finally slunk away. Shortly after that the bears left, too.

Silence fell.

"Not a bad afternoon's entertainment," Mick murmured in her ear some time later. "You can let go now, if you want. Or do you need a hug?" His eyes twinkled with teasing.

Ashley blushed, realizing that had she gripped his arm at some point during the melée and was still clinging to him as if he were her life preserver.

"Sorry." She released him and moved back.

"Don't be. About the hug—"

She shook her head, reprimanding him visually. "I'm fine, Michael. But thank you for offering."

"Not a problem."

His gaze held hers, transmitting an unspoken message that only emphasized the zap of connection she always felt humming between them. The knowledge that he'd read her so easily brought back her blush.

Tati scrambled upright. "Are we going home now, Daddy?"

"I think it's time. It will be dark in a couple of

hours." He gathered up his blankets and Ashley's backpack, climbed down the ladder then waited for them to follow.

Once they were all on the ground, he returned the ladder to its hidden position and walked beside Ashley to the quads with Tati skipping ahead.

"Amazing, isn't it? God's creatures cohabiting with one another, working out the parameters of their relationships. It always makes me wonder why we humans, who are supposed to be the brains on this earth, can't find a better way to live together."

"Maybe it's because we don't all go by the same rules," she murmured as she scanned their surroundings. Shadows, movements, branches swaying—she felt as if a thousand hidden eyes were watching.

"Ashley?" His hand on her arm made her jump.

"Sorry." She faked a smile. "Guess I'm a little nervous."

"There's no need to be. We're perfectly safe. The cougar is gone. I doubt he'd attack a group of three anyway."

"There were three bears," she pointed out.

"Yes, but he didn't attack and even if he had, he would have waited till he'd isolated one of the cubs from its mother, not taken on all three."

She frowned as he stored his blankets in the box of his four-wheeler. "You sound very knowledgeable."

"My father liked to hunt. He taught me to shoot, but after a while he tired of the killing and preferred to take pictures. He'd take me with him to spend a day snapping shots of animals that he sold for postcards. I learned a lot about animal habits, reactions and interactions from those trips with him."

"I would have been terrified to be there with only a camera for defense."

"Animals sense fear, Ashley. If you ever come face-to-face with a bear, don't turn your back or run."

"If my legs would work that'd be my first instinct."

"No." He grasped her shoulders. "You stand your ground, face them and yell at them to go away. If challenged, most of the time an animal will back down unless it's hurt or starving. But if you turn away or run they know you're afraid and they'll attack because they sense a weakness."

"Sounds like some people I've met," she muttered darkly, easing out of his grasp.

"In a way, I think it is a reflection of life. You can't get anywhere if you're afraid to take a risk." Michael's attention seemed focused on some distant feature. "My dad taught me a lot about life during those hours together. Remembering is what helped me after he died."

"I know what you mean. I have some good memories of when my father taught me to swim. No way he was going to live beside a lake with a kid who couldn't keep herself afloat for at least a little while." Ashley smiled, but couldn't shake the sense that someone, or something, was watching them.

Michael touched her arm, waited till her gaze met his. "What is it?"

"I'm not sure I can explain it."

He nodded. "You need to figure out what's causing this fear and try to get past it."

"You don't think I've tried?" She gave him a half smile that was less than heartfelt. "Don't fuss about me, Michael. It's just a silly case of nerves, probably a result of living in the noisy city. I'll get over it. Or I'll leave here and return to my habitat and it won't matter."

She could tell he didn't buy it, but he said no more except to call Tati from her exploration of the denuded berry bushes. The ride home seemed shorter to Ashley. With every mile she lost a little of her jitteriness and relaxed.

By the time they reached his house, Tatiana was noticeably weary. Michael had left meat stewing in a slow cooker and he insisted Ashley share it. Tati fell asleep at the table, her head drooping onto the side of her plate. A pang of sadness echoed inside Ashley at the soft little whisper of "Mommy" when Michael picked her up.

"I'll just be a minute tucking her in," he said. "Don't rush away."

Ashley cleared the table, put the dishes in the dishwasher and stored the remaining food, noting that none of them had seemed very hungry even though they'd been out in the fresh air all day.

After setting the kettle to boil, she wandered into the living room to peer at the row of snapshots he'd lined up on a coffee table. They were all unposed shots of Tati. Mick had caught her happy little smile as she carved a pumpkin, the way the tip of her tongue stuck out when she concentrated on skating, her saucy stance, hands clamped on her hips as she glared at another little girl who looked equally determined. Ashley guessed that was Wanda.

"What do you think?"

"I think that if you want to give up teaching you could probably make a good living doing portraits of kids. These are perfect."

"Easy subject," he said, moving to stand beside her.

"Yes, she is." She turned, but his hand on her arm stopped her. "I should get home." She glanced at him, meeting his stare.

"Ashley, you know there's something there between us. Every time I talk to you, every time I get within a hundred feet of you, it's as if I can feel you pulling me toward you. And we both know it's more than friendship." He reached up, drew a strand of hair from her eyes. His voice dropped to a husky drawl.

"When I'm supposed to be teaching, I'm thinking about you. When I'm reading Tati a story about one of her fairy princesses, I think of you, how your cheek curves, how your hair looks with the light sparkling on it." He leaned closer, touched her lips with his thumb. "You have to feel it, too."

"I do feel it." The whisper slipped out in spite of her determination to remain silent. "I don't want to, but I do."

"You don't want to? Why not?" Understanding dawned; he frowned. "It's because I was married. Because I have Tati?"

"It's because you're dangerous," she corrected, wishing she'd never made that stupid comment to Piper.

"Dangerous—me?" He blinked. A quirky smile tugged at his mouth. "Don't you like to play with fire?"

He was teasing but Ashley was deadly serious.

"No." She shook her head. "I don't do danger, Michael. In fact, I run as far the other way as I can."

"Why?" His fingers moved to brush against her cheek and into her hair.

"Because I'm afraid."

"Of what?" he asked on a whisper. "I'm not going to hurt you."

"No, you're not," she agreed softly, stepping back so his hands dropped away. "Because I won't let you. I c-can't."

Moments stretched between them as he struggled to decipher her meaning. Finally he motioned to the armchair.

"Will you explain that to me, please?"

Ashley perched on the edge of the cushion, wishing she'd gone straight home. But she was as bad as he was—she dreamed about Michael, thought about Michael, imagined Michael.

It would have to stop.

"You're a kind, generous man who deserves to have love and happiness in his life, but I can't be more than your friend, Michael."

He studied her, brow furrowed. "Okay. Can you tell me why?"

"I don't know." It was so hard to put into words. "I'm not…normal."

"Agreed." He smiled at her glare. "Go on."

"I've been engaged twice."

"Ashley, I don't care about your past."

"But you have to. Because it's made me who I am now. It's the reason—" she stopped, regrouped. "I was engaged to a man who was a good friend. I'd known him a long time. I wanted that marriage, wanted it badly. I'd planned my life around being married to him. Then I found out he was in love with someone else, that he was afraid to tell me about her."

"That sounds cowardly."

"It wasn't." She smiled. "It was decent and honorable and very kind of him to believe he had to honor his commitment to me. But it was wrong and I knew it. I broke our engagement off immediately, told him I wanted him to marry the woman he loved, that I intended to be there for his wedding. And I was."

"That took guts." He kept watching her. "Then you were engaged a second time?"

"Yes." She sighed. "Not such a decent and honorable choice this time. I think I knew I'd made a mistake almost immediately but the accident forced me to accept that marriage between us would not work."

He waited and when she said no more, he hunkered down in front of her, clasped her hands in his. "Why did you tell me that, Ashley?"

"So you'd understand."

"Understand that you'd been hurt? That you'd made mistakes. That's part of life."

"That's not what I meant." She stared into his clear brown eyes and prayed for help.

"What *did* you mean?"

"I'm a coward, Michael. I'm afraid of life. I hung on to Parker even though I knew he didn't love me because I was afraid that if I didn't marry him, I'd be left alone. With him I was protected. I didn't have to fear."

"But you figured out it was wrong. You corrected your mistake."

"No, I didn't." She sighed, wishing—but it had to be said. "I latched on to Kent, ignored all the warning signs and told myself somebody was better than nobody. I lent him money, I covered for him, I even lied for him." She hung her head in shame.

"Because you loved him."

She raised her head, met his gaze. "No. Because I *needed* him. As long as I was with him, I wasn't alone. It took a car accident to force me to realize that Kent didn't want *me*. He wanted what he thought he could get from me and he was willing to do anything to get it—even put me in danger."

"What he could get from you?" He looked confused.

"My grandfather left me money. A lot of money. Kent wanted it."

"So you dumped him. Good." He grimaced. "I've made mistakes, too."

"I'm not talking about mistakes." She rose, stepped away from him. "I came to Serenity Bay to heal. Well, in order to really heal what's inside, I'm realizing that I have to learn how to face life without fear."

"You're afraid a relationship between us will turn you into that needy person again, is that it?"

"That's part of it," she admitted softly. "The other part is that you have to be here for your daughter. She needs stability and that comes first. I understand that, I admire that about you and there's no way I would ask or even want you to change that. Tatiana belongs with you."

"Yes, she does. But that doesn't mean—"

"Yes, it does. Because first and foremost you are

Chapter Eight

You have to be crazy to have let yourself be talked
o this, Masters."

Michael glared at the jagged edges of poorly sawn
ywood that were supposed to represent the
rthern lights. Somebody wasn't very good with a
saw. He'd have to fix it. Grumbling to himself, he
t fall against the floor with a loud clap.

Obviously I'm as looney as they come."

think that's a bad sign."

e jerked around, grimaced at Ashley's laughing

nswering yourself, I mean. Talking to yourself
fectly normal."

eally?" He was content to stand there and
his fill.

ybe you need to think about a holiday, Michael."

u tell me where and when and I'll be there,"

her father and she needs you." She stepped in front
of him, cupped his cheek in her hand. "You have a big
heart. You want to help everyone and you think you
can make me better, scare all the bogeymen away for
me. I love you for thinking that, but you can't do it."

"Why?"

"Because I have to figure out my life on my
terms." She leaned her head against his chest and let
him hold her, just for a moment. The words poured
out of their own accord. "The truth is, I've lived in
the shadow of fear for years."

"But how—"

"I managed it. In Vancouver I had my life mapped
out, every step of my day was thought out in delib-
erate detail to cover every eventuality. I thought I was
safe, but now I realize I missed really living. And I
want to."

"Tell me what you want from me."

She leaned back, stared into his eyes.

"I want a friend." She pressed a finger against his
lips, shook her head. "I know you want more, but for
now that's what I need most. And that's all I can give."

"Then that's what you've got." He bent his head
and pressed his lips against hers in a kiss so soft and
gentle it made her want to weep. Then he let his arms
fall away and took a step back.

Ashley watched him, aching to be held, to be protected, yet knowing it wasn't enough.

"I'm here whenever you need me, Ashley. I'll

gladly come if you call, I'll do whatever you ask. But most of all I'll pray for you."

Pray? She hadn't expected that.

"I think you coming home to Serenity Bay is part of God's plan. I don't think it's an accident that God brought us both here to begin again. I don't know what He's got planned, but I do know He wants you to be able to trust Him completely, that your life will only be complete when you stop worrying and start depending on Him. That's what I'm going to pray for. I think we should start right now."

And before she could protest he closed his eyes and began to ask God to show her His love and care. When he was finished Ashley knew she had a lot of thinking to do.

"Thank you," she whispered.

Michael simply smiled, helped her into her coat, handed over her gloves, then waited while she pulled on her boots.

"I'm glad you told me," he said quietly before she opened the door. "Maybe that's the first step to facing whatever you have to face."

"Maybe. Goodnight, Michael. And thanks."

As she drove to Piper's, Ashley automatically slipped into planning mode. Where should she live, what should she do? How could she get past the fear that a future full of unknowns held?

As quickly as the questions came and the worry rose up to choke her, she shoved them away.

"God has not given us a spirit of quoted out loud.

She said it over and over, all the way she tried to believe it.

he muttered, embarrassed that she'd overheard him complaining.

"Christmas isn't that far away."

"Now you sound like Tati." He moved the pieces so they were lined up in sequence. "Does this look right to you?"

"No." She stepped nearer, pulled a paper out of the file she was carrying. "You're missing a section." She held out the paper for him to see.

"That's Marc. I figured his project would take longer than anyone else's. He's not exactly organized. What are you doing here?" He dusted off his hands while his eyes feasted on the woman who hadn't been out of his thoughts for more than half an hour, even though he hadn't seen her in two weeks.

According to Jason, Ashley had taken a trip to Toronto to try to drum up gallery interest in her artists. He couldn't help but wonder how she'd done.

"Checking on your progress. The kids have already started rehearsals. The drama teacher is delighted with the script. He's got a mixture of local talent helping him." She frowned, touched her finger to the end of his nose, showed him the sawdust. "A new fashion statement?"

"Nothing close to yours." He admired the jade-green suit she wore and the high black boots that did great things for her legs. "What's the occasion? My art teacher never dressed like you."

"No class today. I'm working on something else. Something I came to ask your help with."

Michael heard the hesitation and ignored it. "Shoot."

"I need you to look at a house."

"A house?" He raised one eyebrow. "Why?"

"Because I'm thinking about buying it."

"Wow! What brought this on?" She was going to live here permanently? His heart swelled.

"I struck out in Toronto, Montreal, Vancouver and New York. And it makes me furious."

She looked steamed. Her silver-gilt hair danced over her shoulders shooting out sparks where the light hit it.

"They wouldn't agree to a full-scale show," he guessed.

"Not for the weavings, the paintings, the stained glass. Not even all together. Nobody will do more than take a couple of pieces on a trial basis." She flopped down on an upturned crate, her gray eyes steely. "Not a visionary among them. Philistines!"

"I see." Been there, done that. Which made thoughts of his own showing next summer seem an impossibility. "And buying a house will help you because—?"

"I'm going to turn it into a gallery," Ashley said. Her chin jutted out as if she expected an argument. "At least I think I am. If you'll tell me whether the thing is stable and worth renovating. Will you?"

The excitement of her project radiated from her,

lighting her face from within. She'd obviously come to a decision and was now plunging full speed ahead. But Michael couldn't help wondering if she was running into something, or away from something.

"Ashley, I'm not an architect or an engineer," he warned. "You should have the structure checked by a professional."

"I will, after I hear your opinion." Her big gray eyes studied him. "Will you do it? If you'd rather not be involved, just say so."

"Sure, I can look. No problem. I'm just not sure my opinion is worth anything." He dusted off his clothes.

"It is to me," she said quietly.

Michael froze. There it was—an almost-admission that she wanted him in her life—as more than a friend?

"Just look at it, listen to my ideas, and then tell me if you think I'm nuts. That's all I'm asking. P-please?"

The tone of her voice, that soft wobbly note that told him she was having second thoughts, that's what did him in.

"When?"

"Whenever you want."

There was no way he could turn her down, not when she wore that look—the same one Tati got when she begged for another bedtime story.

"We could go now. School's almost out and I don't have a class this period."

"That would be great." Her eyes shone with anticipation. "I'll drive."

"Okay." He had to go back to the staff room to retrieve his coat so he met her in the parking lot. "You're excited about this, aren't you?"

"Yes. For the first time in a long time I feel like I'm being proactive instead of reacting."

"That's good." He noted where they were going, frowning when she turned down a familiar lane. "Isn't this—" Michael paused when she stopped in front of her childhood home.

"I have a kind of love-hate relationship with this house," Ashley explained as she switched off the motor. "When I wasn't here, I wanted to be, and when I got here in the summer, it didn't feel like I thought it should. After a while it became oppressive, the source of bad memories. When my father died, I was glad to sell it."

"But now you want it back?"

"I want to start changing the bad memories, make them into something good."

Michael got out of her vehicle, followed her up the path. He did a quick appraisal of the area as she unlocked the door.

"It's a residential neighborhood. The town council might have something to say about rezoning it for your purposes."

"I've already asked Jason about that. I thought that as mayor he'd know the ins and outs."

"You've thought this through, I see."

"A bit." She grinned. "Since it's a cul de sac, Jason thinks the council probably won't kick up much of a fuss, especially since I intend to buy the lots on either side for parking."

"Big parking lot," he mused.

"I have some other ideas but I'll tell you about them another time." She grasped his arm, drew him into the house. "Imagine this as a big open space. Those walls will come down, of course."

She went on, pointing out changes she'd make, indicating special spots she'd dedicate to sit and look at specific works. Michael followed, trying to visualize through her eyes.

"The kitchen will stay, altered of course, but I want to make it an area where different artists could come and demonstrate, hold a workshop or speak to those interested while others come and go through the rest of the place. If there's a reception or something for a showing it will be handy."

"Good idea."

Ashley walked forward, pushed open a door and waved a hand.

"I'm going to extend this toward the water, screen part of it in." She went on and on, describing a variety of activities that could all be held within the confines of the house.

As they moved through it, Michael checked for repairs that would be needed.

"I could have kids' classes down here," she said, stepping downstairs.

The basement seemed solid, no foundation problems. The second floor seemed equally solid though the roof in one room gave him pause.

"I think you might need new shingles," he murmured, running one hand over the yellow stained plaster. "And someone to fix this."

"Yes, I saw that the other day. I think the bathrooms will have to be redone, too, especially if I intend to stay."

"You'll live here?" he asked, amazed that she'd even consider it.

"I have to live somewhere. I don't want to be at Piper's after she's married. Besides, there's plenty of room here."

"Yes, there is." He studied her, noted the way her fingers gripped the doorknob. She was putting up a brave front, but it was obvious the thought terrified her. "I think it would probably take a while to do the work here. I'm sure Piper and Jason wouldn't mind you staying."

"*I'd* mind. Newlyweds need privacy."

"True." He followed her to the room at the back. She waved a hand.

"This is my room."

"From when you were a child?"

She nodded. "I used to sit in this window seat and dream. Or paint. I've drawn those hills a hundred times."

"They are beautiful," he agreed.

Michael studied the view with her, finally touching her arm. He waited until she faced him.

"This is a really big commitment, Ashley." The sunlight flooding the room turned her hair into a cloud of silver-gold. "Not just of money but of time. Are you sure you want to do it?"

"I have to." Her voice cracked, but she cleared her throat, kept going. "I realize now that I can't go back to the city. Not until I'm free."

That shocked him. "Free of what?"

"Well, I'm still figuring that out." A funny crooked smile touched her lips.

Michael leaned forward, pressed his lips against her forehead, tapped her chin with his fist.

"Good for you." He stepped back. "As far as I can tell the house looks solid, but I'd have someone check it thoroughly before you sign anything. You'll probably want assurances on the rezoning first, too."

She nodded.

"Probably. But I *am* going to buy this house, Michael. If the gallery doesn't work out, I'll move in, live here, make it my home. For a while anyway."

"Why is this house so important to you, Ashley?"

Her shoulders went back, her face tightened. Those big gray eyes, usually so troubled, now seemed to clear.

"I think because this is where it started. It's the first link in the chain, Michael. It's one of the things I've attached negatives to."

"How?" Maybe talking about it would help.

"I thought I was secure here. Then one day everything changed." She sank down on the window seat. "My parents' divorce came as a great shock to me. I knew we didn't live the same as everyone else, but somehow I never twigged on to just how different my family's lives were. Since I've come back to the Bay, I've begun to realize that I never really dealt with my own feelings about their split."

"Because?"

"Good question. Maybe because I was too busy worrying about them." She frowned. "My father seemed like the victim to me. He had nobody else, no other family. He traveled too much to have many close friends. He used to say Serenity Bay was the only place he'd ever retire. It's sad he didn't get to do that."

"You felt guilty because you left him here alone."

"Yes." She blinked quickly to clear the tears that glazed her eyes. "I know I couldn't live here by myself when he was gone. And I really did enjoy school. Rowena and Piper made it fun. Then summer would come."

"They came back here with you, though." He had a hunch he knew what was going on beneath the flawless makeup but Michael probed anyway in hopes of helping her clarify her thoughts.

"We all came back. And we had wonderful times. But for me it was a kind of game, a way to erase the pain of my broken family. I used to pretend I was like Rowena, coming home to my dad."

"But it wasn't the same?"

"No." She stared out the window, pensive. "Rowena's father went away every winter to work in the oil fields. She didn't have a mother. I did."

"So when you were with him you felt guilty?"

She nodded.

"And when I wasn't here I felt guilty. He took the summers off. For two months I was the center of his life, he was here whenever I needed him."

"And you didn't like that?"

"Oh, I loved it, because for a little while I could pretend everything was okay." A tremulous smile lifted her lips. "I adored feeling protected, wanted. More than that, I loved seeing him relax. His face would lose its lines and he'd start to laugh—until the day I had to leave and the sadness returned. Every time I said goodbye I felt like I was abandoning him."

"Ashley, I'm sure your father didn't think that."

"I know. But I did and that's the problem." Ashley traced an invisible line on the window, her voice so quiet he had to lean in to hear.

"Piper's grandparents would take us to school. I'd stand in the living room, in his arms, holding on as long as I could. Then he'd kiss me goodbye and I'd walk out the door and reality would smack me in the face. I was alone again. On my own."

"But you didn't let it hold you back. You went to school, finished your training."

She nodded. "Yes. I *managed* very well. Maybe too well. I'm still managing."

He didn't know what to say, how to help her. So Michael kept up a silent vigil of prayer while he waited for her to continue.

After a while Ashley sighed, offered him an apologetic smile.

"I'm sorry. This must all sound rather silly to you."

"Silly? No. It sounds like a child who did what she had to do to get through her life." He knelt in front of her, took her hands. "There's no shame in that, Ashley. The thing you have to focus on is moving ahead. Getting past whatever has held you back."

She nodded.

"I'm trying. And that's why I want this house." She grasped his hands with hers. "Listen. I was painting this morning and I had the television on. There was a woman speaking. Something she said clicked with me."

This mattered, he could see it in the flash of inner fire that altered her eyes from gray to silver.

"She quoted a Bible verse about walking by faith. And then she said that when we walk in faith we take one step, then another step, then a third. It's a progression, facing each thing and believing God will get us through that, then facing the next one."

"That's true."

"She said faith isn't a big enlightenment we get that lifts us up like a magic-carpet ride and takes us to better things. It's staying in the program, even when it gets rough, believing God will make it better and pressing on."

The clarity of that intrigued him, made him consider his own situation.

"She ended with that verse that says without faith it is impossible to please God. That got me thinking about my faith." Ashley drew her hands from his, motioned around the room. "This house was full of pain because I endowed it with those feelings."

"How does that tie in with faith?" He didn't get where she was going.

"When I get up in the morning questions run through my mind—what if this happens? What if that comes about? That's fear. They're little threats I've been feeding myself for years. If I'm not careful about this, something bad will happen. If my parents divorce, my life will be ruined. If I leave, my dad will suffer."

Her face glowed with newfound knowledge. Michael could see confidence growing in the way her body stance changed. She was beautiful.

"I taught myself to believe the worst would happen and then the panic started. Even when I should have moved on from the divorce I couldn't because I let the fear remain and it kept growing."

He'd never thought of it that way, but now Michael began to apply her ideas to his own life. Is that what he was doing—letting doubt make it impossible to reach his own goal by suspecting God's will for him?

"The fear came because my thinking was wrong, not because what I felt was true." Her eyes widened, she stared at him.

"So what you're saying is—"

"I've let myself believe lies. I told myself lies and I believed them because I was afraid of what might happen. And I think I know why."

"You want to share?"

"Yes, though it might sound jumbled."

"Don't worry about that. Just talk."

In her excitement, Ashley rose, paced across the room and back.

"When I was eight my grandmother came to visit one summer. It was the only time. My parents must have been having problems even then because I recall my mother weeping a lot whenever Dad was gone."

"Go on."

"One night I couldn't sleep. We were having a heat wave that summer. I don't remember where Dad was, but he wasn't home. I could hear voices. Mom and my gran were on the back deck talking— my window was open. I sat on the window seat and listened to them." She jerked to a stop. Her whole body went still.

"Are you okay?"

"Yes. No." She peered at him through the waning light. "Gran was talking."

"About what?"

She looked at him, her face pale. "I don't know. I only remember she said, 'It will ruin Ashley's life, tear apart her world. She'll never recover.' I was so scared. I got back into bed and lay there awake for a long time."

She paused, stared at him.

"I kept expecting something bad to happen. Maybe my parents were sick or I was. But nothing happened. Not all summer. I left for school dreading leaving here."

"And that's when the fear first began?"

"I think so." She stared into the distance, remembering. "I wrote tons of letters that winter. Everything seemed okay. Time went by. Nothing changed—nothing I noticed."

"Maybe you didn't want to."

"Maybe. Anyway, I remember I came home for Easter. I was thirteen that year. That's when they told me." Her face lost all color. "It was the same day that a man grabbed me, t-tried to abduct me."

"It's okay. You're safe." He wrapped his arms around her, held her shaking body until she finally went still. "That's when the fear really grabbed hold, isn't it?"

"Yes," she whispered. She lifted her tear-stained

face, met his gaze. "My mother insisted that I'd made the whole thing up. I was a bit of a drama queen back then."

He brushed the tears from her cheek, stung by her sad little smile.

"She said I'd make them a laughingstock if I told people. She insisted I forget about it. So when the police couldn't find anyone who looked like the man I saw, I finally decided I must have dreamed it." She gulped. "I pushed the memories down, but I still had the nightmares."

"What did she say about the nightmares?"

Ashley shook her head. "I never told her or Dad. I thought that if I didn't make waves, if I was perfect, that somehow I could fix whatever was wrong between them. Because I knew. By then I knew my world was falling apart."

Michael waited until she'd regained her composure, had drawn away from him. Then he asked the question uppermost in his mind.

"So did it really happen, Ashley? Or did you imagine it?"

She kept her head bent, never flinched, never moved a muscle. Her voice emerged whisper-soft, begging him for an answer.

"I've got a better question. If it never happened, how come I keep seeing that same face, seventeen years later? How come I've only ever seen it here, in Serenity Bay?"

Chapter Nine

"I'm sorry. I don't seem to have shed the drama-queen image yet."

Ashley drew a tissue from her pocket, dabbed at her face, embarrassed that she'd dumped her woes all over him.

"Don't."

She forced herself to look at Michael, saw only tenderness in his eyes. A trickle of relief flickered through her. He seemed to understand.

"Tell me how faith figures into this."

"Well," she drew a deep breath. "If I believe God is there, helping me, then I have to believe that He will send what I need. The Bible says He's a rewarder of those who seek Him. That I'm to walk in faith, that I should ask in faith."

"Agreed."

"Asking means I expect God to do something. I

might not see it yet, but I believe it will happen. That's faith." She waited for his nod. "But the thing is, when I let myself worry, when I see how wrong things are, I focus on fear. And that's what prevents my progress on this path of faith."

Michael leaned against the wall, frowning.

"So buying this house, changing it into something good is…what?"

"It's my way of saying I believe God has something wonderful in store for me. That I may have been stuck on what-ifs but I'm changing that to what-could-be. I'm going to start living in this moment, here and now, and stop worrying about what might happen."

"Good for you."

"I don't know if I'll ever see that man again. If I do, I'll deal with it. With God's help. But today I'm moving on."

Michael pushed away from the wall, walked toward her. He stopped when he was just a few inches away. Though he never touched her, his voice reached out to wrap her in a gentle hug of support.

"Do you know how strong you are, Ashley? It takes a lot of nerve to face your fears, to put your ideas into actions. I admire your courage."

"I haven't succeeded yet, so don't congratulate me too soon. The pit of my stomach is still fluttering with nerves. But I think this place—" she waved a hand around "—might be my first turning point. Thanks for coming with me."

"I'm glad you chose me." He glanced at his watch. "Can I take you out for dinner to celebrate?"

The idea held instant appeal. Ashley nodded, then paused. "What about Tati?"

"It's Friday. My mother picks her up from day care and the two are together until tomorrow morning. I think it's facials this week." He wrinkled his nose as if the idea of plastering goop on his cheeks was abhorrent. "And maybe pedicures, too. I didn't pay a lot of attention."

"Hmm, maybe I should join them," she teased. "I haven't had a pedicure in ages."

"Aw, come on! What if I throw in a movie. That new chick flick is in town."

"I saw it with Piper last week."

"Oh."

He looked so disappointed, Ashley had to laugh. "I'd love to have dinner with you, Michael."

"Me, too." His smile hit her squarely in the chest. "Let's go, Ms. New Property Owner."

"I have to make a stop first," she said when they were in her car. "My landlord shipped my skis and I have to pick them up at the freight office."

"You're going skiing?"

She frowned. "Uh-huh. I was going to ask you if I could teach Tatiana."

"You're kidding, right?"

"No. Of course not. Why?"

"Ashley. Dear, sweet Ashley." Michael's knowing

smirk made her frown. "I love my daughter very much but she's about as inept as a kid can be. Whatever genes Carissa passed down, grace wasn't one of them. Put Tati on a ski slope and I can't guarantee you won't be wearing crutches with your bridesmaid's dress."

"She's not inept. She's just—" How to put it delicately? "A bit awkward."

"A *bit?*" He hooted with laughter. "There is none so blind as she who will not see."

"Well, I'd still like to teach her to ski." She pulled up beside his mother's café. "And I don't know where we're going to dinner so I'm stopping here."

"Not here," he begged, after one quick look inside. "Please?"

After a glance at his face, she moved farther down the street. "Is this all right?"

"Better." He took a quick look behind them. "My mother has this cook. Her skill as an interrogator exceeds her skill as a chef, which is very good. Better I don't give her anything to grill me about."

"Oh, good pun." Ashley chuckled at his pained look. "Where shall we go then?"

"How about the steak house just outside of town? You could drop me at the school on the way and I'll pick up my car."

"Okay. Do you mind if I stop at the depot first?"

He shrugged so Ashley parked in front of the delivery building.

"I'll just be a couple of minutes."

Michael got out, and walked beside her. "I'll carry them."

"Thanks." Once the skis were safely stored on her roof rack, Ashley headed for the school. "I'm probably not supposed to say this, but I hope it snows soon."

"Weren't you the one who went off the road not too long ago?" he asked, tongue-in-cheek.

"Yes, but I wasn't prepared. Besides, it was too early for us to have snow then."

"In my opinion, it still is. Thanksgiving is barely past."

"How did the pumpkin cakes go over, by the way?"

"Wanda said they didn't look exactly like pumpkins but they tasted all right," he repeated in a squeaky imitation of his daughter.

"Faint praise indeed." Ashley chuckled. "I'd like to meet this discerner of pumpkins."

"Hang around with Tati for long and you probably will. By the way, you should know that Wanda can ski like a trouper."

"Ah. What about you?" He ducked his head, avoided her glance. "Michael? What did I say wrong?"

"Nothing, but I, uh— My daughter comes by her clumsiness naturally, I'm afraid." He sighed when she didn't give up. "I'm a klutz on the ski hill, okay?"

Ashley giggled at his embarrassment. She was still enjoying his discomfiture when she stopped beside his car.

"No problem. I'll teach you both," she offered. "I used to instruct years ago. I've taught all kinds of klutzes."

"That's very kind but—we'll see." He scrambled out of her car a little too quickly. "I'll follow you to the restaurant, okay?"

"Okay." His rush to leave made her smile for the rest of the drive.

Since they were a bit early, they had their choice of tables to choose from. Michael chose one beside the fireplace, a table for two tucked into a little alcove. Once they'd ordered, Ashley posed the question uppermost in her mind.

"What do you do with your spare time? If you have any, I mean. Do you have a hobby?" She fiddled with the napkin, wishing that hadn't come out sounding quite so nosy.

"Truthfully?" Michael smiled. "There isn't a lot of time to spare when you're a single parent."

"I don't imagine so. But you have tonight and tomorrow. You must have something you want to do. And your evenings, when Tati's asleep. Surely you don't spend all of them checking school work?"

"Not all, no."

It was obvious that he didn't want to tell her. He avoided looking at her, kept his focus on the table.

"Okay, then. Maybe I should change the subject." His snub hurt, especially after she'd shared so much with him. "Your mother told me you lived in New York. You said you studied there. Did you like it?"

He nodded and his face brightened.

"I liked the convenience of having everything accessible without the long drives to Toronto that we have here. The galleries, the plays, the energy—it seems to spark something creative inside, you know?"

"Some cities have a way of doing that."

"After a while it wore a bit thin, though. I guess I'm a country boy at heart. And then with Tati—well, I needed a job and I figured having Mom nearby couldn't hurt. The Bay just seemed like the perfect place."

"Tati's adjusted well. She seems to have accepted you and Serenity Bay as her home."

"For the most part. She still asks the odd question about her mother, but mostly she's busy and happy." He met her steady gaze. "I'm sorry if I seem rude, Ashley. It's just that I don't have a very interesting life. Let's talk about the wedding. You do know I'm Jason's groomsman?"

He was putting her off and Ashley didn't understand why. Did he think she was getting too familiar? Asking too much? But he was the one who'd suggested dinner.

"I know. I think it's going to be a lovely wedding. Jason's taking her to the Caribbean on a honeymoon cruise for two weeks, but don't tell Piper. He had to tell me so I can pack a suitcase for her. She thinks they're going to Toronto."

"Good for Jason."

"I want to plan a shower, a couples' shower. But I'm not really sure how to arrange it."

"Why not ask someone at the church to help? They're both well known there, the fellowship hall would work and you could make it an open invitation."

"But I barely know anyone there. Besides, I want to surprise them."

"You can still do that. Why don't you talk to my mother? She's good at arranging stuff like this. You give me the date and time and I'll make sure the happy couple are both there."

"I appreciate your help, but if you're too busy—"

"I want to help, Ashley. They're my friends, too."

"Okay. Thank you." She pulled a calendar out of her purse. "I thought it should be before Christmas, maybe even before the party season really gets underway. Everyone gets booked up fast at Christmas."

They chose a date, discussed decorations, games and a way to contact everyone without the couple knowing.

When the meal was over, Ashley was delighted to have her plans solidified, even more delighted when thick fluffy snowflakes began to tumble to earth as they left the restaurant.

"If this keeps up, skiing lessons will be sooner than you think." She clapped her hands together.

"Just think, father and daughter, sharing a new healthy experience."

His one look said a thousand words.

"It'll be fun."

"Sure it will." His face brightened. "If I'm to share this fun, I think you should share some new experiences, too. Do you know how to snowshoe, Ashley?"

"No. It's never been a priority living in Vancouver." She stared at him. "Why?"

"Two students of mine have challenged me to race them in the winter festival. Snowshoe racing. I need a partner." He clapped a hand on his hip, his smirk daring her to refuse. "Well?"

"I'd love to learn," she told him, then raised one eyebrow. "If you have time?"

"Touché." He tapped the end of her nose with his finger. "Thanks for sharing my dinner. I enjoyed it."

"I did, too. And thanks again for going through the house with me." Ashley paused at the side of her car. "I appreciate you listening to me. It helped."

"It helped me, too."

"Oh?"

"I'm going to push ahead and practice a little more faith in my own life."

What did that mean?

He moved forward, pressed his lips against hers in a gentle kiss that could have meant so many things. "Good night, Ashley."

"Good night." Half bemused, she climbed into

her car, waited while he got into his. He followed her back to town, then they separated.

Ashley was halfway to Piper's when she noticed the letter. She pulled over, picked it off the floor of her SUV and read his name. Michael must have dropped it. Maybe it was important. Or maybe she just wanted an excuse. She turned around, drove toward his home.

Michael's car wasn't visible when she arrived but car tracks in the dusting of snow led to the garage and the house lights were on so she assumed he was inside.

Leaving the motor running, Ashley collected the letter and walked toward the door. It hadn't completely closed. She stretched out her hand to knock but his voice stopped her.

"No, I haven't told Ashley, Mom, and I'm not going to." He sounded angry, frustrated.

Ashley wanted to turn and run away, but her feet seemed frozen to the stairs. He was speaking again.

"I know you mean well, but if I can't make it on my own, my carvings don't mean anything. Ashley's got money, Mom. She's at home in the art world. Sure, she could be a great help, but she might also hate my work and not want to tell me the truth. I don't want her involved. If I do this showing, I'll do it on my own. Without her interference."

Ashley stepped back as if she'd been struck. She glanced around, saw the mailbox at the edge of the drive. Without a second thought she climbed into her vehicle, drove up beside it and tucked the letter inside. Then she drove away, blocking out all feeling as she rode back to Piper's.

She made small talk with her friend for a few minutes, watched a comedy they both loved and then excused herself for bed. But once she was in her room, the questions wouldn't stop.

Michael hadn't told her about his "hobby" because he didn't trust her. She wondered for a moment what he did, then pushed that away as the pain hit. She was falling for a man who thought she'd interfere.

Once again she'd chosen the wrong man to give her heart to. Michael Masters didn't want her *interference* in the part of his life that mattered so much he kept it a secret.

No one at school had mentioned his carving, she'd seen no sign of it around town. No one in the artists' guild had said anything. Why was it such a secret— especially when she'd shared hers with him? If he couldn't tell her about something he loved, what else was he hiding?

Ashley sank onto the big plushy bed in Piper's home and wondered how long it would take for this hurt to go away. Her gaze fell on the Bible she'd left beside her bed, to the section where she'd left off reading in Corinthians: *For we walk by faith, not by sight…*

"This, too, God?" she asked.

Faith.

Bowing her head, Ashley prayed for the courage and faith to rest in God's promise to keep her safe.

The couples' shower was everything Ashley had hoped it would be.

At least that's what Michael thought. He stood in a corner, watching her lead a game that soon had the room erupting in laughter. He could feel the distance between them even though she'd barely glanced his way.

She'd been cool, standoffish, busy for weeks now. Piper explained it away by saying she'd once again seen the man she was so afraid of. That she'd attempted to follow him this time made his blood run cold. He knew she wanted answers, but to go it alone—

What do you expect? She's not exactly leaning on you for support.

No, she wasn't. In fact, she'd been extraordinarily missing from his life lately. The purchase of the house, the rezoning, the renovations—he knew it all consumed her time.

But she'd made it a point to visit Tati, even tried her on skis. Just not when he was at his mother's.

"You keep staring at her like that, you'll have people talking, buddy," Jason murmured in his ear. He grinned at Michael's jerk of surprise.

"How does a great hulk like you creep up on people?"

"Most of them aren't in a daze. Want to talk about it?"

Jason had become his best friend since he'd moved back here. But Michael wasn't sure he wanted to ask him the questions he needed answers to.

"Aren't you supposed to be in there with your fiancée?"

"Ashley kicked me out for some game they're playing. So talk and make it quick before I have to go back."

"She looks thinner."

"Piper said Emma will have to take Ashley's dress in again." Jason drew him out of the hall into the adjoining cloakroom. "She's been running herself ragged with that house and her plans to make it a gallery."

"I heard." His mother was a regular fountain of information about Ashley Adams.

"How come you haven't been around there?"

"She didn't ask. I invited her to go for a snowmobile ride after we got all that new snow last week, but—" he shrugged "—she said she's too busy right now."

"And the next time you asked?" Jason quirked one eyebrow upward. "Don't tell me you just gave up? Not Mr. Persistence?"

"I've been a little busy building sets for your fiancée's play, Nosy."

"That's an excuse not to call Ashley?" Jason shook his head. "You're nowhere near as bright as I figured."

"She's going through stuff, Jay. Things get a little too personal when we're together."

"And this is a problem because?"

"I was divorced. I have a child."

"Yes, I know. She knows, too. I believe you belonged to both those categories before she met you?"

Michael moved back into the doorway so he could watch her, wishing that smile she lavished on everyone else would flash at him. "That's not the point."

"You gonna tell me what is?"

"No."

"Okay." Jason opened a tin someone had left on a table, picked out a piece of fudge. "Mmm, this is great. Maybe we shouldn't add it to the rest of the stuff in the kitchen. I'll just sneak it out and take it home."

"She's got money, Jason."

"A ton of it. I know." He blinked at Michael's glare. "So?"

"You don't see a problem there?"

"Doesn't matter what I see. I doubt if Ashley cares much about her grandfather's inheritance except that it makes people look at her differently." He raised his eyebrows. "Like you're thinking right now."

"She's opening a gallery in Serenity Bay, Jason.

What am I supposed to say? 'Oh, by the way, I just happen to have some pieces I've been working on. I wonder if you'd show them for me.'"

"Sounds good to me. Honest, forthright. Ow! What?" he asked when Michael thunked him on the shoulder.

"It sounds like I was wangling to get an in with her." He refused the fudge Jason offered. "She'll feel obliged to take them and I'll never know if I could have made it on my own."

"Ah." Jason grinned, his eyes dancing. "Now I get it. We're talking about pride."

"Yes. That and the fact that she doesn't want to get involved while she's still sorting out this fear thing."

"Involved. Oh, my. I didn't realize you were involved." Jason mocked his embarrassment. "Look, man. You're obviously not as experienced as me in matters of the heart so let me give you some advice."

"*You're* giving *me* advice?" Michael wanted to hoot with laughter, but Ashley was in the next room and he didn't want to draw attention to himself so he controlled the urge. "This is going to be good. Go ahead. Share your wisdom, groom."

"Thanks, I will." Jason drew him farther back into the cloakroom where they wouldn't be overheard. "Did you ever think Ashley's fear problems are tied up with her parents' problems?"

"Sure." Michael narrowed his gaze. "Hey! How do you know this?"

"Piper told me. And if you say a word..." he warned, glaring.

"I might have pushed a little too hard," Michael admitted. "She told me she had some issues to work through, that she only wanted to be friends, for now."

"See? That's a good place to start. But friends keep in touch, they don't just disappear because things get busy. Ask her out again. You're my best man, she's a bridesmaid—you can talk about us!"

"Oh, goody." Michael frowned. "It's gone quiet in there. Shouldn't you be back in there with your bride-to-be?"

"Nope."

"Why not?"

"Because I told him not to come back until I said so." Ashley appeared in the doorway, glancing from one to the other. "Hello, Michael."

"Hi, yourself. Sorry I was late."

"No problem." She turned her focus back to Jason, brushed a finger against the dark crumbs on his cheek. Her gaze narrowed. "You've been into that fudge I brought, haven't you? How much is left?"

Since Michael had just watched Jason slip the last piece into his mouth, he knew his friend couldn't speak.

"It's all gone," he said, enjoying his friend's discomfort.

"Jason Franklin, you know very well I was going to use that as a prize!"

"I'm sorry, Ashley but I'm starved. I didn't get any

Chapter Ten

"Seven days till Christmas, folks. If you haven't done your shopping yet, you'd better get to it."

Ashley didn't need the radio deejay's reminder. A square silver box tied with bright red ribbon lying under Piper's tree was a constant reminder that she'd be leaving shortly to spend Christmas with her mother and she needed to make a delivery first. Two of them actually.

She'd spent days stewing over how and when to give Tatiana and Michael the Christmas gifts she'd chosen especially for them. Since she was driving to Toronto tomorrow, procrastination was no longer possible.

Outside, Jason and Piper were supposedly putting Christmas decorations but the peals of laughter made them sound more like kids who'd just been released from school. Ashley tugged on her coat,

dinner and then I had to rush over here. It was too tempting."

"Ooh!"

"Don't kill him yet, Ashley," Michael advised softly, stifling his laughter. "We've got to get them married first. Then it's Piper's job to make him behave."

"Good luck to her. Well, you're going to be the one who provides this prize, Jason. So get thinking about it. Maybe all the sugar will help." She grabbed his arm, drew him forward. "Come on. It's time to face the music and the advice of our panel."

"He can use it," Michael told her, gazing into her eyes. "He has the strangest ideas about love."

"Really." She didn't look away until someone in the audience cleared her throat. Then she launched back into her role of hostess as if it had never been interrupted.

Michael admired her aplomb. He had none. Whenever Ashley looked at him like that, the world stopped. He felt as if he'd been kicked in the stomach. There was a chair against the wall and he sank into it, his knees suddenly too weak to hold him upright.

But as the evening progressed, as the group finally broke for refreshments, his eyes never left Ashley.

Maybe that's why he noticed the exact moment when she almost dropped the tray she was carrying. He got to her as fast as he could, handed the tray to someone else and helped her sit down.

"Breathe, in and out."

She obeyed, but her hands clamped around his like vises. She stared at him and he could see the fear taking control.

"What's wrong?"

"I saw him. He thrust his head around the corner, looked at me, then disappeared. But I saw him!"

"The same man?" he asked knowing exactly who she was referring to.

"Yes. It was him, Michael. He was here. Maybe he followed me."

"Stay here. I'll go check." He eased in and out of the crowd, working his way across the room until he finally got to the door. He stepped outside, raced down the steps and surveyed the church parking lot.

All he saw was a host of cars and trucks, none of them with their lights on or leaving the grounds.

Michael waited several minutes, finally he went back inside.

"Did you find him?" Ashley whispered from just inside the door.

He shook his head.

"He's gone now," he whispered.

She sagged against him, her fingers spread against his chest. Her eyes closed.

"Oh, God," she whispered in a prayer of desperation. "Please help me."

"He will, Ashley. Just keep hanging on to your faith."

But as he stood holding her in the clo tiny doubt flickered through his own min

There had been no one outside. Which be questions—was this man real?

Or was Ashley imagining it all?

snatched up the two gifts and hurried outside before she could change her mind.

"I don't know when I'll be back," she called. "Don't wait up."

Piper waved. Jason threw a snowball that smashed against her windshield.

"You're going to get coal for Christmas," she warned.

"Doesn't matter," he called. "I'm already getting everything I want for New Year's."

Ashley climbed inside the car before he could bombard her with another from the stack of snowballs he had piled beside him. She smiled as Piper caught him off guard, the snow splattering across his face in a wet sopping mess. He retaliated six for her one. When he ran out, he kissed her nose then urged her onto the old sled they'd found. As she whizzed down the hill, Piper squealed with delight, the sound echoing back from the surrounding hills over and over.

Ashley had never seen her friend happier. Their love was as solid and firm as Cathcart House, Piper's grandparents' home. They'd disagree, argue, maybe even hold grudges. But that house would be filled with love.

As it always had been.

"Stop moping about the past, woman. You've made a new beginning. Get on with it."

She drove the roads easily, trying not to check every nook and cranny. She was getting better at trusting. If only she hadn't seen his face at the shower. Everything else was going so well, but she couldn't work her brain past the fear that still clutched her whenever she saw him.

The radio was playing Christmas songs and Ashley sang along as she drove, joy bubbling inside. She loved Christmas, always had. Not being able to open the gallery in time for the season stung, but she'd prayed for the courage to wait.

Wait. That's all she seemed to do lately. Wait for understanding, wait for the gallery work to be finished, wait, wait, wait. Michael had phoned several times, asking her to dinner, hinting that he was ready for his skiing lesson, but Ashley had put him off every time.

She couldn't get past what she'd overheard, and she didn't want to embarrass herself by letting him see that Ashley Adams was infatuated with him—again.

Only it was more than that, and she knew it.

She pulled into his yard, then blinked. There were no tracks. Maybe he wasn't even home.

"I'll just have to leave the gifts, then," she muttered, gathering them up and climbing out of the car. She walked up the steps, struggling not to recall the last time she'd been here.

Tati, still wearing her fuzzy pink nightgown, had the door open before she got to it.

"Ashley, hi! Are those presents?" Her saucer-wide eyes glittered with excitement.

"They sure are. One for you, one for your dad. Can you put them under your tree?"

"We don't have one yet." Tatiana checked the name tags, noted that her present was the largest. Then she pushed them both onto the counter. "Daddy said maybe today. After we bake cookies."

"I said nothing about making cookies, Tati. Oh, hi, Ashley." Michael closed the door behind her. "How are you?"

"I'm fine." He looked tired and a little grumpy. Ashley decided to make it quick. "If you're baking I don't want to intrude. It's just that I'm leaving for Hawaii tomorrow and I wanted to drop these off first. Merry Christmas."

"Thank you. Tati has something for you, too. At least stay long enough for tea. And just so it's very clear, I'm not baking anything. I never said I would. Tati's just trying to talk me into it." He took her coat, hung it up.

"And you're not persuaded?"

"Daddy says he does breakfast, dinner and supper and sometimes pumpkins, but that's it. But he could make cookies. Wanda says her dad helps her mom lots of times."

Exasperation appeared on Michael's face, but he kept his voice gentle.

"I told you that if you could play quietly with your doll for a little while, then after lunch we'd go hunt for a tree. So far you haven't helped me much."

"I will." Tati sat herself at the table. "After I have tea with Ashley."

"Well then, thank you. I'd love to stay for tea. Though I don't usually have it in the morning."

"We slept in a little later today."

"I see." Ashley turned to listen as the little girl described her wish list. "You want quite a lot, don't you?"

"Yeah. I'll get it, too."

"Presents aren't everything, Tati. It's the—"

"Spirit of the season," Tati finished as if she'd heard her father a hundred times before. "I remember." She sighed. "I wish you could have come to my Christmas concert at school, Ashley."

"I did, honey. I was a bit late, but I watched you." Ashley pretended not to see Michael's start of surprise. "I stayed in the back so I wouldn't disturb anyone, but I was so proud of you."

"I didn't forget one word." Tatiana's chest puffed out with pride. "Daddy bought me ice cream to celebrate."

"Good for Daddy." She risked a glance at him, found his gaze on her. "I really liked your angel dress. It was so sparkly."

"Wanda and I both had matching ones. I wish I could have had my special dress to wear."

"Your special one?" Ashley wondered if she should change the subject. Certainly Michael didn't look encouraging.

"Yes. The one I want for Christmas. I'll show you." She clambered down from her seat and dashed out of the room.

"Bad subject?" Ashley whispered.

Michael shook his head. "I've got it covered. Not exactly as shown, though."

She admired the picture of the princess dress, as Tati termed it.

"It reminds me of Piper's wedding dress," Ashley told her. "Wait till you see it." She grabbed a piece of paper and sketched out the lines of the dress. "It floats around her feet just like your princess dress."

"Do all ladies get to wear a dress like that when they have weddings?"

"Not all. Different ladies have different ideas about how they want to get married. Some don't like fancy weddings. When you're a lady you'll be able to choose whatever you want."

Ashley tried to explain about weddings to Tati, but her attention was still fixed on Michael. He kept glancing at his watch, as if she was holding him up.

"I'm sure you're busy," she said, rising as soon as she'd sipped the last of her tea. "I'll let you and Tatiana get on with your day."

"But you could stay and help us bake cookies. Couldn't she, Daddy?" Tati's beseeching voice touched a soft spot in Ashley's heart.

"She's welcome to stay and bake whatever she wants," he said quietly, meeting her glance. "In fact,

I'd really appreciate it if you could stay, Ashley. Unless you're too busy?"

"But this is a time for you and Tati—"

"Daddy said he has to work for two hours," Tatiana complained. "But we could make cookies while he's working. Then we could all go get our Christmas tree. Couldn't we, Daddy?"

Ashley saw the truth as if it was written across his face. No wonder he wasn't planning on baking cookies, he was trying to prepare something for his daughter's first Christmas with him.

"You need a break?"

"I do have some things to do," he admitted. "It's not fair to assume you'll babysit on a moment's notice, though."

"But…?"

He assumed an innocence she knew was a mask.

"But if you did happen to have some time to spare and wanted to help Tati make cookies, I wouldn't try to talk you out of it."

"While you work, I assume." She glared at him, shook her head. "Is it too hard to say, 'Ashley, can you help us out?'"

"Ashley, could you please help us out?" he repeated quietly.

"Of course. Go. Do whatever you need to do. Take all day if you want. We could even go for the tree after supper if that works for you." She stopped when he shook his head adamantly.

"After lunch would be better." Michael asked Tati to get dressed. When she'd left the room he spoke again, his voice lowered so as not to be overheard. "Our neighbor's dog was attacked by a cougar yesterday evening. I don't want to go into the woods after dark unless it's absolutely necessary."

"I see." A shiver of fear whisked across her nerve endings. Ashley shuddered. "How awful."

"Yes, it is. There's a lot of talk about hunting it down before it attacks a human. There have been reports from neighboring counties about adults being chased. One woman even had to fight it off with a stick. Fortunately for her, a deer came by and the cougar found it easier prey."

"I hope they find it before the winter festival. That would really ruin the tourist trade. Many of the events are scheduled after dark."

He nodded but said no more as Tati returned.

"Well, Miss T.," Ashley said, hiding a smile at Tati's lace top, dirty jeans and black patent shoes. "What kind of cookies did you have in mind?"

"Gingerbread men."

Michael mouthed "thank you," then left the room. Ashley assumed he had an office or something at the other end of the house. Not that it mattered.

Thanks to her little helper they were both soon dusted in flour. They made gingerbread boys, chocolate chip mounds, pecan drops and a host of shortbread cutouts. While Tati was engaged in decorating them, Ashley mixed up some gooey chocolate squares, a batch of fudge and a chocolate cake. A withered group of apples huddled at the back of the fridge so she decided to make an apple betty. She managed to almost finish cleaning up before Tati tired of decorating the cookies.

"I'm hungry."

"So am I. Shall we make your dad some lunch?"

"Okay." Tatiana's eyes sparkled. "What should we make?"

"Vegetable soup?" She could use up what was in the fridge and he could stock up on fresh food for the holidays.

"It won't have beets in it, will it? I don't like beets."

"No beets," Ashley promised. She gave the child a peeler and set her to work on the carrots. Soon they had a pot of vegetable soup bubbling on the stove, filling the house with a delicious aroma.

But Michael did not reappear.

When the biscuits were ready, Ashley checked the clock. If they didn't eat soon, there wouldn't be time to go for a tree.

"Your daddy seems to be lost. I wonder if we should find him and tell him lunch is ready."

Tati carefully placed the last spoon on the table. "He always forgets when he's goes in the workshop."

The place of his carving? "Let's go tell him, then."

With Tati leading the way, Ashley followed, until they came to a side door. Tatiana opened it.

"It's lunchtime, Daddy. Me and Ashley made soup."

Ashley didn't hear his response, she was too busy ogling the room. There were faces everywhere. A series of cunning faces arranged on the far wall were particularly fanciful, chiseled out of oddly shaped driftwood. There were larger, chunkier pieces carved out of tree trunks and logs. Thin slices of mahogany, oak and birch lay along a workbench like masks, each expression different from the next.

Entranced by the detail she saw, Ashley moved forward to inspect them more closely.

"*This* is what you do in your spare time." She turned to face him. "They're fantastic!"

"Thank you." He remained still, the chisel motionless in his hand as he watched her.

She could sense his reserve. "Why didn't you tell me?"

Michael shrugged. "I guess it hasn't really come up."

She fixed him with a look. "Hasn't it?"

"I'm hungry. Can't we eat the soup now?" Tati begged.

"We sure can, honey." Michael rose, placed his chisel on his counter, laid his leather work apron on top. But he didn't look at her.

That bothered Ashley more than the fact that he'd kept silent about his art.

She followed Tatiana out of the room, served the soup and biscuits, accepted their praise. But she couldn't get the questions out of her mind. Michael knew she was collecting works for her gallery. Why hadn't he offered some of his? Did he think Serenity Bay was too small-town to show in? Or was it her gallery he thought too small?

"Maybe you and Tatiana should go get your tree by yourselves," she offered quietly when Tati left to wash her hands and get her snow clothes ready. "It's something you should share together, not with me."

"But we'd like you to go with us." Michael shook his head. "I know what you're thinking, Ashley, and it isn't true. But I can't talk now. Wait until later. Please? I promise, there's a good reason why I didn't explain."

Sure there was. He didn't want to hurt her feelings.

She thought about it as they cleared the table together. Then she remembered the cougar.

"I suppose it would be smarter to go together," she agreed. "That way I can keep an eye on Tatiana while you cut down the tree."

"That isn't why I was asking you."

"Isn't it?" Ashley didn't know what to make of Michael's secret. But she did want to hear his explanation. "I've got my ski suit in the car. I'll go get it."

He nodded, but it was what Michael didn't say that mattered.

Chapter Eleven

Michael closed the door to Tati's room with a sigh of relief. Finally he'd get a few minutes alone with Ashley. He prayed for the right words to explain and realized there wasn't a good way to say it.

"The tree looks good, don't you think?" She looked at him with her big silver eyes and his heart started doing somersaults. "Tatiana did a great job with the popcorn strings and her star is very pretty."

"Ashley, I—"

"It's getting late. I should probably get moving." She rose, sidestepped him and headed for the door.

"Wait!"

From the way she came to a stop he knew he'd surprised her but he had to tell her—now.

"Will you let me explain about the carving?"

"You don't owe me any explanations, Michael. Your private life is your own business."

The tinge of hurt frosting the edges of those words hit him hard and he wished he'd handled this before. But regrets did no one any good.

"Please?"

She studied him for several moments, finally nodded. He motioned to the sofa and she sat, but on the edge, as if she couldn't wait to leave.

"I've been trying to carve for ages," he began. "I earned my teaching degree, used it for a few years, but I wanted to carve. So I spent two years in New York working with Hans Leder. Have you heard of him?"

Dumb question.

"Who hasn't?" She tipped her head to one side. "He doesn't usually take students. You must have impressed him. After seeing your work I can understand why."

"I didn't carve faces then. I was more into sculpture. I even had a showing." He swallowed. "It didn't go well."

"First showings often don't." She leaned back in the chair. "Go on."

"Actually it went very badly. Hans tried. He talked to several galleries, even arranged for some of my pieces to be shown along with his. That was a mistake. The reviews were less than kind. I went back to teaching."

"But you didn't quit carving."

"I couldn't. Somehow the wood just kept calling."

He laughed at himself. "That sounds stupid, but it's how I felt."

"It's not an unusual feeling for a creative person."

"I guess. Anyway, I was teaching math then. A girl came into my class midterm. Her name was Maria. She was fourteen and she had brain cancer. Inoperable."

"Oh, no."

"Yes. Maria knew she didn't have much longer, but she wanted to spend as long as she could being what she called 'normal.'" He closed his eyes, tipped his head back and remembered. "I don't think I've ever met a person who touched my spirit so deeply. Her face would wrinkle, she'd get this determined look in her eye and push for an explanation until the concept was clear to her. She was a delight to teach."

He opened his eyes to see if she understood. Ashley sat watching him, her face expressionless, except for those expressive eyes. They shone with unshed tears.

"Maria wasn't pretty but she was beautiful. Do you know what I mean?" Michael saw her nod. "From the inside, radiating out. You'd start out feeling so badly when you saw her return day after day, thinner, paler, wasting away. But Maria would have you laughing in a minute and then she'd join in."

"I wish I'd known her."

"I do, too. Anyway, I became intrigued by her

personality and one evening I was fooling with a piece of wood. I could see her face in it and I began to carve her as I'd first seen her. When I was finished that, I carved another and then another, trying to catch a certain look, a glint, a spark in the likeness. She died two days after school dismissed for the summer."

"The cancer finally took over. That's sad."

"It was. Her death prodded me back into carving in a new way. I began to look at the world through Maria's eyes and because of her I saw things in people's faces, things others ignored."

"Your pieces do have fantastic insight. It's like they ask you to look behind what everyone else sees." Her gaze never left his face. "I understand wanting the time and space to create, Michael, but that doesn't explain why you couldn't tell me. Or why you had to keep it a secret."

"It wasn't really a secret," he muttered. "Okay, it sort of was."

"Because?"

It was confession time. "That showing I told you about—it did a number on my ego."

"I can imagine."

"But it was more than that." He ran his fingers through his hair, remembering the depths his soul had plummeted to. "I was so certain that carving was what I was supposed to do, and so I plunged into it, believed I had a future. When I read those reviews

I felt abandoned, as if God was mocking me. Like everyone else was."

Ashley said nothing, allowing him to feel his way through.

"Maybe that's why I became infatuated with Carissa. She was a success, doing what she loved, acclaimed all over the world."

"And next to her you felt like a failure."

"I *was* a failure." He swallowed. "At first she reminded me of Maria, always laughing, relishing life. I grabbed and held on. It was only after we were married that I saw beneath the mask."

He paused, recalling that day as clearly as yesterday. Carissa had been sitting in the hotel room, so silent he'd wondered about her mental state. Then a fan had arrived.

"Tell me, Michael." Her soft encouragement drew the words from him.

"Carissa came alive when she danced. She lived for the ballet. Without it she was lost. I realized that she'd left New York, and me, because I asked too much of her. I needed too much and she couldn't give it. No one could. It's something I had to find within myself."

"Except that you have a daughter now."

Michael nodded, wishing there was a way to avoid discussing his ex-wife. He never had before. But Ashley was different. He needed her to understand.

"Yes. But with Tati came the same old feelings—

the need to prove that I was good enough, as good as her mother. That I was excellent at one specific thing."

"It sounds like you were in competition with your ex-wife."

Shame washed over his face. "In a way I guess I am."

"Why?"

"Haven't you heard Tati? My mommy this and my mommy that." He felt like a fool saying it, but in another way it was a relief to get it out. "She idolized Carissa. How do I compare to that, Ashley?"

"Why do you have to?" She leaned forward to study him. Her voice dropped. "Carissa is gone. You are Tatiana's father. Every night you get to tuck her into bed, listen to her prayers, kiss her cheek. Isn't that enough?"

"No." He raked a hand through his hair. "I know it sounds stupid, but when she talks about going to the theme park in Paris or spending Christmas in the Alps—I have nothing to compare to that."

"And you want to." She wasn't asking. "You want to hear her brag about you. But she does, Michael."

"Yeah, she talks about the sets we're building or the cupcakes—stuff like that. Stupid little things that—"

"Mean the world to her," she whispered. "You put aside your hopes and dreams, took the teaching job to support you both. When you have a spare moment, you spend it on the wood. There's nothing to be ashamed of in that. You're doing more than a lot of men who have a wife to help them."

She didn't understand. How could she?

"It isn't enough." He was going to come clean and he prayed Ashley would understand. "I had a plan, you see. I figured that if I had enough pieces and a gallery would choose some that I'd risk it again, one last time. I'd hold another showing. If I blew it—well, then I'd know I misread God, that I wasn't good enough, never would be."

"But I could have helped you with that. You know I have connections with a number of galleries. Why didn't you ask?"

He huffed his disgust. "I wasn't going to be another hanger-on, Ashley, like Kent.

"You're nothing like Kent."

He ignored that, begging her to see it through his eyes.

"Since you've come here, how many people have stopped you on the street, asked you to look at what they're doing? How many more since you've started work on the gallery?"

"Lots of them." Her mouth pursed. She shook her head at him. "I'm not going to lie and tell someone their stuff is good if I don't think it is, but at the same time, I want the opportunity to be the first to show artists from Serenity Bay. That's what my gallery is about."

The glint of hurt in her eyes forced him to realize she was on the wrong track. There could be no pretending now. Either he told her the truth and looked a fool or Ashley believed he thought her gallery wasn't good enough.

"I'm scared. Okay?" He kicked his toe against the carpet, hating the words.

"What?" She stared at him as if he'd just asked her to swim in the bay.

"I said I'm scared. I wanted to keep my little secret in the back room, get those carvings done and ship them off to someone who doesn't know me."

"Ah." She actually had the nerve to smile. "I see."

"I don't think it's funny."

"I do. I'm the one who's been confiding her fears and you're telling me you've been keeping your own secret." Ashley wagged a finger at him. "That's not playing fair."

"It's not about fairness. It's about taking the risk, doing what I told myself I'd do and living with the consequences. If what's in there is a lot of garbage, then I'll know and I can forget about my silly dreams."

"It's not garbage, Michael. Far from it."

It was his turn to smile. "Thank you. You're very kind. But you'll forgive me if I don't pin my hopes on that."

"Are you deliberately trying to be offensive?" she demanded. "I've scouted out some of the best pieces for a number of galleries across the country. I think I know what I'm talking about."

"I'm sure you do." He leaned over, brushed his

knuckles against her cheek. "But you're not exactly impartial, Ashley."

"Oh. So I'd lie, tell you it was good even if it wasn't? That's insulting."

"I didn't mean it to be. I just meant—" Michael struggled with the appropriate words. "You wouldn't want to hurt my feelings. Believe me, I appreciate that."

"And if I did?" She rose, stood glaring at him. "If I told you that your work is nice, pretty, but it isn't the kind of work a gallery can promote, not the sort of carving anyone will long to collect—if I told you that, what would you do?"

"Stop carving." He didn't even have to think about it.

"Finally some truth." She slapped her hands on her hips, her eyes frosty. "That's why you kept it a secret, Michael. Not because of any of your silly reasons, but because you're afraid you'll have to hand your dream over, put it in someone else's hands. And if they say it isn't great, you're willing to stop doing what you love. That's really sad."

"I just want to get enough done for a show," he tried to explain, rising to follow as she left the room. "Where are you going?"

He didn't need to ask. She was headed for the workroom. His workroom.

"Ashley, I—"

"Hush!" She quelled his protest with one glare.

He'd never seen her so angry. She picked up a sculpture of Tati. "What were you thinking of when you did this? You weren't thinking of a showing then, were you?"

"No," he admitted.

"I can tell. It's a work from your heart." She set that one down, picked up another of his daughter. "This one is for your show, isn't it?" She inclined her head, waited for his nod. "Do you know how I can tell?"

"No." Her intuition amazed him.

"Then I'll tell you. It's not that it isn't good. It is. Very good. But the sparkle is missing. The little whimsical tilt to the eye or the uplift of the nose—I don't know. It's just not there. This piece is more intricate than the first, much more difficult, I'm sure. But it doesn't have the same presence. I can't hear her laughter when I look at it."

"Oh." Michael sat down, feeling as if he'd been sucker-punched and couldn't catch his breath.

Ashley's face softened. She walked over to stand in front of him, put her hand under his chin to force him to meet her gaze.

"I know you want a showing, Michael. You want to prove that you have what it takes, you want to stuff the critics' words in their faces and show the world. You want the satisfaction that a successful show would give, the approval sticker that you interpreted God's plan for your life correctly."

"Yes."

"But most of all I think you want to give Tati something to brag about, to get yourself onto an equal footing with Carissa, maybe even show her up. Why? Because of the way she handled Tati?"

He said nothing, because he couldn't deny it.

"I'm not saying these pieces wouldn't give you acclaim. Any gallery would take them and be happy to sell them." She leaned in, her breath whispering across his cheek. "But is that enough for you? You have so much more to give. A God-given talent to see beyond, inside, to the heart, and to let us see there too, if we're intuitive enough to look."

Her quiet words humbled him.

"Stop thinking about showing your work, Michael. Think about what's hidden in the wood, what you want to reveal. That's when you'll know you've fallen in with God's plan. That's when the sparkle will burst out of your work and draw in people who just want to see it. That's the reason Tati will be proud."

He rose, drew her into his arms, rested his chin on her head.

"You are a very smart woman, Ashley Adams."

"I know art," she shot back. "Plus, I'm very good at telling other people what they should do. Just not so good at following my own advice. But I'm trying." She tipped her head, met his gaze. "I'm really trying."

He wanted to kiss her.

But a rap on the front door drew them apart.

"Can you see who that is?" he asked. "I'm just going to check on Tati, make sure we haven't disturbed her."

"Okay." She walked out of the room, leaving him alone to get himself together.

Michael closed the studio door and was about to enter Tati's room when a sharp cry pieced the silence of the house.

"Go away!"

His walk toward the front door turned into a run as Ashley's terrified voice begged for help.

"Michael! Make him go away."

Oh God, please help.

Ashley backed away from the door, away from the face that, no matter how much she prayed, never left her dreams. She pasted herself against the wall, slid along it until she came to the kitchen. She ducked inside, grabbed a knife from the block as if it could protect her from the monster at the door.

How had he found her? Why had he come here? To take Tati?

"Ashley? What's wrong?"

"Make him go," she whispered. "Make him go away."

She heard Michael speaking, then he said something and the door closed. A moment later he was beside her, his hands easing the knife from her fingers, drawing on her arms, urging her toward the table.

"Come sit down. Come on, Ashley. You're all right. I'm here."

"Is he gone?" Her voice emerged in a croak. She surveyed the room, dared to look into the living room. No one.

"He's gone now. It's okay. You're safe."

She concentrated on breathing deeply, exhaling slowly, forcing a sense of calm onto her body. Eventually she was able to look at Michael.

"You saw him, didn't you? You saw the man at the door."

"Yes." He frowned, clearly surprised by her outburst.

"It was him! That's the man who grabbed me. Now we can call the police." She rose, reached for the phone. Michael's hand on her arm stopped her from dialing. "What's wrong?"

"Wait a minute. Just let me think this through."

She sat again while Michael frowned.

"That's the man who grabbed you when you were a child?"

"Yes. I told you that." He was acting so strangely. Ashley frowned. "Do you know him?"

"Of course. Ned Ainsworth."

"The police can find him from that." She tried to reach for the phone but again he stopped her.

"Wait!" he ordered when she pulled away.

"Ashley, you can't go accusing this man of abducting you almost twenty years ago."

"Why? He did."

"Are you sure?"

Ashley froze, felt the rise of panic inside. "You don't believe me?"

"Yes, but—" He tried to take her hand, but she pulled away. "It doesn't make sense. Ned's a carver, like I am."

"Where does he live?"

"I don't know. I only met him once. Somewhere up by Cathcart House, I think. But—"

"By Piper's house?" She stared at him as the faith she'd tried so hard to bolster ebbed away. The hairs on her arm rose. "You mean he's been living near me all along? Where?"

"I don't know. That's what I'm saying. I'm not sure anyone knows anything much about Ned. I don't think he lives here year-round. When he is here, he keeps to himself." Michael flushed at her indignant glare. "I know you don't want to hear this, but I can't believe he'd do something like that, Ashley. I just can't. Tati met him when I did. She was never afraid."

"Those are the kind of people you should fear the most." She turned her back, stared at the wall, willing the tears to subside. Of all people, she'd been so sure Mick believed her. "I'd better go."

"Wait, Ashley." He gripped her shoulders, turned

her to face him. "It's not that I don't believe you. It's that I think there has to be some other explanation."

"Like what?"

"I don't know," he admitted, his voice troubled. "If we could find him, you could ask him—"

"I don't ever want to talk to that man again." She struggled to keep a lid on the cauldron of worry that bubbled inside. "Besides, I'm leaving tomorrow."

"Then I'll look while you're gone." He shrugged. "There has to be some explanation. I think he's had a place around here for a long time. I can't imagine he's stayed knowing you could identify him."

"There was never a formal charge."

"No, but he'd have it constantly hanging over his head. If he was some kind of pedophile, wouldn't it have happened again? As far as I know, it hasn't."

"That's true," she admitted quietly. "I checked the newspapers. There haven't been any reports that are similar to what I experienced."

As numbness invaded she pulled on her coat and her boots.

"I'm sorry," he murmured, his face troubled. "You've come so far. And now for this to happen— it's hard."

"Maybe it's the wake-up call I needed," she whispered as she dragged on her gloves.

"What does that mean?"

She looked at him, really looked. He was a man she'd admired, had a crush on, fallen in love with. He had a rare talent for capturing expressions with his carving. He was a wonderful father to a little girl who reached inside and grabbed her heart with both hands.

But when push came to shove he hadn't trusted her. He didn't believe her.

The sting of knowing that she'd trusted wrongly again bit deeply. Ashley forced down the tears with an iron will. She wondered how he'd react to the picture inside the flat box she'd left on the counter.

"I hope you have a very Merry Christmas, Michael. Just do me one favor, will you?"

"If I can."

"Don't let Tatiana out of your sight. If it happened once it could happen again. And I wouldn't wish what I've gone through on my worst enemy."

"Oh, Ashley." He drew her into his arms, kissed her. When she didn't respond he sighed, drew back. "Tati isn't only my child, she belongs to God, as well. He'll protect her."

She nodded, pulled open the door.

"That's what I thought," she whispered. "But look what happened. My attacker is still free. And I'm still afraid."

She closed the door and slowly walked to her car while scanning the yard for signs of the cat that had terrorized the town or the man who still had the power to terrify her.

As always, fear was her companion on the ride home.

"I wonder what Ashley's doing now," Tati murmured as she waited for Michael to braid her hair. "Do they have Christmas in Hawaii?"

"Of course. I'm sure she's getting ready to have dinner with her family, just like we are." The gift he'd shipped overnight express would have arrived by now. He wondered if she'd understand the significance.

"I think she'll go swimming today. That's what I'd do. Wanda says—"

Tuning out Wanda's sage advice, Michael finished braiding Tati's hair, tied on the pink satin ribbons and helped button the dress he'd scoured online catalogs to find.

"You look very pretty, Tati. Just like a princess."

"Thank you, Daddy." She hugged him tightly, then pulled away, her face wistful. "Do you think Mommy's having Christmas?"

He caught his breath at the yearning that washed over her face, struggled to stuff down the imp of jealousy that danced inside.

"I'm sure she's singing carols with the angels, Tati. Or maybe dancing a special ballet for God." It was the best he could do on such short notice. "Now you go watch your new video about Baby Jesus while I get ready, okay?" He debated the next words only for a moment. "And don't open the door for anyone."

"I know, Daddy. You told me a bunch of times." She favored him with a frown then skipped out of the room and down the hall, her shoes tapping a rhythm that expressed her happiness.

Michael climbed into the shower with a prayer that the Christmas spirit would wash away all their cares and worries—if only for today. He'd just lathered his hair when Tati burst into the room.

"Ashley phoned, Daddy! I'm going to talk to her now, but you can have a turn after me."

"I'm coming," he said, to the sound of the bathroom door slamming shut.

Grumbling about her timing while his brain gave praise, Michael rinsed off, pulled on his robe and grabbed the phone by his bed.

"Daddy said we could sleep in today but I didn't sleep in. I was too awake. I was thinking about my mommy." A tiny pause. "But I'm glad you called."

"Me, too, Tati."

"Did you go swimming on Christmas?"

"Yes. I just got out of the water. I pretended it was a big snowbank and that you and I were making snow angels."

"I like swimming. And snow angels. Santa brought me a princess dress, Ashley."

"Are you wearing it now?" an amused voice asked.

"Yes. It's so pretty. It's not white. It's pink. I think that's nicer than white. And I have matching tights and—"

"Merry Christmas, Ashley."

"Merry Christmas, Michael."

Silence lasted about three seconds until Tati burst in again, explaining how much she loved the artist's set Ashley had given her.

"I already did two drawings," she said. "Daddy said they're the best he's ever seen."

"And I love the Christmas picture you gave me. You must do another so I can put it up in my gallery when it opens."

So she was coming back. He felt relief, and a bubbling joy that couldn't be quelled. Michael let his daughter babble on while he got a grip on his emotions, then spoke up.

"Give me a chance now, honey, will you?" he asked.

"Okay, Daddy. Bye, Ashley. Merry Christmas. I love you."

"I love you, too, sweetie."

The phone banged down so hard Michael winced.

"Sorry about that."

"She sounds delighted with her dress."

"Yeah. Some things are easy."

"She was talking about Carissa. Did she have a bad dream?"

"No, nothing like that." They kept the repartee of small talk going but all he wanted to ask her if she'd forgiven him.

"She's adjusting well. I hope all her memories will remain sweet."

"Yeah."

"Are you cooking Christmas dinner?"

"Are you kidding? We're going over to Mom's. The girls are home. It will be bedlam."

"It sounds wonderful."

Another awkward pause.

"I got your gift this morning, Michael. It's beautiful. Thank you."

Disappointment welled up. She hadn't understood the significance of it.

"I called it Faith," he told her quietly.

"Yes, I saw that. It's a beautiful depiction. I don't know how you got the fingers so perfect."

He let that go. "I know I disappointed you, Ashley."

"It doesn't matter."

"Yes, it does. I didn't mean to diminish what you went through but I did and that hurt you. I apologize."

"I didn't make it up, Michael. I'm more certain than ever that it happened."

"I know."

"You believe me?" she asked, her surprise evident. "Really?"

Faith. He'd worked it out while his fingers had smoothed the rough edges of the cypress wood carving of her face. The carving still wasn't quite finished but his decision was made. Either he put his faith in her, wholeheartedly trusted her and moved on from there, or he didn't and Ashley shut him out. He chose the former.

"I believe you, Ashley."

Her silent doubt transmitted clearly across the phone line.

"That's what my carving means. I don't know why Ned did it, what caused his actions. I can't accept that he wanted to harm you, but I do believe that you were abducted by Ned."

"Thank you."

"I also have faith that you're going to get past it." He heard a sniff and his insides melted. "Don't cry," he begged, hurting at the thought of her tears. "This is supposed to be a happy day," he chided, wishing he could hold her.

"It is, isn't it?" The trembling eased out of her voice. "How did you like your gift?"

What gift? He'd seen nothing from her but Tati's present.

"You didn't find it?" she guessed. "But I left it on the counter."

"I'll have another check around. I thought we'd opened everything but the place is such a mess it could be hidden anywhere."

"I hope you like it."

"It's from you, so I know I will." This conversation was too difficult to have over the phone. "When are you coming back?"

"My ticket says the twenty-ninth."

There was that silence again.

"Do you need someone to pick you up at the airport?" he asked, knowing she'd left her car there and was perfectly capable of getting herself back to Serenity Bay.

"I'll be fine, Michael." The lilt was back in her voice. "Send my regards to your mother."

"I will."

"I'd better go. Dinner's ready. Bye."

"Goodbye, Ashley. Take care of yourself."

"You, too."

He hung on to the phone even after she'd hung up, feeling like a schoolboy.

"Aren't we going to Granny's?" Tati asked, standing in the doorway.

"Uh-huh."

"Then you have to get dressed, Daddy. You can't wear that on Christmas."

Michael glanced down, saw the robe. "Two minutes," he promised. "Give me two minutes."

As he pulled up in front of his mother's house, Michael knew exactly how he was going to spend the next few days until Ashley's return.

He was going to find Ned Ainsworth. And when he did, he'd find out the truth.

It was time.

Chapter Twelve

The big grandfather clock chimed twelve times.

"Happy New Year, Michael."

Ashley tilted her punch glass so it tinkled against Michael's and wished this night would never end. After a perfect wedding, Piper and Jason were on their way to a tropical honeymoon. Yet the guests lingered on at Cathcart House, as loathe as she to let the romantic evening end.

"Happy New Year, Ashley."

Michael's eyes glowed as dark as the chocolate fountain dripping behind him. He held her gaze as he sipped from his glass. His regard intensified the tension that always zinged between them, stretching it even more taut as the room faded into oblivion and there were only the two of them.

A moment later he lifted her glass from her hand and set both their glasses down on a nearby table.

"Don't you—"

"Shh…."

The words died in her throat as he touched her lips with the tip of his finger and drew her into his arms. He bent his head and kissed her as if he was starving.

It was a perfect kiss, the kind all teenage girls fantasize over. Ashley had been dreaming about this moment for a long time. She twined her arms around his neck and kissed him back—until the applause grew too loud to ignore.

She peeked over Michael's shoulder and saw her friend, Rowena, clad in a gown identical to her own, holding her own glass aloft in a salute. The rest of the room watched them.

"Go, Ashley!"

Ashley tossed Rowena a look meant to kill. When that didn't work, she hid her burning cheeks against Michael's gleaming white tuxedo shirt. Michael apparently had no problem with them being the center of attention.

"It's midnight and there's mistletoe all over the place," he chided, his grin flashing. "Don't you folks have anything better to do?"

Amid the laughter he drew Ashley across the room, wrapped her cape around her and pulled on his own jacket.

"Let's go outside."

"Okay." Still half bemused, she hugged the velvet

around her neck and stepped through the French doors onto the cleared deck.

"Is it too cold?" His arm found her waist, nestled her against his side.

"It's perfect," she whispered, awed by the glory of a midnight-black sky with stars sprinkled across it like diamonds scattered from a jeweler's pouch.

"You're perfect. You look lovely, Ashley."

"So do you, Mr. Groomsman. We make good wedding attendants." She smiled, but a slight sense of unease gripped her at the blackness of the valley. She twisted a little, so it was out of sight. "It was a beautiful wedding."

"Yes, it was." As if he sensed that she didn't want to talk, Michael fell silent, his gaze flickering across the gilded snow, lit by a full moon.

Ashley studied him. He'd been calling her for days, asking if they could meet, saying they needed to talk. Part of her had longed to go, but the other part fussed and fumed over what he wanted to talk about. So she'd gladly run errands for Piper and used them as an excuse when Michael called again and again.

But tonight there was no escape.

She'd have to tell him. The decisions she'd made at Christmas—to stay in the Bay, open the gallery and let God teach her to keep trusting—that had all changed after a phone call this morning. Now the doubts were tumbling around again. What did God want her to do?

"You're very quiet."

"Sorry. I was thinking about a call I received this morning." She faced him, determined to have truth between them. "I've been offered a job."

"A job? But what about—"

She squeezed his fingers, begging him to wait. Michael clamped his lips together, inclined his head. "Go on."

"It's to manage a gallery. In Paris."

"Paris? As in France?" He swallowed at her nod. "Wow! Big step up."

"Yes."

"Are you going to take it?"

She'd asked herself the same thing a thousand times. "I don't know."

"But you want to."

"Paris is the center of the art world. There is such a vibrant arts culture there. To be part of it—" She let it hang.

He exhaled. His hands dropped from her waist.

"Then you should go."

"Is that what you really think?" she whispered, longing for him to tell her to stay, to point out the negatives about a job in Paris. To tell her she was needed here.

"No."

His admission was so quiet she barely heard it. "Michael, I—"

"I want you to stay, Ashley. I want a chance to go to the winter festival with you, to go sailing in the bay. I want you here when I finally have my showing."

So he was still focused on that. She was glad. Talent like his shouldn't be wasted. Still there was something he wasn't saying. "But?"

"But you have to decide for yourself what you want to do, Ashley. Nobody else can tell you."

"I know that."

"Coming back here, facing the past—that's been very difficult for you. I realize that. Especially since you haven't found the answers you want. I wish I could have helped you there, but I have to admit I've failed."

"What do you mean?" She frowned. Something sad, almost defensive, underlaid his words. "Failed at what?"

"I've been doing some investigating, talking to people. About Ned Ainsworth."

Anger surged up like a geyser. Ashley squeezed her fingers tighter into the soft smooth velvet of her cape but remained silent.

"If you could just talk to him, get his side of the story."

"Do you think anything he said would erase the nightmares I've had?" She met his steady stare, refused to back down. "Do you really imagine some paltry excuse from him would make it better, Michael?" She thrust out her chin. "Not going to happen."

"Sweetheart, what's the alternative? Bury it deep down inside and let it fester a little longer?" He shook his head, his eyes brimming with sympathy, but determination, too. His hands gripped her arms. "This one incident has haunted you for more than half your life, Ashley. You've already said you had bad dreams, that you stayed away from the Bay because of fear. When you did come back, you had to talk yourself into it."

"And you think I should add a little more fear, open myself to the lies and distortions some maniac has to offer?" She jerked out of his grip. "I don't think that's very good advice, *Dr.* Masters."

He stared at her for several moments, the hurt in his eyes visible. But Ashley couldn't back down. The thought of being anywhere near that man—

"Why are you so afraid of the truth?"

She couldn't believe what she'd heard. "You, more than anyone, should know how I've tried to get past my past. How dare you say that to me?"

"I have to say it, Ashley." He cupped her face so she was forced to look at him. "I'm in love with you."

The words, emphatic and clear in the midnight air shocked her. Ashley swallowed, struggled to organize her thoughts. But Michael didn't give her time. He spoke again, his voice earnest.

"I never thought I'd fall in love again, never wanted to even risk the possibility. But I see now that

God had something else in mind, that's why He brought both of us here." One finger traced the angle of her jaw. "I fell in love with you in spite of all my plans, Ashley. You walk into the room and my heart takes off like a jet plane. You're here." He patted his chest. "Inside my heart. I couldn't get you out even if I wanted to. And I don't."

"Michael, I—"

She was afraid of this—afraid of hearing him say what they'd danced around for so long.

"I want to begin thinking about the future, what we can build and share together. I thought you'd come to a decision, that opening the gallery meant you were ready to look beyond—" He stopped, let his hands fall away as he regrouped. His face changed, firmed somehow.

She needed to stop him, to stem words that once spoken couldn't be taken back, but Michael kept going.

"Maybe I was expecting too much too soon. That's okay. I can wait, because I think what we could share is worth waiting for. But I hate seeing you stuck in the past."

"I'm not!"

"Aren't you?" His sad, knowing smile reached out and squeezed her heart. "Your hands shake when your mask slips and you can't cover the fear fast enough, Ashley. Even when you came out here tonight, you did a quick check, just in case there was something bad lurking. Didn't you?"

"I can't help my reactions. I'm trying," she protested trying to ignore the persistent hum of anxiety that never quite went away.

"Are you really trying?"

"Of course."

"Then what is this talk about a new job?" He grasped her hands to stop her from turning away. His dark gaze met hers. His voice dropped to a whisper. "Why now, when you've got the gallery almost ready, would you even consider leaving?"

"It's a great opportunity." Ashley could tell from the look on his face that he wasn't buying that. She scrambled to justify herself. "It's not every day someone dangles a job in Paris in front of my nose. It's something I've wanted to do for a long time."

"Is it?" He didn't look convinced. "I think you're running away."

"Why do you say that? Can't I change my mind?" But there was more to it than that and pretending otherwise was childish.

"What about us, Ashley?"

"I don't know." She frowned, trying to sort it out.

"You told me once before that you had to get the fear sorted out before you could talk about a relationship. I could see the damage the past was doing to you and I agreed. Now I wish I hadn't."

"What damage?" she whispered.

Michael just looked at her. "You know."

She did.

"Maybe it's for the best." He sighed. "If you're this unsure about your future, if you think running to Paris will make you feel safe, then I guess I have my answer."

"I never said I was going…yet. I said I have to think about it. But we can still be friends," she hurried to assure him. "That won't change."

"It already has." His dark eyes brimmed with hurt and anger and a yearning that reached out to touch her soul. "Don't you understand? I want more than just friendship, Ashley. I want to start thinking about a future with you. I want to marry you."

She gasped, shocked to hear him admit it out loud. He smiled.

"I'm not saying we have to get married tomorrow or next week. But I thought—hoped—we could start looking toward the future. I see now that you aren't able to do that."

So soft, so quiet the words. She could hear how much it cost him to admit that.

"I'm sorry, Michael. I really am." She pressed her palm against his chest to emphasize her point. "You know I care for you. More than I've ever cared for anyone. But I'm just not ready to commit to anything more than what we have now."

"And what is it that we have, Ashley?" The chill in his voice worried her. "What exactly is it? A few stolen kisses here and there, you playing house with Tati?"

He sounded angry, bitter. She drew back, hid her

hands inside her cape. "I'm sorry if that isn't enough."

"No, it's not enough," he snapped. "You're creating some kind of fairy-tale world so you'll feel safe. It's not fair to any of us."

"Fairy tale? I don't know what you mean." Ashley began to wonder if she knew him as well as she thought. Those melting eyes hardened into chips of black ice, his face tightened to chiseled marble. She stepped back, shocked by the anger in his next words.

"Do you think I don't hear you with her? You organize each detail, plan and strategize everything. There's no spontaneity because you have to think about all the what-ifs and take precautions in case this monster of fear attacks you." He shoved his hands in his pockets, glared at her. "I've heard you warning her over and over to be careful, to watch out, to check, to make sure."

"There's a cougar out there, in case you've forgotten."

"Yes, there is." He nodded. "And there are rough boys in her day care who could beat her up. Tati might get cut when she goes skating. I might get an incurable disease and not be there for her. They're all possibilities."

"So?" She frowned. This sourness, this wasn't like him.

"Can't you see it, Ashley?"

"See what?"

"How this one thing from your past is impacting everything in your life? Not just how you manage. You cope in your own way, I know that, and maybe that's enough for you. But it's gone beyond just you now. Your fear affects how you deal with everyone else."

The wind picked up. He stepped closer as if to shield her, pushed the hair from her eyes.

"Do you think Tati hasn't picked up on your attitude? She has, Ashley, and it's changed her. She doesn't rush into life the way she once did. Lately she's nervous, fusses if I'm late. At night she asks what-if questions."

"I'm sorry, but I don't think it's a bad thing to be aware." Ashley swallowed her denial when Michael shook his head, his frustration evident.

"I'm not talking about awareness and you know it." He stopped, waited as someone else checked the patio then went back inside. When he spoke again his voice was softer, calmer. "Before Christmas, before you left, you said you were going to try to trust God."

"I am trying. Every day."

"Are you? Really?" Michael's eyes met hers and there was no hiding. "Then why can't you trust God to learn the truth and then to get you through whatever really happened?"

The words hit her like a ton of bricks, each one

breaking through to her subconscious. Like a snake uncoiling, the fear rose inside her, seeping through her body until every nerve was taut.

"I *know* what happened! That's what you don't seem to understand. I was there, Michael. I lived it."

He didn't flinch.

"Then why haven't you gone to the police, Ashley? Filed a report, asked them to investigate Ned—done everything you could to stop him from hurting someone else? If you're so sure his intention was to hurt you, why haven't you done something?"

"It's too long ago—"

"I know all the reasons you'll quote, Ashley." Michael smiled, ticked them off on his fingers. "It happened too long ago, your parents didn't believe you, there's no evidence, my mother didn't see anyone. Everyone thought you imagined it. Even you thought that for a while."

"Why are you doing this?" she whispered as the tears welled. "Why do you keep pushing me?"

"Because I love you and I don't want to see you hurting any more." He didn't touch her physically, but she felt imprisoned by the steady knowing light in his eyes. His breath brushed over her like a caress. "You're afraid to live, Ashley. You've already wasted years letting fear eat away at your life, taking control of who you are, of what you can and can't do."

He held his hands palms up, as if offering her something.

"Aren't you tired of it? Don't you want to be free?"

She shook her head slowly as the truth flared in her brain. "I'll never be free of what happened to me. It's part of who I am."

Michael stepped back as if she'd physically pushed him away. His face whitened, but he remained still. After several moments he spoke, but pain echoed through his low throaty voice.

"It's part of who you *were,* sweetheart. It doesn't have to be part of who you are now. Not unless you let it."

"Michael, I—"

"No, don't say anything else. Let it go." He closed his eyes, shook his head, sighed. "I've been a fool. It doesn't matter what I say, the only way you're going to break free of this snowbank of fear that's got you imprisoned is to face it down. I realize now that you're not ready to do that. I'll pray God will help you, Ashley. I don't think anyone else can."

He looked at her for several moments, as if storing up a mental picture of her. Then he walked toward the door.

"Wait, Michael. What—"

He didn't turn around.

"If you need me, if you decide to stay, if you want to meet with Ned—" His breath whooshed out. "I'm here, Ashley. I love you, and more than anything in the world I want you to be whole. But I can't live looking over one shoulder at the past. When you're ready to look at the future with me, all you have to do is call me. I'll be here."

Then he opened the door, slipped through and closed it quietly behind him. The silence was deafening.

"Daddy?"

"Yes, sweetie?"

"Why doesn't Ashley come to visit me anymore? Did I do something wrong?"

Michael closed his eyes and prayed for the wisdom to be the parent Tatiana needed.

"You didn't do anything wrong, Tati. Ashley's been very busy with her new gallery. And she's helping Piper with the winter festival. She's very busy."

"She said that yesterday."

"You saw her? When?"

"When we went to the library. All the kids get to go on Thursdays, you know that."

Yes, he did. He also knew how many times he'd longed to drive up to the house on the hill and bang on the door, demanding Ashley tell him whether or not she was leaving. But he'd heard nothing from her for weeks.

Maybe it was better that way.

"Tomorrow her gallery is opening. Can we go?"

"Tati, I'm not sure Ashley would want us—"

"She wants me to come. She said I should bring

my picture so she can hang it up. Can we go, Daddy? Please?"

Those big eyes reached into his soul and Michael knew he couldn't deny her. "Okay, we'll go tomorrow afternoon. Grannie's going to take you to the play in the evening while I work backstage. Then we're going to Piper's house for a party. How does that sound?"

"Good!" Tati wrapped her arms around his neck and squeezed as hard as she could. "Thank you, Daddy. I love you this much."

"I love you, too, sweetie. Now it's time to sleep."

"Are you going to work in your shop?" she asked, clouds filling her wise eyes.

"For a while. But I'll have the monitor. If you call, I'll hear you."

"Okay." But she didn't lie back. Instead she scanned the room. "It couldn't get in the window, could it, Daddy? Wanda says cougars can break into a house if they're really hungry."

"Wanda's not right about that," he said, wishing Wanda would keep her thoughts about that marauding cougar to herself. "The glass is too heavy. Anyway, the blinds are closed so he wouldn't be able to tell you're in here. You're safe here with me, sweetheart. And if you start to worry, you know what to do."

She nodded. "Pray."

"That's right. God will always hear you." He tucked her in, gave her a butterfly kiss and waited for the giggle that completed their ritual. "Sleep tight," he whispered as he switched off the light.

Michael waited a few minutes until he was sure Tati was settled, then he entered his workroom, setting the monitor on a table. A cursory glance around the room drew a frown of worry. Were they good enough? Would anyone want to display his work?

Would he ever make it as an artist?

The phone broke through his self-doubts.

"Hi, honey. Are you working?"

"Hi, Mom. Just got Tati to bed. What's up?"

"I've just had word that a friend of mine is going in for major surgery tomorrow afternoon and I'd like to be there for her. But I promised to take care of Tati while you're working the sets for the play. I was wondering if you'd mind if I took her with me. I might stay over."

"Mom, you don't want Tatiana in a hospital."

"Well, you can't keep her backstage, either."

"No." He stifled the sigh. Despite his original protests Michael had come to enjoy the play and the actors, even agreed to be set manager. He couldn't very well quit the day of the final performance. "I'll find someone to watch her, Mom. You go, be with your friend."

"You're sure? I could ask Ashley—"

"I'll handle it. Thanks."

"What happened, son? I thought you cared about her."

"I do. But Ashley doesn't feel the same way."

"Oh. I'm so sorry."

"Yeah. Me, too," he said with heartfelt sadness.

"Keep trusting God, Michael. He'll see you through it."

"Thanks."

"Don't bother looking after the house while I'm gone. Ida Cranbrook will stop over. She and Harold overheard me on the phone at the coffee shop."

"Okay. Have a good trip."

After he'd hung up, he stared at the snapshot he'd pinned to the wall before Christmas—Ashley laughing as she chucked a snowball at him. His heart squeezed at the emptiness of life without her.

Why bring her here if not to heal her fear? Why can't I push her out of my heart if she's not Your choice?

The questions never changed and answers weren't forthcoming. For the first night in a very long time Michael gave up on any idea of carving, switched off the lights, and, after a quick check on Tati, returned to the living room. He lit a fire then sank down beside it with his Bible in hand. It fell open to Ecclesiastes.

"Everything is meaningless," says the Teacher, "utterly meaningless! What do people get for all their hard work? Generations come and go, but nothing really changes."

"That's depressing," Michael mumbled, but he kept reading, hoping for some ray of light that would explain his current predicament. He pressed on through twelve chapters, his heart searching. In the final verse of the final chapter Michael read,

Here is my final conclusion; Fear God and obey His commands, for this is the duty of every person. God will judge us for everything we do, including every secret thing, whether good or bad.

Every secret thing. Every secret thing.

Why did that stick in his mind?

He glanced at the opposite wall where Ashley's Christmas gift, a charcoal drawing of Tati, hung. She'd captured his daughter's every nuance from her tip-tilted nose to her dusty cheeks and mud-spattered overalls, half in, half out of her boots.

Carissa would never have allowed such a picture to hang on her wall. Carissa had been all about perfection. In her dancing, in her costumes, in her life. She'd risen to the top of her field because she gave nothing less than her best. And people applauded that.

Michael froze, caught the thought and held it.

People's applause. Did it really mean so much?

How many times had his daughter raved about her mother and the hordes of fans who asked for her autograph after a performance, the people who flocked to the side doors just to catch a glimpse of her? Carissa, whom adoring fans mourned, whom newspapers applauded, whom his own mother had revered—was he envious of her fame, of her ability to make people notice her?

Michael set aside his Bible, walked back to his workroom and studied the pieces he'd selected to show. Shutting out all emotion he assessed them clinically.

Except for a few, they were showy pieces, larger-than-life faces that didn't require analysis to discern their meaning. The majority were crowd pleasers, faces that would draw a laugh or two.

Yet there, in the middle of them all, sat Maria, staring at him.

The contrast in his work bowled him over. He sank down on his carving stool, stunned by the differences between the pieces. Why? How had he managed to create something totally unique in some and settled for "good enough" in the others?

Ashley's words echoed with haunting clarity.

Stop thinking about showing your work. Think about what's hidden in the wood, what you want to reveal. That's when you'll know you've fallen in with God's plan.

Suddenly he understood why that first showing had been a disaster. He hadn't found the glory because he hadn't given his customers anything to think about. The question was, would another show follow the same path?

Michael turned a piece of mahogany over and over, but no picture sprang to mind. For once his mind was too busy assimilating the truth he'd kept hidden inside for so long.

He couldn't compete with Carissa. He couldn't give his daughter a fine home, fancy clothes, a rich and famous lifestyle. And even if he could, what good would it do to diminish his daughter's mother by trying to outdo her? Tati loved Carissa. She had only memories to cling to. It was his job, as her father, to help her keep those intact.

The truth was, it wasn't just Tati he'd been trying to impress.

What he really wanted was to prove to Ashley Adams that his work—that *he*—was as good as anyone she'd ever find, including whatever was in Paris.

Chapter Thirteen

The Adams Gallery.

Smooth brass letters pressed against the stacked stone wall were classically cool and elegant. Totally Ashley. Michael stepped through the front door and swallowed.

She'd created a home for beauty.

He held tightly to Tatiana's chubby fingers as they stepped out of the foyer into the main rooms. Simple plain walls stood stark and bare save for the pieces Ashley had displayed in a wash of natural and artificial light.

"Daddy, look!"

Tati's tug on his sleeve drew his attention to a long narrow window on the right, in what was once the dining room. Framed by the window stood—Faith?

He couldn't believe it. He moved nearer to get a better look. The sculpture he'd given her for Christmas perched atop a white cube, catching the light from outside and reflecting it back.

Michael stared at the polished black walnut, his fingers curling as he remembered how he'd felt releasing the image. A hand reached upward, into the light, pressing through a heavy covering of black so that each fingertip, each knuckle, each flexing muscle was revealed.

"It's beautiful, isn't it?" a woman said. "I've looked at it from many different angles and I see something new each time." She pointed to the palm of the hand cupping the little bit of paper he'd enclosed at the last minute, naming his gift. "It's called Faith. I wonder who the artist is."

"My daddy—"

Michael shushed Tati before she could say anything. The woman smiled then moved away to examine a brilliant blue weaving. Only then did Michael notice the small plaque on the clear plastic case covering Faith. Not for sale.

"Hi Ashley." Tati's cheerful voice drew his attention.

Michael turned, saw the woman who inhabited his dreams standing across the room, speaking to someone. He was about to hush his daughter again when Ashley grinned, waved and after murmuring something to her guest, hurried toward them.

"Hello, sweetie," she said, hugging Tati. "Michael." Her gaze never quite met his. "Did you bring your picture, Tatiana?"

"Yes." Tati waved the sheet she'd created.

"Good. Let's you and I go hang it up while your daddy has a look around." She glanced at him. "It's okay, isn't it?"

"If you have time." He watched them leave, his heart thumping madly as he noted the hollows in her cheeks and the narrowness of her waist. Clearly she hadn't yet resolved her problems. But at least Ashley was still here and not in Paris.

"Excuse me." The man Ashley had been speaking to touched his arm. "I understand you're Faith's creator."

Michael smiled. "I think that distinction belongs to God. But if you mean the sculpture, yes, it's mine. Or rather Ashley's. I gave it to her."

"Nice gift." He thrust out a hand. "Ferris Strang."

"Michael Masters. You're visiting Serenity Bay for the winter festival?"

"Mostly to see Ashley's gallery. I was half hoping it would be horrible and she'd have to come back and work for me. I should have known better."

"She's certainly talented." Michael moved from one exhibit to the next, amazed by the details she'd thought to include. Nothing had been left to chance.

Strang followed him through the building, pointing out things Michael wouldn't have noticed.

"Clever to hide the lights in here," he said when they moved down the hall. "The natural light is great but on a cloudy day the pieces need a boost. The ordinary person wouldn't notice the subtleties but Ashley has a way of honing in on these things. I've never met anyone more adept at display."

By the time they arrived in the sunroom where Ashley was just emerging from the kitchen, Michael had to agree.

"It's perfect," he told her quietly. "You've done a fantastic job."

"Thank you." She motioned toward the kitchen. "I've just put on a pot of coffee. Are you two interested?"

"I'm more interested in what else your friend has done," Ferris hinted.

"Of course. Michael, why don't you—"

"Actually, I don't have anything I want to show at the moment," he interrupted, ignoring Ashley's surprised look. "I'm in the middle of revising my approach."

"From the looks of that piece out there, I don't think you should. It's an amazing work. I interpret it as an inner struggle, to break free of the doubts and believe. Am I close?"

"Exactly," Michael nodded. He accepted the coffee from Ashley, sat where she indicated. Tati was busy at the table creating a new picture, her tongue peeking out from between her lips.

"Ashley mentioned you're a teacher."

"Yes, I teach a shop class at the high school. We built the sets for the play that's starting tonight."

"I see." His nose turned up just the tiniest bit. "Will you send me some pieces when you're ready? I'd be interested in seeing them."

Michael couldn't look away from Ashley, though she barely looked at him.

"That's a good idea, Michael. You have some great pieces and Ferris puts on wonderful shows. I know that's what you were working toward…"

The words flowed past, but he barely heard them. His mind was too busy realizing that she was distancing herself. He faced the truth. She would leave, move on as best she could, still carrying that daunting fear, never quite free. Managing.

He couldn't bear to think of all she'd miss.

In that instant Michael made up his mind to do the only thing he could for a woman he would always hold in his heart.

"Tell you what, Ashley. I'll give the Adams Gallery first dibs if I decide to sell. If you think any would suit Ferris, you go ahead. Minus your commission, of course."

"But I wouldn't dream of—" A customer interrupted and Ashley left to deal with her inquiry, but only after frowning at him.

Michael ignored her glower, rose, set his cup in the sink and picked up his daughter's jacket. "Come on, Tati. I've got to go to the school and get the sets organized for the play tonight."

"But I'm not finished with my picture." Her cupid's mouth set in the stubborn line that spelled trouble.

Michael wasn't in the mood to bargain.

"You can finish it there. The art kit Ashley gave you for Christmas is in the car. Okay? Now let's go." He zipped up her jacket, pulled on her mittens and buttoned his own coat. "Nice to meet you, Ferris. I hope we see you at the party tonight."

"Well, I don't know—"

"Good. See you." Michael didn't stick around to hear the rest of it. An idea flickered at the back of his mind. He needed to get out of here, needed time and space to think things through.

Ashley frowned, fluttered a hand when Tati called goodbye, though she didn't move from her patron. That was okay with Michael. He just wanted to escape.

He drove toward the school with thoughts circling his brain like bees near honey. The dress rehearsal plodded on with a thousand flaws. He listened to each request the director made, adjusted the sets as best he could, all the while watching Tati busily drawing her picture.

When everything was set, every last detail in place, he gathered up his daughter and packed her and her art supplies into the car.

"This isn't the way home. Where are we going, Daddy?"

"We're going on a little errand. It shouldn't take long."

He pulled up in front of the town office, his mother's voice echoing. Ida Cranbrook. Why hadn't he thought of her before? Ida made it her business to know everything that had anything to do with Serenity Bay. As town clerk she certainly ought to be able to tell him where to find Ned Ainsworth.

It took Ida four phone calls to adjacent counties and a talk with one of the oldest members of Serenity Bay, but by the time Michael left he had a piece of paper with a name and a phone number.

"Please let it be enough," he prayed as he headed for the fast-food joint that would fulfil Tati's demand for supper. While they were there they met Wanda and her mother.

God must have approved Mick's plan because his daughter was invited for a sleepover at her best friend's home, leaving him free to carry out his idea.

Cathcart House teemed with people. Piper and Jason had invited everyone who'd assisted in any way with the winter festival, and it seemed that no one had declined.

Ashley refilled coffee carafes, stacked canapes on platters and generally assisted as best she could until Piper caught her and insisted Rowena do something to get their friend to mingle among the guests.

"This is a night to celebrate. Don't you dare let her hide out in the kitchen, Row."

"Yes, ma'am!" Rowena slipped her hand through

Ashley's arm and drew her among the milling crowd. "It's quite a tribute to our Pip, isn't it?"

"She deserves it. She's put in hours on this project. Jason, too." Ashley sipped her fruit punch, trying to pretend a nonchalance she didn't feel.

"He's over in the corner, watching you."

"Who?"

Rowena shook her head. "Oh, Ash. Don't you know you can't fool me? I know you." She tugged on her arm. "Come on, you can reintroduce me to Michael. I must say he's improved a lot over the past ten or so years."

"No!" Ashley jerked to a halt, grimaced at the sticky sweetness that spilled over onto her fingers from the punch glass. "Stop teasing, Row. It's not funny."

"No, I can see that." Rowena met her glare, warm sympathy lurking in the depths of her eyes. "I'm sorry, sweetie. I know you care about him."

"I don't want to talk about it." She motioned to the left. "Did you meet the man who plays the lead in the play? He's right over here." Ashley drew her friend toward the burly bearded fellow who'd brought the stage to life.

"We'll talk later," Row whispered before she was drawn into another conversation.

Ashley ignored that, kept herself busy moving from group to group, accepting compliments on the gallery, speaking to the friends she'd made. But her eyes disobeyed and kept returning to Michael.

He finally approached her when the crowd had thinned out and only a few people were left.

"Ashley, I need to talk to you. It's important."

She wore a white mohair sweater and matching wool slacks that were fully lined but still she felt a cold shiver of apprehension crawl up her nerves.

"You didn't bring Tatiana?"

"No, she's staying with Wanda. A sleepover." He frowned. "Can we talk? In the den?"

"I thought we'd said it all last time," she murmured, praying her friends would be too busy to notice them.

"Not quite." He had her arm and was leading her toward the study.

Ashley followed, wondering what more there was to add. He'd basically told her goodbye on New Year's Eve.

He drew her into the room, closed the door and stood in front of it. She frowned, wondering at the odd look on his face. She followed his glance, gasped and reached for the doorknob as panic filled her body.

"Get him out!" she panted. "Get him out of here."

"Wait a minute. Just hear me out. Ned didn't kidnap you, Ashley. I asked him and he said—"

"What does it take to get through to you?" she snapped, shoving her shaking hands into her pockets as she gauged the distance between herself and her nemesis. She glared at Mick. "I do not want to talk to this man. Ever. I do not care what he has to say. I do not care what you have to say."

"But if you'd only listen."

"*You* listen, Michael Masters." She moved until she was only inches from him. "You know how I feel." She didn't care that her voice sounded raw, only that her heart was breaking. "You of all people know. The fact that you could bring him here, into this house where I'm living—" She shook her head, fought for a measure of control.

"Ashley, listen."

She pushed past him, gripped the doorknob and pulled open the door as she drew a calming breath.

"I trusted you, Michael. How could you do this?"

"I wish you would trust me, Ashley. But more than that, I wish you'd trust God."

"Get out. And don't come back. Either of you."

She pulled the door closed behind her, turned into the hall and climbed the stairs. Once inside her room she locked the door. A long time later Piper knocked and asked if she was all right.

"I'm fine, Pip. It was a lovely party. I'm going to sleep."

"Okay."

Silence. Then Rowena scrabbled at the door.

"I won't go away until you open it."

She'd expected that. Ashley rose, calmly walked across the room and opened the door.

"I'm fine, Rowena. Really. Just a little tired. I'll see you in the morning, okay?"

"You're sure? Michael said—"

"I'll *see* you in the morning." She quietly closed the door, twisted the lock. Then she prepared for bed, but before she climbed into the big four-poster she checked the window lock and rechecked the door.

He knew where she was. He'd actually been here. That was bad enough.

But the deep twisting hurt of knowing that Michael had led him straight to her burned more deeply than she could have dreamed.

She curled up into a ball under the downy quilt and pretended to sleep.

Tomorrow she'd leave for Paris.

Chapter Fourteen

"Ashley! Ashley, wake up. Please wake up."

The panic in Piper's voice drew her back from the edge of the nightmare. She flicked on the lamp, hurried to open the door.

"What's wrong?"

"It's Tati. She and Wanda are missing."

"Missing?" She tried to comprehend what Piper was saying.

"The girls were having a sleepover at Wanda's. Wanda's mom said they went outside to play on the new swing set. When she went to check they were gone. With a storm blowing in and all those cougar reports, everybody's worried. A search party has been formed. They're going out to look. I thought you might like to help."

"Yes." Ashley scrambled for clothes.

"Jason and I are supposed to coordinate things so

we're leaving immediately. Once you're ready, you and Rowena can check in and see where you'd be needed most. She's making coffee."

"Okay. Thanks."

"Pray, Ash. They're just little girls and they've already been gone for over an hour." Piper didn't say all the things that could go wrong. She didn't have to. Her face telegraphed her worry.

Ashley knew the dangers of being lost in these woods as well as she. The nights were frigid. Hypothermia was only a matter of time. And then there was that cougar. There had been reports of stalking, animals ravaged. If they didn't find the girls soon…

A new thought rushed in, supplanting all the others. Ashley grabbed her socks, rushed downstairs.

"Piper," she called as her friend was about to close the front door. "Where is Wanda's home?"

"If you didn't take the turn at the top of the hill that leads here but kept going across the hills you'd come to it. There." She pointed.

"Okay. Just one more thing."

Piper frowned, but waited.

"Do you know where Ned Ainsworth lives?"

"That's funny. I'd never heard of him until Ida was talking about him yesterday," Piper mused. "Why do you want to know?"

"Just tell me," she begged, unwilling to get into it now.

"I can't. I don't know. Hang on." She pulled out

her cell phone, dialed. "Ida, can you tell me where Ned Ainsworth lives? You were talking about him yesterday. Michael did? Oh. Okay. Thanks." She flipped the phone closed. "He's on an acreage past Prime Vista Road."

"Where's that? I've never heard of it."

"It's only recently been opened to public traffic. Past Lookout Point somewhere."

"Piper?" Jason stuck his head in the door. "We have to go, honey."

"I'm coming." She hugged Ashley. "You and Row take your cell phones. The coordinating center is my number at the town office. If you find anything, call there. Be careful, okay?"

"You, too."

The door closed behind her. Ashley bent to pull on her thick socks, dragged on ski pants, then a pair of warm hiking boots she'd purchased a few weeks ago. She turned to find Rowena capping a couple of thermoses.

"How long till you're ready?"

"Just have to put on my coat." She pushed cups, thermoses, some cookies and a couple of wrapped sandwiches into a backpack. "In case we find them and they're hungry."

"Good thinking. I'll get my car. Meet you out there."

Thankfully, Ashley remembered she had a full tank of gas. Rowena had barely closed the car door before they were heading out of the yard and down the road Piper had indicated.

"Um, do you know where we're going?" Row asked as she buckled her seat belt.

"I have a hunch I want to check out." Even the thought of it kept her fingers clenched around the steering wheel, but though the old clammy fear threatened to swamp her, Ashley refused to back down. Not now. If he'd taken the girls she was going to know, and then she was going to stop him.

For good.

Rowena said nothing more as they bumped and slid down the rutted hill, perhaps because she was too busy hanging onto the armrest. When they finally came to a small narrow track, Ashley shifted into four-wheel drive.

"Ash, are you sure this is where you want to go?"

"I'm sure." Then, because she couldn't bottle it inside anymore she told the whole story, how she'd seen Ned several times, how the fear had overtaken her life, driven a wedge between her and Michael. "It's probably a stupid idea and one I'll regret, but I'm going to face down Ned Ainsworth, Row. If it is him, if he's taken the girls, I'm going to get them back. And then I'll make sure he never does it again."

"And if it isn't him? What if you're wrong?"

Ashley didn't have an answer to that. She pulled into the yard, turned off the engine.

"I have to do this, Row. For Tati, for Michael, but most of all for me. I should have done it long ago."

"Your hands are shaking."

"Everything I own is shaking. I'm scared stiff and I can't catch my breath, but I'm not leaving here until I know." She glanced at her friend. "Will you come with me to the door?"

"Try and stop me."

They walked through the drifting snow that blew off the roof and covered the path. Ashley rapped on the door, then stepped back, praying as she never had before.

"Nobody seems to be home. But there's a truck in the shed." Rowena tried the door handle of the house. "It's open." She pushed inside, glanced around. "There's a fire going. I'd guess he's around here somewhere."

Ashley remained glued to the doorstep. Suddenly she heard a noise. She wheeled around. Across the yard at the edge of a cliff, a hand appeared. Ned. Grabbing onto the saplings he pulled himself up. A child lay across his shoulders.

"Rowena!"

Ashley raced across the snow, falling several times in the swirling drifts, but each time picking herself up until she was within three feet. Then fear took over and she froze.

"Help her," he gasped.

"What have you done? Oh, what have you done?"

She lifted the child from his arms, pushed back the hood. It wasn't Tatiana.

"Take her to the house, Ash. I'll help him," Rowena ordered.

Ashley didn't understand why he needed help, but she did understand the splint on the little girl's arm. She pushed inside the house, laid the child on a sofa.

"Are you okay, sweetheart?" she whispered as the eyelashes fluttered. "What's your name?"

"Wanda. You have to help Tati. She hurt her head when we fell into the water."

"Water?" Ashley's blood ran cold. The falls were near here, weren't they? Tons of rushing water—enough to sweep away a little girl if someone didn't stop her.

"We didn't mean to go out of the yard," Wanda sobbed. "We only wanted to get one of the big sticks from the tree—for the snowman's arms. I slid down the hill and Tati had to rescue me. But we couldn't stop. She went in the water and then I couldn't see her for a while. When she got out she had a big cut on her head. She said her tummy hurt."

Ashley shared a worried look with Row, who was helping Ned sit. How badly? she wanted to ask.

"They must have fallen down a ridge," Ned's gruff voice explained. "I found tracks to a cave. I'm pretty sure the other child is in there." He rose, wavered a little, grabbed a chair to support himself. "It's rough terrain. I slipped myself."

That's when Ashley saw his blood-soaked leg and the gash that needed stitches.

"I can't get her alone. One of you will have to help me."

"I'll do it." Rowena found the first aid kit he pointed out and began wrapping his leg.

Ashley took a deep breath. "No, I'll go. She doesn't know you, Row."

"Whichever of you is going, we have to hurry. I saw cougar tracks following hers." Ned reached for his rifle but grabbed the mantel instead, then collapsed in a chair. "You'd better call for help," he whispered just before his head lolled back.

"He's out," Rowena muttered. She made sure his leg was elevated then began removing Wanda's coat. "Let's have a look at you, sweetie."

Ashley heard and saw everything as if through a fog. Her gaze rested on the man who'd filled her dreams for years. That coat—she knew that coat. It was older, more ragged now, but it was the same horrid shade of green.

She gasped at the sight of the faded, shabby crest on the right arm, thought back to that April day. It was as if she was young again. She felt those arms close around her, relived the terror of being shoved in that car.

"Ash, what's wrong with you? Call Piper. Get us some help up here."

Ashley dialed automatically, explained.

"Ned Ainsworth's. We have Wanda. Her arm, I think. We need Michael, some rescue people and some medical help. I'm going after Tati," she whispered, staring at Ned's unconscious body.

"No. Stay where you are."

"I can't. Ned says he saw cougar tracks. I have to get Tati. I have to, Piper." She hung up, slipped the phone into her pocket and pulled on her gloves.

"Ashley, you can't go down there by yourself," Rowena protested. "You have to wait for help."

"I can't leave her alone, not with that cat out there. I'll use the rope he used to climb down."

"Take the rifle."

"I don't know how to use it, Row. And even if I did, I can't climb with it. I'll figure out something else to keep her safe. Just get some help down there as fast as you can." She saw a box of matches and a flashlight on the mantel. They went into her pocket. She zipped it closed, saw Wanda's dry coat and tucked it into a bag that she slung over one shoulder. "To keep her warm. Okay. I'm going."

Rowena hugged her. "I'll be praying, Ash. You know that. God will be there with you. Just call on Him."

"I have been since we left Piper's." She glanced around once more, then let herself out.

The snow fell harder now. The wind swirled it around, almost obliterating Ned's bloody tracks. She gulped down her fear, kept her focus on the point where she'd watched him climb over the ridge. Once there, Ashley dug the rope out of the snow and began her climb down.

"Our relationship wasn't a total write-off, Kent. At least you taught me the basics of rock-climbing," she muttered as she lowered herself over the precipice and began feeling with her boot for something to use as a toehold.

Slowly, carefully, she crept down, thankful for the security of the rope to support her. Her arms ached like fire. Finally she was at the bottom. She whispered a breath of thanks. It was darker here, somehow colder, though the wind wasn't nearly as sharp. Ashley eased away from the wall, took her bearings then sought for something to show her where to go.

A cave, he'd said. She glanced around, thought about calling, then decided that might draw the cat's attention, if it wasn't already nearby.

"Lord, I don't know where to go. Please help me find Tati. And bring Michael soon."

She stepped forward, saw drops of blood and decided she was on the right track. The rocks were slippery, the loud rush of water blocking out most sounds. It was getting more and more difficult to see, too. The forest above shielded out so much light. She moved quietly, praying constantly for help.

When she found nothing Ashley's hope began to flicker. Where was Tati?

Out of the corner of her eye she caught movement. The cougar? She couldn't tell right away, not until it snarled a warning.

"Where is she, God? Please help."

Fear, the nemesis she'd never been able to shake, crept upon her, more cunning than the cougar. She could hardly breathe, her throat began to close as her fingers clenched inside her gloves. Every nerve tautened until she wanted to run.

But that would draw the cougar.

I am holding you by your right hand—I the Lord your God—and I say to you, Don't be afraid; I am here to help you.

The words she'd read last night returned with crystal clarity.

"Don't be afraid," she whispered, forcing her eyes to peer straight ahead. "Don't be afraid. God is here."

Like a beam of sunshine, peace crept into her heart and swelled as she repeated the words over and over.

And then she heard it, softer, quieter than usual, but that sweet lilting voice was Tati's.

"And God if you could s-send Ashley, too, I'd really like it. She knows about being scared and I'm really s-scared right now."

"Tati?" Ashley crept forward, into the opening of a cave so small she had to bend to get inside. "Honey, are you in here?"

"Yes."

"Why don't you crawl over here so I can see you?"

Silence, then a little sob.

"I don't want to. It hurts too bad."

"Okay, you stay put." She crawled on hands and knees toward the voice. "Tell me where it hurts, sweetie."

"My head. And my side. I fell into the water. I'm c-cold."

"I know. Wanda told us. I brought her jacket. Do you think we can take yours off so you can wear hers?" Finally she reached the little girl who was lying on the ground. "Hi." She grinned, so relieved to see that precious face.

She removed Wanda's coat from the bag and with the utmost care helped Tati remove her damp sweater and jacket. She zipped up the dry one, pulled the hood over her head.

"Now you just wait there. I've got some matches and I"m going to try to light a fire to keep us warm. Okay?"

"I want my daddy."

"Oh, he's coming. He didn't know you were here so he was looking for you somewhere else, but I phoned Piper and told her and she said he'd come right away."

"W-Wanda doesn't like o-other kids to wear her stuff."

"She won't mind this time." Was her voice quieter? Ashley wished she'd thought to tuck Row's snack into this bag. "I have to get some bark to start the fire. I'll be just outside the cave so if you need me, you yell and I'll come. Okay?"

"Uh-huh. But I won't be afraid now that you're here."

"Good."

Ashley crawled back out of the cave, gathered a few branches and some twigs and carried them back. Twice she thought she saw the cat sneaking through the woods nearby, twice she repeated the words that had comforted her and broken the grip on the fear that had obsessed her.

Something else glimmered in the back of her mind, some memory that hadn't quite cleared. There was no time now to think about it, but later…

"Ashley?"

She hurried back to the cave, found Tati weeping.

"Sweetheart, what's wrong?"

"An animal, it was looking at me."

The cougar was getting braver. She had to get a fire going.

Cold seeped through her clothes. Her fingers were growing numb but still Ashley kept foraging, searching for bits of anything she could burn. Finally she had a small pile of debris gathered in the bag she'd brought. It was time to snap down some larger dead branches to feed the fire, keep it going long enough to warm them both until help came.

She backed into the cave, sensing the animal following her, feeling its feral study of every move she made. It was waiting, she knew that. Biding its time until it could strike.

"Oh, God, protect us. Keep Tati safe," she whispered.

"Is it still there?" Tati's voice, weaker now, came from the back of the cave.

"Yes. It's still here." Fear clawed its way through her body as Ashley caught the glint of eyes studying them, the snap of teeth that could tear apart a deer. She shuddered, fought to remain calm as she prayed without speaking.

And suddenly she realized that the fear she'd lived with for so long was like that cougar. It had already robbed her of so much. If left to prowl her mind it would devour everything, her security, peace, joy. All the things she as a Christian was supposed to have had been diminished because of fear. Even the love she'd found in Serenity Bay would be gone because she hadn't dealt with the root that grew its tentacles around her spirit.

Now she understood why Michael had pushed so hard, why he'd insisted she talk to Ned. With a clarity she'd never found before, Ashley realized that the only way to live, to fully engage in life, was to challenge the fear, to meet it head-on. Freedom from fear lay in facing the worst and dealing with whatever happened next.

She'd been told that before, of course. But until

this moment she'd never quite understood how important taking a stance and holding her ground would be.

Ashley made up her mind. She would do it. The moment she got out of here she would face Ned and ask for an explanation. A wisp of uncertainty trembled on the edge of her mind, but she pushed it away. She would know the truth. And perhaps it would set her free.

But that would come later.

Right now she had to find a way to hold off the cat.

She huddled down on the ground, assembled her pitiful stash of materials. But she kept one eye on the opening. Removing the box of matches, she opened it carefully, lifted out one, struck it against the side of the box. It flared. She quickly set it against the bed of pine needles and bark she'd placed in a tiny heap, but a whisper of wind blew out the yellow-orange flame before it could take.

"It didn't work," Tati rasped.

"Not this time. I'll try again." She did, striking match after match but with no success. "Paper. I need some paper."

Ashley rifled through the pockets of her ski pants, found a tissue. She tucked it under the needles, lit another match. The tissue caught, flamed, then went out as quickly, barely skimming the needles.

"Light," she begged. "Please light."

But either the material was too wet or she wasn't doing it right because one by one the matches lit up the darkness for a second, maybe two, then went out. Soon she had only three left.

"Ashley?"

Tati's hushed whisper drew her attention to the cave opening. The big cat stealthily approached, his ominous growl sending shivers over her body.

"Get out of here! Go!" She grabbed a big branch and waved it wildly, jabbing forward in thrusts aimed at him as she yelled. The cougar backed down, turned and moved back. But it didn't leave.

Ashley knelt, tried another match. But her fingers were shaking too badly and the match went out. The others fell to the damp ground as the big cat edged stealthily closer.

Forget the fire. She had to fight him with what she had.

Ashley grabbed a thick straight stick and jabbed at the glow of eyes. She hit something. The cat growled, backed away, but soon slunk forward again. She jabbed harder and kept at it, even though she had to crawl on hands and knees.

And she prayed.

Finally she'd backed it up to the cave opening. Just a few more feet, then she could stand, use the fallen willow as a weapon. She swung once, twice, then slipped on the rock.

In slow motion she felt herself go down, down,

until she hit rock and the stick flew out of her hand. She felt the swipe of a paw against her arm, felt the fabric of her jacket tear.

In that second she thought to bury her head, protect her face. But Michael's words rang clearly through her mind.

Don't ever show your fear. Face it head-on.

She lifted her head, glared at the cat as she scrabbled behind her for something to strike with. She felt a small stick, grabbed hold and swung with all her might, striking the animal so it backed off long enough for her to rise.

"Get out of here," she hollered as loudly as she could. "Go!"

But the cougar knew his advantage. He moved forward, closer, closer.

"I tried, Michael," she whispered as the cougar prepared to pounce. "I really tried."

In a flash of fur the animal jumped toward her.

Now!

Michael inhaled, took his shot and pressed the trigger.

The big cat fell directly on top of Ashley and for a moment he thought he'd missed. He tore through the bushes and brambles, uncaring of the scratches they left. He had to get to her.

She lay almost covered by the cougar's thick fur coat. One check ensured he'd caught his prey squarely between the eyes, then he dragged it off her, lifted her head.

"Ashley? Come on, sweetheart. Talk to me."

"Tati," she whispered. "Inside the cave. She's hurt."

Michael's blood ran cold at the scratch on her cheek that could have been so much worse. He grabbed his radio and asked for two stretchers.

"Not for me," she husked, dragging herself into a sitting position. "But Tati needs one. I think she hurt her ribs." She pushed him toward the mouth of the cave. "In there."

"Stay here," he whispered, brushing his lips across her forehead. "Someone will help in a minute."

She nodded, twisted to touch her arm. Blood.

"You're hurt."

"I'm fine, Michael. Now go get Tati."

Because her voice was so strong he did as she asked, hunkered down and eased inside the cave.

"Tati? It's Daddy. Where are you, brave girl?"

"Here." Her voice was faint, her face so pale his throat clogged in terror. "I hurt, Daddy."

"I know you do, sweetie. Just lie still while I check." His measly first aid course wasn't much help but he guessed ribs, too. "I'll put my coat over you so you'll warm up." He stripped it off, laid it over her. "There. Pretty soon some men will bring a little bed and we'll get you out of here."

"Why can't you carry me, Daddy? Did it hurt you?"

"No. I'm fine." He brushed the hair back off her face. "I just want to make sure you don't have some broken bones before we go up the hill. Wanda hurt her arm. She went to the hospital but she said to tell you she's not mad that you wore her coat."

"Where's Ashley?" Tati tried to sit, moaned and put her head back down.

"Ashley's waiting for you just outside. She stopped the cougar from coming in. It scratched her, but she's going to be okay."

"Are you sure?"

"Positive." He heard a noise. "I'm going to go tell the men we're hiding in here. Will you be okay by yourself for a minute?"

"Yes. I prayed, Daddy. I prayed really hard for you to come. I was scared."

"I know, baby. But you're safe now." He went outside, used his radio and waited until he saw someone heading toward them. Then after a shared look with Ashley he slipped back inside the cave to wait by Tati's side.

"We didn't mean to disobey, Daddy. We fell down the hill."

"I know. It's all right. Here's the doctor." He moved aside, pointed to his ribs to indicate the injury. The paramedic, a young man obviously at ease with children, soon had Tati cared for and fastened to a stretcher. Michael slid his coat back on while the others moved her out slowly, careful not to jar her.

Ashley sat outside with another man who held a thick pad of gauze against her arm as he taped it.

"How bad?" he asked the medic.

"Several stitches and a tetanus shot. She was very lucky."

"Luck had nothing to do with it." Ashley might be hurting but she'd lost none of her spunk. "I had a whole lot of help from the Man upstairs. And from this guy right here." She grinned at him.

"If you knew how long it's been since I shot a gun—" Michael shook his head, helped her stand. "We are going to need a second stretcher," he said. "There's no way Ashley can climb with that arm."

"You always have to be right," she complained as she accepted his help to get across the rocks. "You okay, Tati?" she asked, leaning over the bundled little form.

"Yes." But she looked terrified.

Ashley kissed her forehead. "You're going to get a ride up this big hill now," she explained.

"I'm scared," she whispered as they began to fasten the ropes that would help carry her to the top.

"That's okay. We all get scared sometimes. You just close your eyes and pretend you're sitting in your dad's lap and he's rocking you to sleep."

"Is that what you did when you got scared? Really?"

Ashley nodded. "Really."

"Okay." Tati closed her eyes. A tiny smile curved her blue-white lips. "See you at the top, Daddy."

"Yes, you will, baby. I love you."

He stood back, let the rescuers do what they were trained to do. Then he helped fasten Ashley into another harness.

"When did you start dreaming of rocking in your father's arms?" he asked, prolonging the moment before they took her away.

"Fairly recently." She grinned. "About two seconds before you shot that rifle, when I thought heaven was pretty close. Thanks for being there."

He shook his head. "You saved my daughter." His eyes sought hers. "I'll talk to you later," he promised before kissing her.

"Count on it." And for the first time Ashley kissed him back without restraint.

The search-and-rescue guys snickered as they elbowed him out of the way. "Can you folks maybe pick this up later?"

"Absolutely."

While they pulled Ashley topside, Michael grabbed a free line and began climbing up. Only when he'd reached the top did he remember.

"I left Ned's rifle at the bottom," he told Bud Neely, the police chief.

"I'll see that it's put back in his cabin. They took him to the hospital. His leg's bad." He looked grim. "I'm glad you got that creature. Now you'd better go with your little girl."

"Yes." Tati lay in the ambulance. He climbed in beside her, looked around for Ashley.

"Her friends said they'd take her," the paramedic told him. "She said you needed time with your little girl."

"Thanks." He and Tati did need time. But that didn't mean he would let Ashley leave, not without begging her, one last time, to stay where she belonged—with him.

Chapter Fifteen

Ashley eased into the room, trying not to make a sound.

The man she'd feared for so long lay on the narrow white bed covered by a thin sheet and a pale blanket.

She stared at his face, went over each detail in her mind. As it had with the cougar, fear crept forward, tried to take over. She didn't fight it. She invited it, let herself imagine all the things it promised.

And when none of them came to pass, it quietly died.

"Hello." Ned peered at her through the gloom. "Is the little girl okay?"

"She's fine. Bruised ribs, a cut on her forehead and very cold, but otherwise she's fine."

A smile flickered across his face. "I'm glad."

"Me, too." She didn't know where to start. "How are you?"

"Tougher than old boots. They had to do some work on my leg but it will heal. Word is the girl's father shot the cat."

"Yes."

"I'm glad. Every so often you get one like that. Gets a taste of humans and won't quit until it's stopped." His face changed, saddened. "One of them attacked my granddaughter once. Killed her."

"Oh, I'm so sorry." A wave of empathy filled her.

"She was a beautiful child. Happy, easy to be with. And boy, did she ask questions. I'd let her come with me to my cabin for a few days every summer. That child loved the woods as much as me." He fell silent, reminiscing.

"Did she fall down that ravine? Is that how you knew where to look for Wanda and Tatiana?"

"No. She was playing in a sandbox I'd made her, waiting for me to pack some sandwiches so we could go to the brook and fish." He gulped, paused, then continued, his voice broken. "I heard her scream. Couldn't think what was the matter. Raced outside and there it was, tearing at her poor little body."

Oh, God, forgive me for causing this man any pain. The silent prayer burst from Ashley's heart.

"I got her to the hospital as fast as I could. She lived for three days but she'd lost too much blood. I was too late."

"I'm so sorry, Ned."

"Yeah. I went to Toronto for her funeral. Then I

came back here and I hunted for that monster." His face blanched, his teeth clenched. "I looked all over the place, spent weeks searching, but I couldn't find the thing. Not one sign. I'd given up, was leaving town the day I saw you."

"By the apple blossom tree," she whispered, closing her fingers around the hard steel of the bed frame as her throat tightened and her knees melted.

"Yes. You were crying. I was going to drive past until I saw it."

"A cougar?"

He nodded. "Crouched behind you about fifty feet, deciding whether he could get you or not. It was the same animal. I recognized the marks on his left hind."

"I didn't know," she whispered, aghast at the thought of what could have happened. "I didn't hear a thing."

"You wouldn't. They're good hunters." His finger played with the coverlet. "My rifle was in the trunk, I didn't have time to get help. All I could think of was to get you out of there."

"So you grabbed me, shoved me in your car." Suddenly she remembered the way he'd kept looking in his rearview mirror. "When I got out at the coffee shop, why didn't you come in, explain?"

"I had to get that cat. I couldn't risk letting it take another child. I tracked it and I shot it. I thought I'd feel better." He shook his head. "But it didn't bring my granddaughter back. I knew I had to get out of there if I was ever going to put it behind me. I never came back. Then last summer I got a letter. Someone wanted to buy the old cabin."

"You decided to sell?"

"I was going to. But I had to come back one more time." He shook his head. "I'm retired now. No job I have to get to, my time's my own."

Ashley said nothing. It was enough to absorb each word, fit them together and see the truth.

"A lot of time has gone past. When I got back last June, the first thing I saw were the wildflowers. Lara always called them bluebells. Then I found the sundial we'd made. I listened to the waterfall and I thought I could hear her laughter."

"It was your healing place," she whispered.

Ned nodded. "I used to carve things. I thought I'd try that again. Not to sell, just for something to do. Summer passed, fall went and winter came and I decided I didn't want to leave. I liked feeling close to God, talking to Him, listening to the ways He talked back to me. I decided to stay through the winter."

"I'm so glad you did."

He blinked, studied her.

"I never meant to hurt you. If I'd known what you thought—I never realized you'd be so scared or I'd have come back, explained. But I thought you'd know. I'm very sorry."

"Don't be sorry. You saved my life. I would never

have known that if I hadn't come back to Serenity Bay, stayed here and faced my fear."

"And I couldn't have found peace about Lara if I hadn't come back," he whispered.

Awe filled Ashley at the wonder of God's ways.

"Thank you," she whispered when she'd finally absorbed it all. "Thank you so much."

"I second that, Ned. I don't know what we'd have done if you hadn't been there." Michael stood behind her.

"God would have found another way. His plans for us are good and right. He always follows through on His promises."

"Yes."

The nurse hurried in and asked them to leave so the patient could rest. After assuring Ned that they'd be back, Ashley followed Mick out of the room, to a waiting area.

"Tati?" she asked quietly.

"Is asleep. I'm going to hang around here tonight."

"Of course you are. That's what loving parents do." She reached up, touched his cheek.

"I do love her. More than anything." His face glowed. "I'd do anything for her, Ashley. I'd die for her if she needed that."

"She doesn't. Tati needs you to live, to love her, to be there for her. She doesn't care whether you're famous or not, whether you've had the most success-ful showing in North America. All any little girl really wants is to know that her daddy will be there for her."

"I know. And I will be," he promised. "What about you, Ashley Adams? What do you need?"

She took her time before answering. "Not a job in Paris."

"Oh?"

"Nope. Too far. And I don't need a sports car or a big strong he-man like Kent to protect me, either." She smiled, let him see her joy. "I've got God. I'm free, Michael. Free. I faced the monster—and it was me."

He didn't ask questions, didn't need an explanation. He simply smiled, opened his arms and said, "I'm glad."

She relaxed into the warmth of his hold, tucked her head under his chin and told her daddy in heaven how much she loved this man.

"You didn't answer my question. What do *you* need, Ashley?"

She picked up the challenge without a qualm, leaning back in his arms to study his dear face.

"I'll tell you what I need, Michael Masters. I need love. Real love, not the pretend stuff that wears off during the tough times. I need a man who isn't afraid to tell me the truth, to push me until I figure out the hard parts. I need a man who won't let me get away with skating by on life, a guy who will insist I dig in and live every moment."

"I think I might know someone like that," he murmured, his eyes dark and melting.

"So do I." She drew him close. "I love you. When I was fifteen I had a crush on you. Who would have guessed it would last all this time and then blossom into love?"

"I always thought you were a very discerning fifteen-year-old when you were hiding behind my mother's ficus plant."

"Say it," she begged.

"I love you, Ashley Adams." He bent his head, covered her lips with his as he told her how much he cared. And he never used a single word.

By the time she drew away Ashley was breathless— and happier than she'd ever thought she could be.

"When are you going to marry me?"

She stared at him as the events of the past months fluttered through her mind. What an amazing God they served.

"Ashley? You are going to marry me?"

"Of course I am. In the spring, under the apple blossom tree. And I'm going to ask Ned to give me away. Fitting, don't you think?"

"Perfect," he said.

"You do realize I have to okay all the wedding plans with Tati first?" Ashley grinned.

He didn't say anything for a moment, which was unusual for Michael. Then he touched her cheek. "Thank you," he whispered.

"Excuse me, Mr. Masters?"

"Yes?"

The nurse beckoned. "Your daughter would like to speak to you."

"Ashley's coming, too. We're getting married."

"Congratulations."

They broke the news to Tati who was so excited she couldn't get back to sleep. Finally Ashley leaned down to whisper something in her ear.

"But you have to keep it a secret and you have to go to sleep now so you can get better. Promise?"

Tati's eyes closed immediately.

Epilogue

April in cottage country could be iffy. Sudden snow squalls, frosts, high winds. Anything could happen.

But on April twenty-sixth the weather turned out to be better than any fairy tale could have promised. Fresh spring flowers bloomed all around Serenity Bay, but especially in front of the old church by the brook, next to the radiantly blooming apple tree.

The wedding took place outdoors with white chairs dotting the church lawn, balloons tied to the streetlamp and big pots of tulips and daffodils blooming all over. Folks said the bride's best friend had hauled them all the way from Toronto.

At precisely two-thirty in the afternoon, a small electric organ sounded the "Wedding March." All the guests rose as the very handsome groom took his place beside the minister. Next, two beautiful women emerged from the church. The first they knew as their own economic development officer, Piper Franklin. Her husband, the mayor, stood beside the groom.

Following her, a slim redhead moved gracefully down the aisle clad in a sleeveless gown of the palest pink imaginable. Each woman carried a small round bouquet of baby's breath and tiny pink rosebuds.

Once they'd taken their places a hush descended on the group as a small girl stepped out of the church. Her dark curls gleamed in the sunlight, a perfect foil for the tiny seed pearls sprinkled among the curls. She stepped down the aisle in a frilly white organza dress nipped in at the waist by wide satin ribbons. Her full rustling skirt burst out like a flower in full bloom all the way to her shiny white shoes. She carried a small white wicker basket and from it she chose tiny pink rosebuds to drop all the way down the aisle. Then she took her place beside her father who just happened to be the handsome groom.

"Aren't I pretty, Daddy? Wanda said I couldn't do it, but I did!" At which point she dropped her basket.

Her daddy only smiled, lifted her into his arms and kissed her cheek. Then they all waited.

Finally the bride emerged from the church, tall and slim. She walked very slowly, perhaps because of the very high heels she wore. Rumor had it the groom had chosen the shoes.

Everyone in Serenity Bay knew that the bride could have shopped in Paris but had instead asked their very own Emma to make her dress. And what a dress! Gossamer silk, as delicate as butterfly wings, swathed around Ashley's creamy shoulders framing her beautiful face. Then it tucked in, caressed her model-thin figure in a smooth elegant flow of pearly iridescence that tumbled down to skim the tips of her white sandals.

The bride didn't wear a veil but had instead tucked a few white rosebuds into her upswept silver-blond hair. She carried a single long-stemmed pink rose in one hand. The other clung to the arm of a tall man wearing a plain black suit. Friends claimed the pearl earrings she wore were a gift from Ned Ainsworth.

He walked with her down the aisle then passed her hand from his to her betrothed when the minister asked, "Who gives this woman to be married?"

He turned and took a seat beside the bride's mother in the front row while the groom set down the flower girl and nodded at his mother to watch her.

"Dearly beloved, we are gathered here—"

Tears welled in many eyes as the ceremony that joined a man and a woman neared the exchanging of rings.

"Is it time now, Daddy?" the little girl asked loudly.

He nodded and she dug in her basket, found what she wanted and handed it to him. The groom slipped a perfect wooden circlet onto the bride's ring finger. Those in the know said he'd painstakingly carved it from a piece of the old oak tree that had once stood in the backyard of her childhood home.

"I now pronounce you husband and wife. You may kiss your bride."

A torrent of "oohs" filled the little glade as the couple sealed their pledges in an age-old fashion. Then a torrent of rice filled the air as Ashley and Michael Masters walked down the aisle, Tatiana skipping happily behind them.

Folks from the Bay said the afternoon was a delight of funny stories, good food and love. Around five the bride prepared to throw her bouquet until the flower girl, who'd been having the time of her life, suddenly yelled, "Wait!"

She rushed up to the bride, pulled at her skirt until Ashley leaned down to listen to hear her whisper. The bride nodded once, kissed her rosy cheek and brushed away a smudge of dirt.

Tatiana ordered everyone into a circle, and when they had complied she gave the bride a signal. The single pink rose was held up high as the bride turned her back and tossed it way up into the air.

The little girl followed its progress down as she darted here and there among the guests. At the last moment she bumped against one of them knocking her out of the way so the rose landed in the hands of bridesmaid Rowena Davis.

Tatiana and the bride share a grin of fulfillment before the groom kissed his daughter goodbye.

"You do what Uncle Ned and your grannies tell you to do. No disobeying. Right?"

"Yes, Daddy. I will." She waited, then hugged Ashley, whispered something in her ear.

"You're welcome, sweetheart. I think you look exactly like Snow White."

"Me, too," Wanda said in utter amazement.

Tati glowed.

"Daddy and I are going to send you a card and a present so be sure you check the mail every day."

"Goodbye!"

"Goodbye!"

The groom held the door while the bride climbed into the sports car. They drove down the road, empty cans rattling behind them. After a moment they paused, looked back and saw Tatiana and Wanda picking icing roses off what was left of the wedding cake.

The groom turned his attention to Ashley.

"Welcome to my world, Mrs. Masters."

"Welcome to mine, Mr. Masters."

He kissed his new wife, cast one last frown at his icing-covered daughter, then shrugged.

"Is marriage anything like you expected?" she asked.

"It's getting better by the moment." He lifted his arm so she could snuggle against his side. "Let's keep it that way for the next sixty years or so."

"Piece of cake," she told him.

Their laughter carried into the hills and the valleys of Serenity Bay, and bounced right up to the Father who had arranged it all.

* * * * *

Dear Reader,

Welcome back to Serenity Bay! Don't you just love getting away for a while, escaping the phones and duties and just relaxing, enjoying life? Serenity Bay is that kind of place. Small town, lake, lots of beach. But for Ashley, it also held dark places, trepidation and fears she could never quite escape.

Our lives mirror Ashley's in many ways. Each of us has dreads and terrors we choose to live with, adapt to and work around. Instead of facing them we often choose to deny their existence. And our lives are poorer because we refuse to live fully, in the moment. We miss out on some of God's richest blessings.

As you search your own heart and pull out the weeds of fear, I pray you'll find hope and comfort in knowing that nothing is ever hidden from God. That He sees, He knows and He loves you anyway.

I hope you'll come back to the Bay next month for Rowena's story. Until then, I wish you renewed faith, everlasting hope and a love that spreads through your life and brings you true serenity.

*Lois
Richer*

P.S.: You can reach me anytime at
www.loisricher.com or loisricher@yahoo.com.

QUESTIONS FOR DISCUSSION

1. People in therapy often learn that an event in their childhood can affect them later. Discuss how Ashley misconstrued things and how it caused later problems for her. List ways we can deal with children to help prevent these situations.

2. Ashley thought Serenity Bay would be safer than Vancouver. Do you think there are "safe" places? Share your thoughts on making life safe, whether we should try, or whether it matters if we trust God.

3. Divorce has a huge effect on adults and children. Sometimes these effects are manifested in surprising ways. Talk about behaviors you've noticed in children from divorced families and ways that you and your church could reach out to show love to those impacted by divorce.

4. Each of us has secret fears. Talk about reasons that we are so hesitant to share this part of ourselves with others.

5. Growth in faith often occurs most during our worst trials. Why would this be so? Discuss how we can use these times to prepare ourselves for the next trouble spot in life.

6. Someone once said, "When God closes a door, He opens a window." In Ashley's case she lost her job but became her own boss. Have there been times in your own life when you've found this to be true? What happened after you crawled through the window?

7. Raising children is hard work. Raising them as a single parent is even tougher. Michael found several difficulties raising his daughter—little private time, juggling parental duties, career demands. Does your church reach out to support single parents? Consider ways it could do so.

8. Facing fear means knowing what you're afraid of and being willing to risk figuring out why. An old therapy exercise requires the group to gather around one member. That person closes their eyes and allows themselves to fall backward, confident that the members of their group will catch them. The ease with which you can let go is reflected in your trust of those around you. You might want to try this in your discussion group. List ways to build trust in those relationships around you—friends, spouse, children. Commit to trying just one in the next week.

2 Love Inspired novels and 2 mystery gifts… Absolutely FREE!

Visit

www.LoveInspiredBooks.com

for your two FREE books, sent directly to you!

BONUS: Choose between regular print or our NEW larger print format!

There's no catch! You're under no obligation to buy anything. We charge nothing—ZERO—for your first shipment. And you don't have to make any minimum number of purchases.

You'll like the convenience of home delivery at our special discount prices, and you'll love your free subscription to Steeple Hill News, our members-only newsletter.

We hope that after receiving your free books, you'll want to remain a subscriber. But the choice is yours—to continue or cancel, anytime at all! So why not take us up on our invitation, with no risk of any kind!

Love Inspired®